"I—I didn't come here to have a fling with a handsome Italian,"

Casey said.

"So would you settle for an ugly Sicilian?"

Rico was such a flirt. "I think you know how handsome you are," Casey responded, "so I'm not going to pump up your ego any more. It's just that I—I don't want to, uh, embarrass your family by—"

"Nothing human embarrasses my family."

"I don't want to be indiscreet."

He whispered naughtily, "So we'll be discreet, then."

"Rico!" But his audacity delighted her, and she knew he could see it.

Now his dark eyes grew serious. "Listen to me. I am not a fling."

"No, you're not," she agreed softly. The memory of him would stay with her a long time. She knew that already. "You'd be easier to handle if you were."

Dear Reader,

Welcome to **Silhouette Special Edition** . . . welcome to romance. Each month, **Silhouette Special Edition** publishes six novels with you in mind—stories of love and life, tales that you can identify with—romance with that little "something special" added in.

And this month, we have a star-spangled surprise for you. To help celebrate the Fourth of July, we have two books that are dedicated to the Navy—and our country's valiant armed services. *Under Fire* by Lindsay McKenna is part of the thrilling WOMEN OF GLORY series—the hero and heroine are both naval pilots. *Navy Woman* by Debbie Macomber is set at a naval submarine base in the state of Washington—the hero is the commander of a vast fleet, and the heroine is a busy naval attorney. Three cheers for the red, white and blue—and the Navy! We're protected in the air as well as by sea! Happy Fourth of July.

Rounding out July are books by Ada Steward, Laura Leone and Carole Halston. And, as an added bonus, July brings the initial story of the compelling series SONNY'S GIRLS—*All Those Years Ago,* by Emilie Richards. The next installments in SONNY'S GIRLS due out in August and September, respectively, are *Don't Look Back* by Celeste Hamilton and *Longer Than . . .* by Erica Spindler. Don't miss these poignant tales!

In each **Silhouette Special Edition**, we're dedicated to bringing you the romances that you dream about—the type of stories that delight as well as bring a tear to the eye. And that's what **Silhouette Special Edition** is all about—special books by special authors for special readers!

I hope you enjoy this book and all of the stories to come.

Sincerely,

Tara Gavin
Senior Editor

LAURA LEONE
The Bandit King

Silhouette Special Edition

Published by Silhouette Books New York

America's Publisher of Contemporary Romance

This is for all my friends in Sicily,
may they forgive me my trespasses—
not to mention my impertinence

SILHOUETTE BOOKS
300 East 42nd St., New York, N.Y. 10017

THE BANDIT KING

ISBN: 0-373-09681-X

First Silhouette Books printing July 1991

Printed in the U.S.A.

LAURA LEONE

has been an unemployed actress, an unqualified language teacher and an undisciplined student. She has lived and worked in five countries and hopes to quadruple that number before she retires. Named the Best New Series Author of 1989 by *Romantic Times,* Laura likes writing for a living because she can sleep late, avoid rush-hour traffic and work in her slippers.

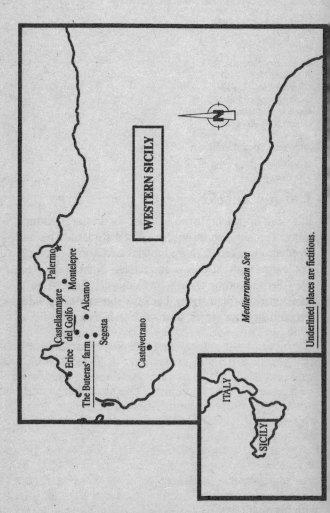

WESTERN SICILY

Palermo
Montelepre
Castellammare
del Golfo • Alcamo
Erice •
The Buteras' farm • Segesta

Castelvetrano

Mediterranean Sea

Underlined places are fictitious.

ITALY

SICILY

Prologue

The ripening fields of western Sicily spread before him like a virgin land, fresh and verdant under a sky more fiercely blue than any other. For a brief moment, gazing at the lush, blossoming, fruitful spectacle of spring in his native hills, he could almost forget that this land had suffered rape, pillage and plunder since the beginning of recorded time.

The hot Mediterranean sun caressed his shoulders, and the breeze carried to him the scent of wisteria, perfumed and heavy in the quiet siesta hour of sleep and shadow play.

This was a cherished moment, the pleasure he permitted himself every time he returned to his family's home between the ancient ruins of Segesta and the azure waters of the Golfo di Castellammare.

Two hours ago he had been ready to quit his job. He was so frustrated he had even threatened to leave Sicily, to accept a position in northern Italy, or even to return to America where he had received his master's degree. A man with his qualifications could get work anywhere—as he had vehemently reminded the government bureaucrats who were responsible for today's headaches.

But now he could stand here, near the cool walls of the house, near the familiar lemon and olive groves, near the timeless harmony that his life in Palermo lacked, and here he could always understand in a deep, instinctive, illogical way why he couldn't leave Sicily—no matter how many times he threatened to.

The years in America had been worthwhile and enjoyable, but the need to come home had sung in his veins every hour that he spent overseas. Perhaps it was a hereditary problem, he mused wryly, since his father, many years before, had also left the promised land of America to come home to Sicily—at a time when he even risked death or imprisonment by returning.

"Rico, is that you?"

Enrico Butera heard his father's voice calling to him from the inside of the family's rustic stone house. Like many old Sicilians, his father preferred to speak to friends and family in the thick, guttural syllables of his local dialect. Italian was "good" language, reserved for strangers, like Sunday clothes and the best grappa.

After one last glance at the hills rolling majestically toward the sea, Rico turned to the house. As he entered the back door which was already open to catch the spring breeze, he called, "Yes, Papa, it's me. I'm sorry I'm so late."

He found his father sitting, as usual, in the shaded *salone,* where the open windows displayed the beautiful vista in the west while awnings sheltered the room from direct sunlight.

"Rico!" Antonio Butera threw his hands up in a gesture that expressed his exasperation. "We have already eaten, and your sister has taken the children upstairs for their siesta. She said that you are always late, so why wait for you? She is right!"

Rico kissed both of the old man's cheeks in greeting and gave him a sheepish smile. "Sorry, I ran into some trouble at work this morning. And traffic coming out of Palermo was murder. Is there any food left?''

"Of course. Help me up, I'll show you."

"No, I'll get it."

Since his father's stroke, which had occurred shortly after the death of Rico's mother a year ago, the old man had been weak and feeble. It tormented Rico to see his tough, barrel-chested father fading before his eyes, to see him struggle with simple tasks where once he had been full of power and vibrant energy.

"Help me up," the old man insisted. "I will sit with you in the kitchen while you eat."

"Yes, Papa."

Rico didn't want to argue. His father looked better today than he had for months. Renewed, as if the blossoming of spring had restored some of his joy in life. Nevertheless, Rico's heart ached as he studied the old man surreptitiously while they made unsteady progress together toward the kitchen. Despite the glow of alertness in his dark eyes, his steps were slow and uncertain, his breath ragged. And Rico noticed the tremor in his limbs, though he didn't mention it.

In the kitchen, Rico helped himself to some *caponata*— a vegetable dish—and some of the pasta his sister, Daniela, had kept covered and warm in the oven for him. The bread was fresh and crusty, the food spicy and delicious. His sister's husband was a lucky man, he reflected. Their mother had taught her only daughter all her secrets. Ah, to have a woman at home, Rico thought wistfully, cooking as your mother used to, putting fresh flowers in the *salone* and fresh sheets on the bed, nurturing your children every day and lying in your arms every night....

As if reading his thoughts, his father said, "You miss your sister's cooking when you are not here, eh? If you could trouble yourself to get a wife, maybe Daniela could teach her some of Mamma's recipes."

"I went to the department store just this week, Papa. They're fresh out of wives," Rico said blandly.

"Do you think I will wait forever to see your children?" the old man demanded.

"Sorry, Papa. They were having a special on grandchildren. If I had known you wanted some, I would have picked up a couple." Rico deftly twirled some *buccatini* on his fork and stuck it in his mouth.

"Don't be so disrespectful! How much longer do you expect me to live? A man wants to see all his children married and settled before he dies."

"Papa, please—" Although the chant was familiar, it made Rico feel uneasy to hear his father talk of death when it lurked so near his frail body. It seemed like a bad omen.

"The most beautiful women in the world live in Sicily. The best cooks, the most loving mothers, the most loyal wives." Rico smiled at his father's conviction.

"You should have told that to my brother before he married a northerner," Rico replied mischievously.

"Don't change the subject! It seems to me that if you cannot find what you are looking for here, then you are a fool.

"To tell the truth, Papa, I guess I haven't been looking all that hard. The bread is very good today, don't you think?"

"In June you will be thirty-four. A man should be married at your age."

"*You* weren't married at my age," Rico reminded him.

"That was different!"

"Yes, Papa, it was." Rico leaned forward and said confidentially, "*I* haven't shot anybody yet."

The old man snorted with annoyance for a moment, then chuckled and clapped his palm gently against the side of Rico's face. "Eat," he said. "Your sister is always afraid you are starving in Palermo." Then just for good measure, just so he could have the last word, he added, "It's not natural to live alone."

Rico returned his attention to his meal, knowing that their usual opening discussion was concluded. It was the right of a man's family to worry about him; it was normal and warm and comfortable. It was also, he acknowledged silently, tiring after such a rotten day of once again wrestling with the interrelated problems of criminality, government misconduct, bureaucratic indifference and sheer incompetence that kept Sicily in such a state of chaos. He watched his father get up shakily to retrieve a corkscrew from the kitchen counter and frowned.

"Papa, you shouldn't have that," he protested when his father opened a bottle of local wine, white and dry and cold.

His father grunted with a dismissive gesture. "So I will die a day sooner. Can one day more or less matter so much now?"

"Don't—" Rico began.

"You have some, too."

"The doctor said—"

"I have an interesting letter from America," the old man said grumpily, "and I would like to discuss it while we drink."

Rico stopped himself in the act of taking the bottle away from his father. The old man's eyes glinted with enthusiasm and the first real interest he had shown for months in anything besides the family.

Rico relinquished the bottle and said, "Good news?"

His father maintained an important silence while filling two glasses to the brim with wine. But his expression was growing more animated by the moment. Whatever the news was, Rico was glad his father had found something to bring him pleasure again. He accepted his wineglass solemnly and waited.

After a long sip of the forbidden wine and a sigh of pleasure, the old man leaned forward and said grandly, "A journalist wants to come all the way from America to interview me."

Rico's fork stopped halfway to his mouth. "What?"

"She wants to write a story about my life."

His appetite suddenly forgotten, Rico pushed his plate aside and peered at the piece of paper that his father pulled out of his pocket, unfolded and spread before him on the heavy wooden table.

"This letter," his father explained seriously, "is from the very famous American journalist, K. C. McConnell, who works for the prestigious publication, *Sentinel Magazine*, which is a division of..." He frowned and consulted the letterhead.

"Yes, Papa, I have heard of it." Rico suppressed a smile at his father's use of adjectives. He had never heard of the "very famous" journalist, and while *Sentinel* was a reasonably good American magazine of news and human-interest stories, the words "prestigious publication" were a little too lofty. He nevertheless tried to look properly impressed.

"And this journalist wants to come here to interview you?" he asked, picking up the letter and glancing over it.

"Yes. Read it, Rico, read it for me. There are some words I don't understand."

"Of course, Papa."

Antonio Butera had lived in America for several years before returning to Sicily to marry and have children, and his spoken English was still proficient. However, he had learned English through practical experience rather than through formal schooling, and he couldn't read it well. Rico, who had completed his higher education in America, perused the letter quickly.

It was gracious and professional, expressing respect for Antonio Butera's wish for privacy while at the same time urging him to break his silence after more than forty years and finally tell the public about his days as a Sicilian bandit and companion of the notorious Salvatore Giuliano.

Rico was just finishing the letter when he heard steps behind him. He looked up to see his sister, Daniela, standing in the doorway. "You know about this?" he asked.

Daniela nodded and sat down with them at the table. "It came four days ago. The following day I purchased a copy of *Sentinel* at the big newsstand in Piazza Castelnuovo in Palermo."

Rico knew the place. It was one of the few newsstands in all of Sicily that sold foreign language journals. "And did the magazine have a story by this—" he glanced at the letter "—K. C. McConnell?"

"Yes. And a little information about her at the end of the story," Daniela added with sparkling eyes.

"It's a woman?" Rico asked with some surprise.

"You see? An old man still has his charms, my son." Frowning thoughtfully, the elder Butera said, "What funny names these Americans have."

Rico smiled as he studied the expression on his father's face. "Do you want to do this?"

"Oh, yes, Rico! He must!" Daniela exclaimed.

"I asked Papa," Rico said with a palms-up gesture of impatience, though he agreed with Daniela. If this journalist could so renew their father's interest in life, then she must come to Sicily.

"Yes, I want to do it," was the answer after one final moment of consideration. Then he added, "If you think it's a good idea."

Rico slid the letter toward his father, who folded it and put it back in his pocket. As he watched the careful, possessive way the old man handled it, Rico said, "It seems perfectly legitimate, Papa. I am just curious about why you're suddenly willing to talk after all this time."

His father's face clouded. His lids fluttered down to cover his eyes, and he shrugged. "I'm an old man now, Rico. When I am dead, who will be able to tell about those days?"

For a moment, Rico wondered if the old man was lying. His expression was suddenly closed, and there was a forced casualness in his voice that struck Rico as strange. Then Rico shrugged away the feeling, attributing it to his own crankiness and wired nerves. He knew his father felt the weight of his own mortality, had felt it ever since the death of his wife last year. The old man had undergone many changes, and this willingness to tell the story of his lawless youth was undoubtedly the most surprising change of all.

"Yes, Papa. I think you should do it," he said, knowing that his disapproval might have stopped his father, and that his approval was what finalized the old man's affirmative decision. Daniela may have already expressed her wholehearted approval, but it was the son's approval that mattered. "So, do you want me to help you write your response?"

His father smiled again. "Yes! After we finish our drink together."

As soon as he had said it, he clapped a hand over his mouth. That was when Daniela noticed the half-empty wineglass sitting by her father's right elbow. She let out a stream of loud accusations against Rico for encouraging his father's bad habits, and a torrent of warnings to the old man about where he was likely to wind up if he kept sneaking cigarettes and alcohol every time her back was turned.

Rico finished his pasta while they argued, half listening to them and idly wondering why an American journalist would come all the way to rural Sicily to talk about things that had happened more than forty years ago.

Chapter One

"'*M*ules are very numerous in Sicily.... The mule is the mode of transport by which the poor man rides to work.'" Nolan Fisher stopped reading aloud and stared at the page. "Good God, what kind of place are we going to?"

"What on earth are you reading?" Casey McConnell asked, glancing at the photographer who was stuffed into the window seat beside her. She had foolishly hoped *Sentinel* would spring for first-class airplane tickets since it was such a long trip. But no, she and Nolan were sitting in coach, uncomfortable and restless after nearly twelve hours of travel.

Nolan showed her the cover of his book. "*An Alphabetised Guide to Sicily and Its Environs, 1913*, by Miss Winnifred Hampton."

"What environs? It's an island."

"According to Winnifred, there are a lot of islands around it. Pantelleria, Mozia, Ustica, Lampedusa, the Aeolians, the Aegades.... Hey, give me back my book!"

Casey eluded his grasp and glanced through Miss Winnifred Hampton's ancient publication. "You mean the entire book is compiled of alphabetical listings and her...rather unique definitions?"

"I doubt if it made the bestseller list," Nolan admitted, "but it's fun reading."

"Well, don't worry about the mules, Nolan. I'm sure things have changed a bit since 1913," Casey said, idly leafing through the guidebook. Then she chuckled. "Listen to this. '*Plumbing* is an unknown phenomenon in Sicily.'"

Nolan grimaced. "I suppose it's too late to turn back?"

"Absolutely." She skimmed another page and let out a low whistle.

"What?" Nolan demanded.

"'*Corpses* are hung out to dry at the...'" She paused over the pronunciation. "'At the *Convento dei Cappuccini* in Palermo, dressed in their best Sunday attire. The custom began—'"

"No way," Nolan protested, forcibly grabbing the book back from Casey. "Let me see that!"

"Hey, you lost something," Casey said, leaning down to snatch up a folded piece of paper that had fluttered out of the book and had fallen to the floor between them. She handed it to Nolan.

He frowned briefly, unfolded the paper to read it, then cursed and slapped his forehead.

"Problems?" Casey asked mildly. Nolan had a tendency to dramatize, and she suspected the note was nothing more important than an overdue dry-cleaning bill.

"I'm sorry, Casey. It slipped my mind. The receptionist handed this to me just as I was leaving the office yesterday evening. You were already down in the street getting us a cab to the airport, and what with the rain, and the hassle, and that pervert on the corner of 56th Street who tried to—"

"Get to the point," she urged.

"This is for you. I forgot to give it to you. I'm really sorry."

"For me?" She took it from his fingers and opened it. The moment she read the brief message, her lips tightened. It was the only show of emotion she would permit herself.

"It's from your father," Nolan said unnecessarily.

"Yes." She shoved it into the loose pocket of her trousers.

"Are you gonna return his call?"

"Not from Sicily, I'm not."

"When we get back?"

"No."

"Come on, Casey," Nolan urged, rushing in where wise men wouldn't have dared to tread.

"Drop it."

"He's your *father,* Casey. Maybe he—"

"Forget it, Nolan. The man is a liar, an adulterer and a smooth talker. He's got about as much moral fiber as cream cheese. What's more..." She took a steadying breath, aware that her voice had risen. "What's more, the fact that he's trying to contact me for the first time in years can only mean he needs money, help, or ego boosting."

Nolan held up both hands. "Okay, okay, sorry I mentioned it."

After a long moment, Casey said, "Sorry I snapped at you."

"It's okay."

The subject of Casey's father came up seldom, but it always made her tense and irritable. She didn't want to think or talk about him. He was history as far as she was concerned.

She was glad Nolan was ready to let it drop. They had worked together often enough to be able to blow off steam without offending each other, and to recognize when to back off. It was one of the reasons she had requested that the magazine assign Nolan to accompany her to Sicily.

The airplane was descending rapidly, and Casey tightened her seat belt fractionally, anticipating a rough landing since they were fighting a strong wind from the south. When the plane touched down ten minutes later, all the Italians on board—virtually everyone except Casey and Nolan—gave a loud cheer. The Italian passengers had done the same thing on the connecting flight from New York when it had landed in Rome. Casey thought it was a nice custom.

As the plane taxied toward the main building of Palermo's airport, Casey said, "I wonder what Miss Winnifred would have said about Giuliano."

"My guess would be, 'Salvatore Giuliano, a rogue, a bandit and a scoundrel.'"

Casey shook her head. "No, even Winnifred probably couldn't have resisted romanticizing him. 'Salvatore Giuliano, a modern-day Robin Hood, living wild in the hills of western Sicily, stealing from the rich and giving to the poor.' Or maybe she would have considered him a freedom fighter."

"Well, since Giuliano was a bandit about thirty years after Winnifred was a tourist, we'll never know."

When the plane taxied to a halt, they gathered together their carry-on luggage—Casey's books, notebooks and tape recorder, and Nolan's cameras, lenses and film—and deplaned, descending a dozen or so steps to the pavement. The wind was blowing fiercely, assaulting them with a fine layer of red dust. They followed the crowd of bustling Sicilians into the large, squat building nearby.

They were admitted through a large open doorway where they passed a number of uniformed men who either smiled and waved or else ignored the passengers. Then they entered the main section of the airport.

"This is like Grand Central Station before Labor Day weekend," Nolan exclaimed. "How will we find Butera in the middle of this?"

The airport was indeed a confusing place. Hundreds upon hundreds of people, many pushing and shoving their way through, surrounded Casey and Nolan in a fleshy sea of humanity. There was a great deal of noise and shouting, all of it competing with some construction that was taking place at the far end of the building.

"We won't find him. He'll find us," Casey assured Nolan.

"How?" he demanded.

"I gave his father a description. He said we'll be impossible to miss."

Judging by the stares they were already receiving, Casey suspected old Signor Butera had known what he was talking about. Everyone in sight was short, dark-haired, dark-eyed and olive-skinned. At five foot nine with golden blond hair, blue eyes, pale skin and a long, angular face, Casey couldn't have stood out more if she were carrying a neon sign advertising her foreign status.

Standing beside her, Nolan Fisher almost qualified as the neon sign. The *Sentinel* photographer was well over six feet tall, with long flaming red hair tied back in a ponytail. A quick glance around the crowded airport indicated that shoulder-length hair was distinctly unusual for men in Sicily.

Casey glanced at her watch. "He should be here. It's already twenty minutes past the time we were supposed to meet."

"You keep an eye out for him, I'll get our luggage. Okay?"

Casey nodded and watched Nolan walk away. Having finalized her travel arrangements the week before, she had telephoned the Butera household. Although she had fully expected to get a taxi at the airport and check into the Hotel of the Palms, old Signor Butera had assured her that that wasn't the Sicilian way of doing things. Since she was coming to see him, she and Nolan would be his guests, and his son would collect them at the airport.

Her editor was uneasy about the idea. After all, Casey was interviewing Antonio Butera because he had once been an outlaw, a criminal, a bandit who rode with the notorious Salvatore Giuliano. Annoyed by this overprotective attitude—being a "helpless female" had already cost her the most important assignment of her career—Casey had pointed out that Giuliano was a great folk hero in western Sicily and that Butera probably fell into the same category. Her editor pointed out that Giuliano's band had killed well over one hundred people. Casey reminded him that that had all happened more than forty years ago.

In any event, Signor Butera had made it clear he would be offended if Casey and Nolan didn't stay with him. Since she wanted a cooperative interview subject, she had agreed. It should be quite an adventure, she reflected, being the guest of a man who had actually been a bandit on horseback, living wild in the hills with one of the most intriguing figures in modern history, stealing from the rich and giving to the poor.

Of course, there was more to it than that, as Casey knew from her research. Though an idealist, Giuliano had been a puppet of the Mafia and of corrupt political parties vying for supremacy in postwar Italy. She wondered how much Butera knew of Giuliano's powerful connections in those days. She wondered even more how much he knew about Giuliano's mysterious death.

It's going to be a good story, she promised herself encouragingly. She had been peripherally interested in doing it for some time, though her busy schedule and Butera's own cultivated anonymity had made her doubt more than once that she would ever have the opportunity to conduct the interview. Then, when the story that should have been hers was given to someone else and she had threatened to quit, *Sentinel* had given Casey carte blanche to do "the Sicilian thing," hoping it would appease her. Miraculously, Butera had responded affirmatively to the letter she had sent him, after she'd finally tracked him down.

Casey was still trying to work out whether she had done the wise thing in remaining with the magazine, or had merely sold out. Either way, she was determined that this would be the best damned story *Sentinel* published all year.

Perhaps this wasn't as strong and contemporary a topic as the story for which she had been passed over, but Giuliano was an intriguing figure and Butera had shared his lawless life for a number of years. Surely the old man must know something that no one else knew. And she would convince him to tell it to her.

Something disturbed the intensity of her thoughts—a sudden tingle of awareness, a slight surge of empathy. She glanced around and suddenly saw what else, besides a great story, a hardworking female journalist could want from life.

He was unusually tall for a Sicilian, if the crowd around him was anything to go by. His broad shoulders tapered down to narrow hips, and his long legs, encased in tight blue jeans, looked muscular and capable. His sea-green cotton shirt was open at the throat, and the sleeves were rolled up, displaying strong forearms with a light dusting of dark hair.

Casey's eyes flashed up to his face. The Moorish ancestry of the Sicilians showed up clearly in his liquid dark eyes, so brown they were nearly black, velvety and shining, fringed with long, thick lashes and emphasized by the dramatic arch of his black brows. They were eyes a woman might have envied—tender yet sparkling with fire, languid yet dramatic. But the harsh strength of his face, with its high cheekbones, long jaw and straight nose, gave his expression a solid masculinity that the eyes softened but couldn't diminish. The darkening shadow of a beard on his jaw made him look slightly dangerous.

He stood with his arms folded across his chest, studying her with open curiosity for a moment that seemed to last forever. Casey suddenly remembered that they were in a Mediterranean country now, and her idle interest in the stranger—according to her guidebook—would probably be taken as an open invitation.

She had only just realized that, when a friendly, confident grin split the stranger's face, flashing healthy, even white teeth in his dark visage, and he slowly stalked toward her. Casey rolled her eyes and wondered what to do next. She could handle herself perfectly well under normal circumstances, but she didn't know the Italian translation for "get lost."

When he was within two feet of her, he unexpectedly stuck out his hand and said, "Miss McConnell. Welcome to Sicily."

Casey stared at him. "Signor Butera?"

He nodded. "Please call me Rico. My father told you I would pick you up, didn't he?"

"Yes." Casey took his hand. Her palm met his, which was warm and hard and slightly callused, and his long slim fingers closed strongly around hers. Casey realized she was staring again. To cover it, she said, "Your father was right. You spotted me immediately."

"You were impossible to miss." The sparkling light in his eyes made the comment complimentary as he swept her over with a glance.

"Oh." She smiled tentatively. "You speak English very well."

He rose one dark brow to acknowledge the compliment. "Thank you. I have spent some time in America."

"Oh, really?" Casey pulled her hand out of his. The glide of his flesh against hers made the gesture seem too intimate. "What part of America?"

"New York mostly." He gazed at her for another moment, his expression frank, assessing and openly intrigued. Then he glanced around, his eyes bright and alert. His onyx-black hair curled crisply around his head and shone healthily under the artificial lights of the airport terminal. "I thought you were to be traveling with a man."

"I am." Casey looked around. "He— There he is! Nolan!"

Nolan approached them looking confused and exasperated. "You're Signor Butera?" he asked, interrupting Casey's polite attempt at an introduction. "Thank God. Perhaps you can have a word with these guys about our luggage. There's something wrong, but I'll be damned if I can figure out what's going on.''

''Ahh.'' Rico nodded sagely and said, ''I will take care of it. Where are your bags?''

''Something's wrong?'' Casey interrupted. ''What could be wrong?''

''I'm sure it's nothing. I'll handle it for you. Trust me,'' Rico intervened.

Casey stared at him doubtfully for a moment. Trust him? She had only just met him. There was a knowing gleam of mischief in his smile that tugged briefly at her before she looked away. She had something important to determine here, before they took another step. ''Nolan, what do you mean, you can't understand—''

''Casey, could we talk about this later?'' Nolan pleaded. ''When I left our suitcases, they were attracting a small congregation.'' He spun around and headed back toward the baggage-claim area.

Casey watched him walk away with a vague feeling of alarm. *Another* important reason for requesting Nolan as her photographer on this trip was that he had studied Italian in college and supposedly spoke it with reasonable accuracy. At least he had always told *her* that he spoke it. Since her command of the language was limited to a couple of phrases pulled out of her guidebook and whatever else she could glean based on her proficient Spanish, she could be handicapped if Nolan's Italian proved to be rustier than expected.

Rico started to follow Nolan toward the baggage-claim area, then turned and glanced at Casey. He shook his head, took three smooth steps toward her, slipped his arm through hers in a curiously old-fashioned gesture, and pulled her along.

''You will soon discover,'' he said in his deep, lightly accented voice, ''that a blond woman standing around alone in Sicily only remains alone for a few seconds.''

He was a good four or five inches taller than her, and the look he flashed at her from beneath his heavy lashes was both amused and flattering. It was a combination that made her smile foolishly, even though she didn't quite understand his comment.

He walked with a smooth animal grace, and his grip on her arm was unselfconscious and firm. A natural toucher, she thought. She wasn't a toucher, and she was unaccustomed to this virtual stranger's easy assumption that he could simply drag her along with him. However, he was clearly such an expert at negotiating through the aggressive throng of pushing, shouting Sicilians that she decided to cooperate. They trailed behind Nolan as Rico smoothly steered and maneuvered her in the general direction of their bags.

"I don't get it," Casey muttered when she saw three uniformed men hovering over their luggage and arguing. "There was no problem whatsoever when we came through customs in Rome."

"This is not Rome," Rico said simply.

Upon spotting Nolan—who was hard to miss in that Mediterranean crowd—the three Italians turned toward him with a flurry of excited gesticulations and exclamations.

"I can't make out a word of this," Nolan said, casting a pleading look in Rico's direction.

Rico released Casey and held his hands out, palms forward, in an apparent effort to stem the flood of speech pouring forth from the three officials. The three men all wore different uniforms, and they were carrying a variety of weapons and communications devices. Rico listened to them courteously for a few moments, nodding and murmuring *"sì."* Then things got a little confusing.

Two of the guards started arguing ferociously with each other, shouting a great deal, waving their arms and making specific gestures whose meanings were a mystery to Casey but which apparently represented an extreme form of exasperation. The third guard appeared to take sides with first one, then the other, switching his loyalties every thirty seconds or so.

Casey and Nolan exchanged a worried glance. What could they possibly be carrying that could cause so much alarm? The Rome-to-Palermo trip was a domestic flight, completely routine as far as Casey knew. There was nothing in Casey's ordinary, well-worn gray suitcase except clothing and personal items, and she knew Nolan well enough to firmly believe that his luggage was equally innocuous.

Accustomed to taking control of difficult situations, Casey said, "All right, gentlemen, let's all stay calm."

She had no idea if they had actually understood her, but the very act of her verbal intervention sparked a combustion of angry gestures directed toward their bags and more general shouting.

smiled with unabashed delight when she recoiled,

palms apart to gesture toward Casey, Nolan, or the baggage which still sat innocently on the dirty floor.

Apparently his argument was convincing. After a few more minutes, the guards were all nodding their heads and murmuring things that sounded conciliatory to Casey's unaccustomed ears. Someone must have cracked a joke, because the four of them all started laughing. They seemed to become great buddies at that point, for there was a whole lot of back patting and rib jabbing, and a few more jokes.

Then the three men all shook Rico's hand. This was followed by a clear request to be introduced to Casey and Nolan. Rico performed the introductions entirely in Italian, so Casey just nodded and smiled and hoped he was saying something remotely accurate about her. Then there was a great deal of handshaking and smiling, and prett
things got so merry Casey even found her

Casey walked wearily behind Rico, who promised her that the car was parked very close to the main entrance. It was unnerving, at the end of nearly a day's journey, to have found herself under suspicion of God-only-knew-what in a strange country where she knew no one and couldn't speak the language.

"No wonder overseas assignments are considered so stressful," she mumbled.

"*Cosa?*" Rico glanced her way inquisitively. *What?*

"Nothing." She smiled blandly. As soon as they were safely inside the car, she was going to insist he explain what had just happened.

"Just a little farther," Rico said encouragingly, turning around and striding ahead of her.

He strode very nicely, she thought. Although he had the body of a young man and his hair was a pure coal black with no trace of gray, his face had the hard maturity of a man in his thirties.

She wondered what kind of work he did. He carried the weight of her bags easily, and beneath his well-fitted shirt she could see the bunch and flow of thick, developed triceps and deltoids. There was a toughness about his body and his stance that made her believe he hadn't developed that physique in the sterile confines of a health club, just as there was a quick energy about his actions that made her suspect he didn't spend all day in an office.

"We're almost there," Rico assured her, looking back briefly again. Casey was beginning to suspect he had a slightly different definition than she about what qualified as "close to the main entrance," but she was in no position to complain. A little walking, she decided, would be good for the thighs she had recently decided were showing signs of too many hours at her desk. The "active life" of a *Sentinel* reporter, she had discovered over the past few years, meant long hours, fast food and emotional stress, rather than physical activity and healthy exertion.

The hot Mediterranean sun beat down on her as she continued to follow Rico Butera. It had been raining and chilly in New York the night before, so she appreciated the warmth of spring in this climate. However, a hot gusting wind was blowing thin layers of red dust all around them. By the time they finally reached the car, Casey felt like a cast member of *Lawrence of Arabia,* caked in dust and disheveled by the wind.

Rico opened the passenger door for her and said, *"Prego."*

Casey looked at the new red Citroën—also covered in dust—and then back at Rico. "I thought you said the car was parked near the entrance." They had been walking for over five minutes.

Seeing that she didn't intend to get into the car just yet, he walked back to the trunk, opened it and hoisted her luggage inside. Then he glanced up at her. A hint of laughter glittered in his eyes, adding buoyancy and mischief to the austerity of his desert-prince features. "I lied," he said simply. When her eyes narrowed, he added, "Here comes your colleague."

Casey turned to see Nolan straggling along, tugging his battered suitcase behind him. As he neared the car, he said accusingly to Rico, "I thought you said the car was parked near the entrance."

"He lied," Casey said flatly.

Rico shrugged. Casey noticed that the gesture seemed to ripple through his whole body. "After your eventful arrival, I didn't think it wise to leave you two alone while I went to get the car."

"He has a point," Nolan admitted to Casey.

"I thought you said you spoke Italian," Casey said reproachfully to Nolan.

Rico glanced over his shoulder at them as he tossed Nolan's suitcase into the trunk. "You speak Italian?" Without waiting for an answer, he continued, "That's good. She will have enough trouble outside my father's house without struggling against a language barrier, as well." He slammed the trunk shut and said confidentially to Nolan, ignoring Casey. "You must go everywhere with her, you understand me?"

Casey opened her mouth to object to a number of things, but Rico was already rounding the car to open his door. He called cheerfully across the roof to Nolan, "So where did you learn to speak Italian?"

Nolan grinned at Casey's sour expression before shrugging and answering, "I took Italian in college and spent part of my junior year in Florence. I've been to northern Italy twice since then. I mean, I expected to be a little rusty, but that conversation back there barely sounded like Italian to me."

"Ahh." Rico nodded knowingly and smiled again. "This is not northern Italy. You will find things a little different down here."

"I'll say," Nolan said. "Was that dialect?"

"No, Italian." Rico opened the driver's door and got in the car.

Following his example, Casey made herself comfortable and then turned to look at Nolan in the back seat. "What do you mean by dialect?"

"Well, there's standard Italian, which is taught in schools and spoken on TV. Then there's everything else," Nolan said vaguely.

"Italy was only unified in 1860, Miss McConnell, nearly a century after your own country. We're still working out a few things," Rico explained casually, putting the car into gear.

"I do know my basic history," she said. "And call me Casey."

"Casey?"

He looked at her with those dark, liquid eyes, revealing interest and a certain impertinent charm that made Casey want to squirm. He had very full lips, she noticed suddenly. Firm and sensual and expressive. She lowered her eyes when she realized she was staring at him again.

"Yeah, and I'm Nolan," came a cheerful voice from the back seat.

When Rico turned his attention back to the road, Casey returned to her initial concern. "So if they were speaking Italian, Nolan, why couldn't you understand it?"

"The accent was very thick. And they were talking a mile a minute, and all at once."

Rico nodded. "You will find it difficult at first, Nolan," he confirmed. "In Florence they speak a very pure form of Italian. The farther from Florence you get, the more it changes. And in Sicily, we have a certain way of speaking that baffles most outsiders."

"But he'll eventually get the hang of it?" Casey persisted doggedly.

"Eventually," Rico confirmed. Then he winked teasingly. "But perhaps not before you're ready to go back to America."

How reassuring, Casey thought, hoping that she wouldn't need to rely on Nolan at all. "Well, I love a challenge," she murmured.

"Then you're in the right place," Rico replied laconically.

Casey maintained a diplomatic silence while Rico followed the signs leading from the airport to the main road. As soon as they seemed to be on some kind of thoroughfare, however, she brought up another subject of concern. "What happened back there with our suitcases?"

"Yeah! That's what I'd like to know," Nolan said. "It's funny how scared you can be when you're perfectly innocent."

"Oh, nothing serious," Rico said dismissively. He paused briefly at a fork in the road, then chose the route heading west.

Casey saw a road sign for Alcamo, and she knew from her background research that the town was in the general direction of the Butera farm. "Nothing serious? Then what was all that shouting about?"

She saw the subtle curve of Rico's lips which she was already learning meant he was trying not to smile. "A bit of theatrics, that's all. It was a dull day at the airport, and they wanted to liven things up a little."

"What?" Casey said incredulously.

"The excuse was that they were concerned that your suitcases were improperly labeled. Foreigners always receive more attention here, as they are so noticeable."

"*What?*" she repeated. "They held us up for twenty minutes, and they had me convinced that *Sentinel Magazine* would have to bail us out of jail on smuggling charges—and all because they wanted a little entertainment?"

"Well, put that way it does sound pretty bad," Rico admitted, "but I assure you, there was nothing to worry about."

"But what if you hadn't been there?" Casey demanded.

"But I *was* there," he said simply.

"But can they *do* that? I mean, can't we complain to someone?" she asked, angry now that she had been so inconvenienced for no reason at all.

"Well, we could," Rico admitted blithely, "but it would be more of the same thing. Just more theater."

"So how did you convince them to let us go on our way?"

"I told them a good story," he said vaguely.

Casey wasn't satisfied. "What, precisely?"

He glanced sideways at her. "I told them that you were my fiancée, and that you had come to Sicily to marry me against the wishes of your employer, who had not given you sufficient time to prepare for the journey. We talked for a while about how insensitive these big American companies are to the needs of the family, what terrible stress you have been under, about what a fine journalist you are, about how good it was of your cousin here," he nodded to Nolan in the back seat, "to accompany you on this long journey." Rico shrugged philosophically. "A good story."

"In short," Casey said, "you lied."

He met her critical gaze easily. "I told a good story," he repeated.

"Why didn't you just tell the truth?" she persisted.

He grinned at that. "The truth is not something a Sicilian gives away. Anyhow, they wanted—"

"A bit of theatrics," Casey finished wearily. She hoped the elder Signor Butera wasn't so circumspect, or the interview would be a total waste of time. She took a deep breath. "I find this extraordinary."

He looked at her again, his expression a strange combination of amusement and sympathetic understanding. "You will find that most things here are incomprehensible to outsiders. Even after they're explained."

"How reassuring," Casey muttered.

She remained silent for the next twenty minutes or so, concentrating on trying not to scream. In an active and varied life, she had never encountered anything like traffic in Sicily. Everyone on the road, including Rico, drove at a breakneck speed that would have gotten them locked up in America. The drivers all seemed to operate on instinct, with a proud contempt for turn signals, road signs and lane dividers. More than once, a car swerved directly in front of them with no warning, or braked suddenly when it was only a dozen feet ahead of them.

Rico drove with an electric alertness that made Casey want to leap out of the car the first chance she got. Like everyone else on the road, he swerved quickly and unexpectedly in and out of lanes, turned without using his indicators, stomped on the brake suddenly and then, just as suddenly, accelerated without caution.

Casey gripped the door handle with her right hand and continually checked and rechecked the fastening of her seat belt with her left hand. Of course, the seat belt probably wouldn't save her in the multivehicle pileup that seemed imminent, but it could at least offer some small measure of reassurance.

She wondered briefly if Rico Butera's driving had given his father his stroke. She had intended to ask Rico about his father before arriving at the Butera farm, but she was far too agitated to talk right now. She squeezed her eyes shut, hoping Rico wouldn't be offended if he noticed.

She finally became aware of the car slowing down and turning more regularly. When the car came to a stop and Rico killed the engine, Casey opened her eyes quickly and looked around. They were on a narrow street surrounded by pale stone buildings, all the same color as the rocky tan and golden hills through which they had driven.

"Where are we?" she asked breathlessly.

"Alcamo. I promised my sister we would stop to get bread for lunch." Rico's voice was distracted.

Casey looked over her shoulder at Nolan. Evidently she wasn't the only one unbalanced by local traffic. He was staring into space with a glazed expression, and a light film of sweat covered his face. "Are we nearly there?" he asked weakly.

Casey shrugged and looked at Rico. He was looking directly ahead. A puzzled, apprehensive frown drew his dark brows down and gave his face an expression quite unlike the friendly, lively one he had worn at the airport. Casey looked curiously in the same direction.

There was a huge crowd of people blocking the street, all pushing, shoving and trying to get closer to something beyond Casey's line of vision. She looked up. Every building had several balconies, and every balcony was full of people looking down into the street.

"Nolan, something's happening," she said. She opened the door and touched one foot to the pavement.

"Casey, no," Rico said quickly, putting a hand on her arm to restrain her.

She shook him off and stepped out of the car. Behind her, Nolan hopped out of the car and slung a camera around his neck. She and Nolan hadn't gotten their jobs at *Sentinel* by letting events pass them by.

Rico got out of the car and looked at her over the hood. "I want you to stay in the car." It was not a request.

"What's happening here?" Casey asked. She would choose a quieter moment to tell him he shouldn't give her orders or talk about her to Nolan as if she weren't there, much less lie about her to strangers.

Nolan hurried past her and pushed forward into the swelling crowd. People were milling around in all directions. Some tried to get closer to the hidden scene. Those who had apparently seen all they wanted to hurried away, no doubt running home to tell the news to the families standing on the balconies. As they approached the nucleus of the crowd, Casey realized that there were nearly a dozen policemen there. Whatever the problem was, it was evidently pretty serious.

One of the policemen saw Casey and Nolan. He came toward them swiftly, shaking his fingers and shouting angrily, pushing them back into the crowd as he did so.

"Can you understand him?" Casey asked worriedly.

"He's telling me I can't take photographs."

Casey turned and sought Rico in the crowd. She spotted him just a few feet behind her talking to a young man. She pushed toward him and demanded, "What's going on here?"

"Come away from here, Casey," he said very seriously.

"Why? What's happened?" She glanced inquisitively at the man who had been talking to him.

"L'hanno ucciso," the young man said gravely to her. *"Capisce? È morto. L'hanno ucciso."*

"You should not see this," Rico insisted quietly, taking her arm and trying to pull her away.

She glanced past him at Nolan, who was still trying to get close enough for a photograph. "What does that mean?" she asked Rico. *"L'hanno... l'hanno...."*

"Casey, there's been a killing. Come, we must go now. My father would not want you to see this."

She yanked her arm free of his annoying tugging and snapped, "Stop it!"

"This is not—"

"I'm not—"

"Hey, guys, maybe we should split," Nolan interrupted uneasily. "Those cops are making threatening gestures at my camera."

Casey took a sharp breath and bit back her next comment. She was surprised to find her hand was clenched in a fist and Rico's fingers were wrapped around her upper arm like a vise. Before she knew what was happening, he had dragged her back to the car and helped her inside.

"Sorry, Casey," Nolan said as he climbed into the car. "It's not our story, anyhow."

"No," she agreed tightly, nevertheless frustrated. As soon as Rico was sitting next to her she demanded, "What exactly does it mean?"

"*L'hanno ucciso?*" he said without looking at her. "It means, 'They have killed him.'"

"They have killed him," Casey repeated. The sentence struck her as implying a certain amount of foreknowledge. "Who has killed whom?"

There was a heavy silence. Casey heard a rustling noise and glanced back to find Nolan leafing through his guidebook. "Rico?" she prodded.

"I don't know who *he* was. But," he added grimly, "everyone in Alcamo knows who *they* are."

"The Mafia?"

"Welcome to Sicily," Rico said with heavy irony.

"Ah-ha! Here it is," Nolan exclaimed.

"What?" Casey asked.

"'*Murder.*'" Nolan held up Winnifred Hampton's guide to Sicily and read aloud. "'Murders are not uncommon, though they are usually reserved for *vendetta* (see entry). Foreigners are hardly ever murdered in Sicily.'"

"How reassuring," Casey muttered.

Chapter Two

They completed the rest of the drive in virtual silence. Rico made only one effort at conversation, and that was to ask about the notebook in which Casey started scribbling as soon as they were back on the road. It was a thick, sturdy spiral one, small enough to fit in her big purse. She always took notes assiduously, about everything, and her notebook was seldom out of reach. Rather than sharing this information with Rico, however, she was still annoyed enough to offer a clipped response that effectively eliminated conversation for the rest of the journey.

Nolan was shifting restlessly in the back seat of the car. Their arrival had so far been more eventful than either of them had anticipated, and she suspected that Nolan was beginning to realize that Sicily was a whole different world from the one he had known as a student and tourist in northern Italy.

While she had covered plenty of murders early in her journalistic career, Casey was still astonished to come upon the scene of a violent crime in a relatively small town in broad daylight.

It was quickly becoming apparent that her visit to this island would be anything but dull. She had a number of questions, but she would wait until later to pose them. After putting away her notebook, she contented herself with looking at the scenery. The austere, jutting cliffs she had admired upon leaving the airport now gave way to rolling green hills, lush with ripening crops under the cobalt-blue sky. Only the dusty wind kept the scenery from being perfect.

Rico's driving was slower and more sedate than before, though still a bit too flamboyant for Casey's taste, so the rest of the drive passed without any more stress to her system.

Eventually, they pulled into a little gravel lane that was evidently the Buteras' driveway. As they approached the house, Casey's lips curved in a soft smile of delight. She couldn't have imagined a better setting for a retired bandit. The house was a rambling, rustic, very old structure, probably eighteenth-century, although it appeared to have been modernized somewhat. It sat comfortably atop a hill overlooking the rolling fields around it, and its walls were covered with a cheerfully chaotic assortment of vines and flowers.

"Your father's home is beautiful," she said sincerely.

"Yes." Rico's expression expanded with pride. *"Bellissimo."*

As soon as he killed the engine, the entire family seemed to burst forth from the interior of the house. Casey and Nolan got out of the car and met their hosts halfway.

A beautiful, slender, sloe-eyed woman came rushing forward with both hands outstretched. "Miss McConnell, yes?"

"Yes," Casey admitted.

"We are so happy you are safely here," the woman assured her enthusiastically in English that was slightly slower and much more heavily accented than Rico's. "I am Daniela."

"How do you do?" Casey had spoken briefly to Daniela on two separate occasions after receiving the letter Rico and his father had written inviting her to come to Sicily for an interview.

"Come! Come into the house!" Daniela insisted. "My father is so excited you are here, I had to make him promise not to get up."

Two children and a grown man had also emerged from the house with Daniela. The children, a small boy and girl, were virtually dancing around Rico, shouting and laughing with obvious delight at his presence.

"*Bambini!*" Daniela shouted. *Children!* She shouted more things that Casey didn't catch, but the gist of it seemed to be that they should stop pestering their uncle and should come meet the American lady. The two of them scrambled over to Daniela and stood solemnly before her, tiny images of their mother, with big dark eyes, oval faces and curly black hair. "These are my children," Daniela said with obvious maternal pride. "Franco and Maria."

Each child took Casey and Nolan's hands in firm, adult little handshakes, murmuring the greeting *"piacere"* with polite, breathless formality. Then the boy laughed, the girl squealed and they both ran back to Rico, the excitement of visitors forgotten in the splendor of their uncle's smile.

His smile *was* splendid, Casey noticed with a ripple of something pleasant. Franco grabbed Rico's tight jeans and seemed to swarm up his body like a monkey until, with a little help from Rico, he was perched high on his uncle's shoulders. Little Maria's squeal turned to a high-pitched whine, which Rico quieted with words Casey couldn't understand. The tone, however, made it unmistakably clear that Maria could ride on Rico's shoulders as soon as her brother was finished.

Rico shook hands with the final member of the group, a stout, friendly-faced man in his late thirties who hung back a bit. Rico gestured briefly toward Casey and Nolan and drew the other man forward.

"Casey, Nolan," he said, "this is Daniela's husband, Paolo. He speaks no English, I'm afraid."

Casey stuck out her hand for the obligatory handshake and said, "Please tell him I'm sorry I can't speak Italian."

This statement was immediately followed by a long, earnest discourse from Paolo, who appeared to be either explaining that he was sorry he didn't speak English or else that he didn't mind that she spoke no Italian. His introduction to Nolan was equally loquacious, interrupted only by a brief exclamation of delighted surprise.

"What's he saying?" Casey asked in confusion.

"He's delighted that Nolan speaks Italian," Rico explained.

"Well, I don't exactly—" Nolan began uneasily.

"We are all standing here while Papa is shivering with excitement!" Daniela exclaimed suddenly. She said something to Paolo, evidently a request that he take care of the luggage, then led the party into the cool, airy interior of the old house.

Antonio Butera sat in a big easy chair in what appeared to be the living room. It was beautifully decorated with rugged, well-worn antiques, heavy wooden furniture and paintings that showed an eclectic and discerning taste in art. The old man was wearing a black sweater, a well-pressed white cotton shirt, and formal black trousers. His white hair shone softly in the sunlight pouring through the wide windows.

Casey had the impression that he had fussed all morning and tried to look his best for this meeting, and that made him seem endearing already. The dark eyes sparkling through his wrinkled, heavy features reminded her of Rico's.

"Signor Butera," she said softly, feeling like Stanley discovering Livingstone. From a brief hint over a year ago that one of Giuliano's original band of followers might still be living in Sicily—one that had avoided both death and jail—she had tracked him down until this face-to-face confrontation had become a reality. It was almost enough to make her forget her recent humiliation at *Sentinel*. Almost.

He reached toward her, clasping her palm between both of his big-knuckled, thick-fingered hands. He patted her hand several times, seeming too excited to speak, then he finally said, "Miss McConnell."

"Please call me Casey."

"And you must call me Totò."

"Totò?" she repeated with astonishment. When he nodded, she smiled and glanced at Nolan. "I think we're not in Kansas anymore."

To her surprise, Totò wheezed with laughter. "That is one of my favorite films," he said finally.

Nolan introduced himself and then asked, "Why Totò, sir?"

Helping his nephew slide to the floor, Rico answered, "It's for Antonio. We are great believers in nicknames here."

"A trait Sicilians have evidently carried with them to my country," Casey murmured.

"Ah, yes," Rico said, curiosity sparking in his eyes. "What do your initials stand for, K. C. McConnell?"

"Oh, it's a long story," Casey said dismissively.

"I'm not in a hurry." The way he arched his dark brows and folded his arms across his chest made him look extremely impertinent.

"*Imbecile!* If she wants to tell you, she will," Totò scolded good-naturedly. He added apologetically to Casey, "He has no refinement."

"I see." Casey felt her mouth curve as her eyes held Rico's. She saw the same warmth there that he showed toward his niece and nephew, a teasing look that charmed her against her better judgment. She sternly reminded herself that Italian men were notorious for their flattering but shallow attraction to foreign blondes.

At that point, Daniela insisted they all sit down to lunch, which was nearly ready. Since Casey couldn't abide airplane food and hadn't eaten much en route, she was starved and felt immensely relieved to know the family had apparently counted on this. Paolo carried their suitcases upstairs, then hustled the children off to the bathroom to wash up. Rico helped his father to the dining room with a gentleness and devotion to the old man that Casey found touching.

Her own family relationships were a world apart from the obvious affection and intimacy she had already noticed among the Buteras. She wondered what it was like to be so close.

"I had hoped we could enjoy our first meal together outside in the *cortile*," Daniela said to Casey and Nolan, "but unfortunately, we have *scirocco* today."

"You have what?" Casey asked, taking a seat at the long dining room table.

"*Scirocco,*" Rico repeated, sitting directly across from Casey. "Hot winds from the south. They carry the dust of the Sahara straight up from Africa."

"Oh, you mean it's not always this windy?" Casey said with a feeling of enormous relief.

"Only when there is *scirocco,*" Totò said. "Once or twice a month. It lasts for a few days, then comes the rain."

"It sounds a lot more predictable than weather back home," Nolan said agreeably.

After few confusing exchanges during which everyone translated for everyone else, Paolo finally insisted that they speak only English for the benefit of their guests, assuring them that he wouldn't mind. Casey knew this because he spent five minutes explaining it to her in his friendly, earnest way, and then Rico gave her a brief, condensed translation.

Daniela piled some fabulous-looking pasta into their individual bowls, explaining that the sauce was *pesto trapanese*, a specialty of western Sicily. Whatever it was, it melted in Casey's mouth and was so delicious she had trouble not gobbling it like a growing teenager.

She was digging into her portion with gusto when Daniela said suddenly, "Rico, didn't you remember to get bread?"

Casey's head shot up and she looked across the big table at Rico. He went still as he met her eyes. They stared at each other for a long, silent moment, and there was a fierceness in his expression that burned straight through her.

Finally Rico put down his fork and met his sister's curious gaze. After a glance at his father, he said, "We stopped in Alcamo for only a moment. There had been a killing right outside the *panificio,* so I came straight home without going in for bread."

Rico met Casey's eyes again briefly, and she suddenly wondered if he would have even mentioned the scene to his family if she and Nolan hadn't been there.

Totò grunted and stabbed his pasta with his fork. "Terrible! This is a terrible thing for you to see, so soon after your arrival."

"Are such things common?" Casey asked. "Public killings in broad daylight?"

"They are not *un*common," Daniela admitted unhappily. "But this is shocking! One sees such things in the newspapers almost every day, but seldom in person. How terrible for you!"

"What's the cause?" Nolan asked.

"Mostly drug wars, isn't it?" Casey asked. She had read up on Sicily as much as time would permit before coming here. Most of her research, however, had concerned events of forty years ago, and she had only a superficial knowledge of current problems.

"Yes," Daniela said. "*Mafiosi* and their drug wars."

"*Mafiosi?*" Casey repeated. "That means members of the Mafia?"

"*Sì.* But these young men, they are savages," Totò said contemptuously. "It is not like it used to be."

"Not like what?" Rico said critically. "Like the old days? Stop it, Papa. These men were *always* savages. They were always brutal, violent killers and extortionists, and you are wrong to pretend they used to have some sort of feudal integrity."

"We would not be here, if it were not for the honor of certain men," Totò responded, shaking a finger at Rico.

"Those 'men of honor' would have sacrificed you without blinking, had you not made it worth their while to help you," Rico said cynically.

Casey wanted to ask them to clarify a few points, but within moments Rico and Totò had forgotten about their guests and started arguing in rapid Italian, punctuating their angry remarks with expressive gestures, frequently interrupting each other or even talking at the same time.

What would have been an embarrassing outburst in an American family seemed to be taken as a matter of course in this family. Paolo tried to answer the children's questions, Daniela sided with Totò and Rico argued with everybody. Casey listened in confused fascination as the decibel levels rose, but apparently only she and Nolan thought shouting at the table was at all unusual. She had thought it would be too rude to bring her notebook to the table with her, so she reminded herself to make a note after lunch about what had led up to this incomprehensible argument and to ask about it later.

Finally, Totò chuckled and looked across at Casey. "He is a rebel, our Enrico."

"Really?" Casey asked. "Like his father?"

Totò chuckled again. Rico rolled his eyes, and shook his head. "My father was a bandit, not a rebel," he reminded her with a slight curve to his full lips. "Which is perhaps," he added, obviously wanting to have the last word, "why he is so lenient when he talks about men who were basically thieves and killers."

"Rico works very hard against the Mafia," Daniela explained seriously, "so he is very opinionated. Please eat some more."

Casey guiltily accepted another plateful of pasta, trying not to think about her thighs. "What kind of work do you do, Rico?"

"I'm a civil engineer."

Casey frowned. "What does engineering have to do with the struggle against organized crime?"

"In this country, everything," he said wearily.

"Please," Totò interjected, "don't encourage him to tell you this story. It goes on forever."

Rico cast his father an exasperated look before saying, "No, of course not. Better we should talk about some crazy patriot who died of stupidity forty years ago. Why trouble a visiting journalist with the real problems of our country?"

"Rico!" Daniela scolded, obviously shocked at this irreverent reference to the esteemed Salvatore Giuliano.

"Casey came to see me, not you," Totò reminded Rico austerely. Rico made an irritable gesture of acquiescence and turned his attention to his pasta.

Casey fell silent again, beginning to think it would be easier to tackle the Buteras one at a time. They were certainly a volatile family. They had already dropped numerous interesting hints into her lap, and lunch wasn't even over. Natural curiosity was one of her greatest professional assets, but she knew when to pursue and when to back off—which was another important professional asset. So she concentrated on her delicious pasta accompanied by a fabulous dry white wine that she was told came from their own little vineyard.

When she had finished her second heaping helping of pasta, she sat back in her chair feeling replete and at peace with the world. Daniela and Paolo cleared the table together, refusing any offers of help. At that point, Casey decided to try a different angle.

"Why do you keep referring to Sicily as a country, Rico? Isn't it a province of Italy?"

He shrugged. "Sicily is a province of Italy, true, but we were granted a certain amount of autonomy in 1947 to appease our, uh, separatist instincts. Sicily has been dominated by many foreign conquerors, of which the Italians are merely the most recent. However, Sicily couldn't survive as a separate nation in the modern world. Perhaps it never could have," he added pensively. "But most people here will tell you that we are a distinct and separate people from the Italians, despite the obvious similarities. And most Italians would agree."

"I know that after his early years as a bandit, Giuliano was made Colonel Giuliano, the western region commander of the Army for Sicilian Independence—backed by the Separatist Party," Casey said slowly. She asked Totò, "Were you a Separatist?"

"Perhaps," Totò said vaguely. "It's hard to remember what I believed as a young man, and in such different circumstances. I know that I hated the government in Rome, but I don't think I ever really considered the realistic alternatives in those days. However, Giuliano was a Separatist, and he was a very convincing man. And times were very, very bad in Sicily."

"Tell me how it began," Casey urged. Although she didn't have her notebook handy, she could always ask him to repeat pertinent information at another time. She knew the historical facts, but Totò's personal reminiscences would be the essence of her article. "I read that Giuliano became a bandit in 1943 when he shot and killed a soldier."

"Not a soldier," Totò said. "A *carabiniere.*"

"What's the difference?" asked Nolan.

"The *carabinieri* are the national police. The *polizia* are the local police. The *vigili urbani*... Well, it gets confusing, and they are not part of this story anyhow," Rico said.

"We were all very hungry in 1943. Western Sicily was nearing starvation," Totò said, his face bearing the sad memories.

"Why?" Casey asked. On the way here, the local farms had looked fruitful to her city-bred eyes.

Rico interrupted his father to explain passionately, "Sicily has always suffered chronic poverty. That's why there are so many Sicilians in America. Mismanagement of land, greedy aristocrats and powerful *mafiosi*, corrupt officials and an impotent bureaucracy, water wastage—"

"Rico, she asked Papa," Daniela said, interrupting.

Totò cleared his throat. "There was not enough food for the poor even in the best of times, and 1943 was not the best of times. During their retreat, the Germans took as much food from Sicily as they could carry. The supplies that remained were looted in the confusion that followed the collapse of the Fascist government. The offices responsible for allocating food were scarcely functioning under those circumstances, and there was also so much destruction due to the war—highways, railroads, even Palermo itself."

Totò shook his head in remembered sorrow and added, "So poor people couldn't get bread and pasta, let alone meat. And in Montelepre, where Giuliano and I lived, we were all poor."

"Of course, the *mafiosi* continued to eat well," Rico added persistently.

Totò ignored him. "Salvatore Giuliano was a good boy who knew how to take care of his family." He paused and took a deep breath. "The *carabinieri* caught him smuggling a couple of sacks of black-market grain, transporting it back to Montelepre. He resisted arrest, knowing his family would starve if he were in prison."

"Of course he cared nothing for himself," Rico said with just enough sincerity to sound dreadfully sarcastic.

Totò was evidently used to it, for he ignored him again. "During his escape he was severely wounded, and he accidentally killed a *carabiniere* with his pistol."

"And that was the beginning of his career as an outlaw," Casey murmured.

"Yes," Totò confirmed. "He was a bandit from that moment until his death in 1950."

"And when exactly did you join him?"

Rico began speaking softly with his niece and nephew who were clearly getting bored, but Casey sensed he was still paying attention to the discussion. Despite his attitude, she suspected that he was drawn to the intriguing story of the romanticized bandit and his own father's lawless youth.

"Shortly after Giuliano became an outlaw, the *carabinieri* came to Montelepre to search for him. I was his friend, and I lived not far away. They rounded up more than two dozen of us and arrested us with no evidence. And they insulted our mothers!"

Rico glanced at Casey and said, "You should know, Casey, that *la mamma* is the most sacred icon in Sicilian society."

She wondered where Rico's *mamma* was. Was Totò a widower? "How could this happen, Totò? How could the *carabinieri* simply conduct a house-to-house search and arrest so many of you without proof of collusion?"

"Ahh," Rico said. "Perhaps you are starting to understand why so many Sicilians wanted to secede from the government in Rome."

"You mean this was all legal?" Casey asked.

"It was the way of things here, in that time," Totò said.

"So you were all arrested?"

"*Sì.* Near Christmas, 1943. We were imprisoned in Monreale, in the hills above Palermo. And in January, Giuliano freed us from our prison."

"And that was when you joined him and became an outlaw," Casey said.

"Yes. Perhaps if times were different..." Totò shook his head. "But who can ever say what might have been? I was an escaped prisoner of the state, my family were starving and I knew there would be no justice. Especially not for me, for I had wounded a *carabiniere* during the arrest. And so I became an outlaw."

Casey knew they would have to go over this again later so that she could fit Totò's unrecorded story in with the known names, dates and places. But for the moment, she was content to start shaping the big picture in her mind. It was a story straight out of the old American West, a story of a good man wronged, of a strong people oppressed. The article would be great. Resting her palm against her full belly, she contemplated her next question.

"Here we are!" Daniela and Paolo entered the room and swooped down upon them, bearing enormous platters piled high with hot, aromatic food.

"There's more?" Casey croaked, watching Daniela fill her plate anew.

Daniela saw her startled face and laughed. "Of course! You didn't think we would serve you just pasta, did you?"

"Food is served one course at a time in Italy," Rico said, watching Casey's dismay with an expression of vast amusement.

"Yes, you Americans eat it all at once, don't you?" Daniela said, moving on to Nolan's plate. "I don't understand how you can digest properly. Now these are Sicilian *involtini,* and I think you will like them very much. That," she added, nodding toward the platter Paolo carried, "is *caponata.* It's my mother's special recipe."

"Be sure to eat a lot, Casey, or Daniela will be offended," Rico warned solemnly.

Casey glared at him, then looked at her plate in dismay. How many more courses would there be? She was beginning to feel very sorry for pigging out on Daniela's delicious pasta.

The *involtini,* thin slices of beef wrapped around the most delectable stuffing Casey had ever tasted, were indeed delicious as was the *caponata* which was made of eggplant, tomatoes, olives, capers, celery and a very generous amount of garlic. This was followed by fresh salad lightly flavored with olive oil, fresh lemons, salt and ground pepper. Then Daniela brought out a basket of fruit and a tray of *cannoli,* tubes of fried pastry filled with ricotta cheese mixed with sugar, bits of chocolate and candied citrus peel.

Fearing she would never again fit into her clothes, Casey tried to refuse dessert. She was shouted down and forced to try "just a little," lest she faint from hunger between now and the evening meal. By the time Paolo brought out little cups of *espresso* sweetened with generous spoonfuls of sugar, Casey began to see how eating could take up a major part of any Sicilian's day. She was also starting to realize that the unconditional Sicilian hospitality mentioned in her guidebook was no exaggeration.

"My poor thighs," she muttered to herself, thinking of all the aerobics classes she would have to squeeze into her crowded schedule when she returned to New York.

"Now it is time for siesta," Daniela announced when Casey finished licking the last bit of powdered sugar from her fingers. "You must be very tired after such a long journey."

Feasting and sleeping, Casey thought. This was obviously not a society for workaholics. "Well, I guess I could stand to lie down for an hour or two."

"I won't wake you. You sleep as long as you like," Daniela said maternally, rising from the table to show Casey and Nolan to their rooms.

As she climbed the stairs and strolled toward the back of the house, Casey realized that it was bigger than she had thought. She counted five bedrooms. She protested when she realized that she had taken little Maria's room, who would be forced to sleep in her brother Franco's room for the duration of Casey's visit. However, these objections were quickly overruled by her hosts.

Nolan settled into a room down the hall from Casey's. Of the remaining two bedrooms, one was for Daniela and Paolo, and the other was Totò's. Casey briefly wondered how the old man managed the stairs every morning and night, for he looked more feeble than she had expected.

Casey washed up, spoke briefly to Nolan, then entered her own room and closed the door behind her. This was the first quiet moment alone she had enjoyed since yesterday morning in her cramped apartment in New York.

She opened her suitcase, shook out a few clothes and started undressing. Then for no particular reason, she wondered where Rico slept. Did he live here or elsewhere? He wore no wedding ring, and since the Buteras were hardly a reticent family, she assumed she would have heard about a wife by now if he had one.

He had an intriguing magnetism, she reflected, as she brushed out her shoulder-length hair. Unlike the men she had known most of her life, he seemed totally natural, completely at ease with himself and his emotions. Feelings seemed to ripple out of him with refreshing grace and honesty. Well, perhaps *honesty* was the wrong word, she decided, recalling his casual unconcern for the truth.

Casey finished unpacking, putting her clothes in the spaces Daniela had made for her in the closet or the dresser. She slipped off her bra and drew a large T-shirt over her head.

Despite Rico's obvious charm, she had nevertheless found his protective this-isn't-fit-for-the-eyes-of-a-woman attitude extremely annoying today. She also wondered again why he had seemed reluctant to tell his family about the Mafia killing in Alcamo. She would ask him as soon as she had the opportunity.

She opened the shutters of her charming, simple room to gaze out at the expanse of hills and fields. Then she closed the shutters quickly as she was assailed by a wave of hot wind and fine dust. She coughed briefly, then began arranging her background reading materials and notebooks on the bedside table.

It might be interesting to include Rico's viewpoint in her article, since he seemed to disagree so vehemently with his father about a number of things. She would give it some thought, she decided.

Maybe, she admitted wryly as she settled down into the clean, crisp sheets of the bed, she was just trying to rationalize her fascination with his desert-prince looks. After all, it wasn't very often she met a man who looked like the embodiment of . . . well, of the harshly beautiful cliffs of the windswept island of Sicily.

"That'll sound pretty good in the article," she murmured before rolling over to hug her pillow.

Chapter Three

Rico relaxed quietly in the shadows of the garden, smoking a cigarette and trying to ease his restlessness. Nearby, he could see and hear Daniela nagging their father, urging him to lie down and rest for an hour. Her Italian was elegant and impeccable, as their mother had always encouraged. Their father answered her in dialect, irritably insisting that he was too excited to rest. But her nagging, he added, might give him another stroke.

Daniela finally gave up. She waved her arms around, chastising the sky for having cursed her with such a stubborn father, then she finally went inside. Within a few moments Rico heard her bedroom door slam and knew she had joined the rest of the household for an afternoon nap.

The courtyard was silent at last, disturbed only by the sounds of the wind playing against the shutters and teasing the fruit-laden trees. The musical tinkle of the small fountain was soothing and familiar. He inhaled deeply on his cigarette, then rubbed it out beneath one booted foot.

The scent and sound and memory of his mother was here, in the leafy shadows of the small garden she had planted around the fringes of the old courtyard. Rico knew his father habitually spent a great deal of time here since her death. The old man missed her terribly and had become pensive and moody since losing her. But today he had sparkled with some of his old vitality. Rico was glad he had advised Totò to go ahead and accept the interview with Casey McConnell.

Thinking of Casey made him restless again. He let out a heavy sigh, pushed himself away from the stone wall behind the fig tree, and stepped out into the sunlight.

"Rico!" Totò exclaimed. "Do you want me to also have a heart attack? Why do you sneak around like a thief in the night?"

"Sorry, Papa," Rico said blandly.

Totò's eyes narrowed suspiciously. "You were having a cigarette!" he accused.

"Yes, Papa. I was."

"It would kill you to share with your father?" Totò grumbled. "It would be so wrong for us to sit and have a cigarette together, the way we used to?"

"Papa, you know what the doctors—" Rico stopped speaking when Totò made a rude gesture that expressed his opinion of doctors. Instead he said, "You shouldn't be sitting out here in the wind, should you?"

Totò shrugged. "The sun feels good. And there will be rain in a day or two." There was a companionable silence before Totò said, "So what do you think of our American journalist?"

"She isn't what I expected," Rico hedged, squinting into the sky and wondering if Totò could be right about the rain.

"No," Totò agreed sagely. "I thought she would be like a television star. But I like her anyhow."

Rico smiled slightly. No, Casey McConnell wasn't at all like the plastic-looking television journalists he remembered from his years in America. She was younger than he had supposed, and certainly much prettier.

She had rumpled golden hair that escaped from her ponytail to fly about her face like a halo. She had lively, curious, inquisitive blue eyes that assessed her surroundings with quick intelligence, yet there was a subtle vulnerability in them that made him want to protect her. And despite the American mania for skinny women that Rico had never understood, she was shaped like a real woman—smooth and strong and ripely curved.

He fumbled absently for the cigarette packet in his shirt pocket again, reminding himself—as he already had several times today—that there would be no point getting interested in a foreign journalist who wouldn't be around for long.

"I don't think she's married," said Totò. "No ring."

"No," Rico agreed. He struck a match, cupping his hand around it as he lit another cigarette in the windy courtyard. He reminded himself that American women lived very independently, just because Casey wore no wedding or engagement ring, didn't mean that there wasn't a man waiting for her back in America.

"Strange that her mamma should let her travel so far from home by herself," Totò mused, his eyes riveted on Rico's cigarette.

"She's not alone. The photographer came with her."

"He's a nice boy, but..." Totò rolled his eyes, silently expressing his lack of faith in the photographer's ability as a protector.

Rico grinned. "They do things differently in America. She doesn't need her mamma's permission to go far away. Her mamma may not even know she's here. You must remember what it was like there."

"They are a strange people," Totò admitted, shrugging to show his tolerance of the culture that had sheltered him for several years. "But someone should look after Casey. She is so young."

Rico suppressed a smile at Totò's fatherly concern. Casey was still a young woman, but she was certainly no child. She was perhaps thirty years old, perhaps a little less. But her skin was smooth, and only laugh lines around the eyes gave away her age. Her voice was warm and feminine, and when she walked, her hips swayed with a naturally provocative rhythm that drew his fascinated gaze again and again.

Enough, he warned himself. Surely she would be around only long enough that to render any interest in her would be an exercise in frustration. Aware that he was doing his father no good, he gave in to the longing look in Totò's dark eyes and passed his cigarette to him. While Totò was contentedly taking a long, deep drag on it, Rico asked, "How long did you say the Americans will be here?"

"One week." Totò held his breath for a moment, then released a puff of smoke on a long, pleasure-filled sigh. He jerked his arm away when Rico tried to take the cigarette back. "Show some respect!" he snapped. "A man gets a little ill, his family think they can push him around."

"Two more puffs, and that's all," Rico said sternly, thinking guiltily of how Daniela would scold if she could see them now.

Totò grunted. "I had thought they would send someone older."

Rico shrugged. "I'm sure she knows her job, Papa."

"She looks too much like a girl," Totò protested. "I don't know if I can tell her ugly things."

Rico glanced curiously at him. "Do you have ugly things to tell?" His father had said more to him about the past than to Daniela, but Rico sometimes wondered what secrets the old man had kept all these years and was apparently now ready to reveal.

"I... Yes. Ugly things, my son. Dangerous things." Totò took another heavy drag on the cigarette and looked away from Rico's suddenly piercing stare.

"I didn't know you had such serious intentions for this interview," Rico said carefully.

Totò seemed not to have heard him. Instead he shook his head slowly, staring at the tip of the cigarette and muttering, "I thought she would look very big and tough. I thought an important American journalist would be more like...well, less like Casey, anyhow.''

''You don't have to tell her anything you don't want to, Papa,'' Rico reminded him quietly, aware that Totò's breath was suddenly a little harsh.

''But I do! I brought her here to tell all! But she is just a woman, a soft woman with pretty blue eyes and a white throat. She is not a big American magazine. By herself she is not this *Sentinel*.... I just don't know what to do!''

Rico took the cigarette away from Totò, cursing himself for having given it to him in the first place. His father was drawing air in short, harsh little gasps now.

''Papa, shh. Calm down,'' he urged. ''Take a deep, steady breath, that's it. Shh, don't think about the interview right now, just close your eyes and take a nice, slow breath.''

It was several minutes before Totò had calmed down enough for Rico to help him upstairs to his bedroom. After leaving the old man napping fitfully, Rico finally began to doubt that the excitement of the *Sentinel* interview was the best thing for his father.

It was dark when Casey awoke. She cursed and slid out of bed, feeling both annoyed and guilty that she had already wasted most of her first day in Sicily by eating and sleeping. The long journey, the series of turbulent events that had followed, the enormous meal and the delicious wine with which Totò kept refilling her glass had combined to virtually knock her out for—she checked her watch—five hours.

She dressed quickly, slipping into dark olive-colored slacks and a pale yellow blouse. When she left her room and went into the bathroom to wash up and put on some lipstick, she noticed how terribly quiet the house seemed. Someone had thoughtfully left a light burning for her at the top of the uneven staircase. She descended it and looked into the *salone* and the dining room. No one appeared to be home.

"Hello?" she called. Where had they all gone? She stepped into the kitchen and tried again. "Hello?"

A tall, menacing figure loomed large in the doorway, blocking out the meager light of the moon. Casey fell back with a silent gasp, then let her breath out on a sigh of sheepish relief. "Rico! You startled me."

"*Scusa,*" he said. "I heard you call."

"Where is everyone?"

He tilted his head consideringly, but she couldn't see his expression in the darkened doorway. "Daniela and the children went to visit our cousins. There's to be a wedding, and there are many plans to make. Paolo took Papa into the village so he could sit in the piazza with all the men and brag about the important American journalist who has come to learn the story of his life."

Casey smiled at the fond amusement in his voice. "And Nolan?"

"He awoke as they were leaving and asked to go, too. He will find the conversation quite incomprehensible," Rico added. "Naturally my father wanted to take you with him, but Daniela said we must let you sleep, so Nolan was most welcome."

"As proof that I really exist?"

"Certainly. My father has been known to tell a few tales in his time."

Like his son. "Why didn't you go along?"

"Are we savages with no manners?" he asked lightly. "Someone needed to be here to entertain you when you woke up."

"And you drew the short straw?"

She saw the flash of his grin in the shadows. "Not exactly. I had just returned home, and they told me to look after you as I was heading for the shower."

"Oh." She wondered where he had gone while she slept.

After a brief silence he said, "Please, come out into the *cortile.* It is a beautiful evening."

He stepped aside and led her out of the sheltering house. The *cortile* was a charming courtyard, walled in by the house on three sides and overlooking a garden on the fourth side. Farther down the gently sloping hill was another wall with a wooden gate.

The courtyard was paved with pale, rough stones and contained a table and several scattered chairs. The surrounding walls were covered with vines and riotously colorful blossoming plants. An enormous tree dominated the courtyard whose charm was made complete by the small fountain at its center. A statue, presumably portraying an ancient goddess, spread her voluptuous arms wide, palms facing the ground. Water sprinkled from her fingertips to fall delicately into the basin surrounding her feet.

"Oh, this is beautiful. This is like a tiny piece of paradise," Casey exclaimed. "I love fountains!"

"Then Italy is the country for you," Rico said, enjoying her pleasure. "Even when water is rationed, even when crops are dying, we always manage to find enough water for our fountains."

She walked to the fountain and bent over to let her fingers trail through the tiny fall of rain created by the goddess. Rico noticed, perhaps not entirely against his will, how her dark trousers outlined her lovely rounded bottom. She looked very firm, as if she walked a lot. Well, he supposed that reporters did walk a lot. The smooth cheeks of her bottom would fit his hands nicely, and her thighs would cushion him.... *Basta,* he chided himself, *that's enough.*

Casey turned to face him, idly shaking her fingers dry. He thought how exotic she looked under the rising moon, under the borning stars of the Mediterranean sky. Her hair shone like golden strands of the finest silk, her skin looked as aristocratically white as the foaming, fresh milk in the sturdy wooden buckets of his childhood. How he had loved the taste of fresh milk....

"The wind has died down," Casey said.

Her voice sounded breathless to him. He realized he was staring. He tried to think of something to say, wondering why his usual glibness had deserted him. "Yes. *Scirocco* is gone. It has left only a clear night and the scent of the desert.''

Casey drew in a deep breath and stretched, drawing the soft fabric of her pale blouse across her breasts. Rico closed his eyes, trying to ignore his senses. ''The desert?'' she said languidly. ''It smells more like flowers to me. What is that smell?''

He smiled. She looked sleepy-eyed and lazy as she spun in a slow circle, looking for the source of that scent. ''It's wisteria,'' he said, gesturing to the creeping plants covering the walls. ''Those purple blossoms.''

''They smell divine.'' She drew another deep breath and sighed. ''Who planted all these flowers and that garden over there?''

''My mother started it. Daniela keeps it going.''

''Then the farm belongs to your father?''

''It belongs to the family,'' he said vaguely.

She leaned against the edge of the fountain and regarded him steadily, apparently becoming more alert. ''Your mother planted these things? Is she... Is Totò a widower?''

''Yes. Since last year.''

''I'm so sorry.'' She had a throaty way of making the trite phrase carry meaning. She sounded truly sorry. ''How did she die?''

''Hit-and-run driver in Palermo,'' he said shortly.

''Oh, Rico, how terrible!'' No wonder Totò's face bore heavy marks of grief.

''Yes,'' he agreed, his face showing a flash of pain as vivid as his usual smiles.

The thought of sudden death reminded her of some of the questions she had stored up for him. ''I wanted to ask you about today. The killing in Alcamo.''

Rico shifted restlessly and reached into his pocket. ''Do you smoke?'' he asked, offering her a cigarette.

''No.''

''Americans usually don't, do they?''

"Fewer and fewer." She watched him light up and then said, "How much do you know about today?"

He looked surprised. "What makes you think I know anything?"

"You wouldn't have mentioned it to your family if I hadn't been there, would you?" At his sharp stare, she nodded and confirmed, "I noticed. And yet Daniela said such things are not uncommon."

He took a long drag on his cigarette before saying with disgust, "That is a gross understatement. At one point the area between the three towns of Bagheria, Casteldaccia and Villabate was labeled *il triangolo della morte*—the triangle of death—by the press, because a Mafia feud there produced a corpse a day for several weeks running. And Palermo is known for its 'illustrious corpses'—the bodies of magistrates, investigators and government officials found riddled by bullets or blown up by car bombs."

She stared at him for a moment, then gestured to their peaceful, pastoral surroundings in the moonlit night. "It's hard to reconcile that level of violence with this setting, isn't it?" She frowned thoughtfully. "Did you want to avoid upsetting your father by mentioning it?"

Rico blew out a long stream of smoke. "Believe it or not, I wanted to avoid arguing with my father." His dark eyes glinted. "But of course, I failed."

"Why do you argue about Mafia killings?" she asked curiously.

"We don't argue about the killings. We argue about the 'old' Mafia and the 'young' Mafia, about the way things are and the way my father imagines they were." He flicked an ash off the end of his cigarette before he added wearily, "Mostly we argue about *omertà*."

"I've heard that word before," Casey said.

He made a dismissive gesture. "Probably in silly movies and novels that glorify it."

"*Omertà*," she murmured, remembering her reading. "To be a man."

He grimaced at the definition. "That is without a doubt how it is perceived, and we will only be free when that changes."

"Then it doesn't mean manliness to you?" It was a reporter's question, an attempt to make him expand his ideas, express them aloud. But it was asked with more than professional interest.

"*Omertà* is the greatest sickness in Sicily," he said, studying the glowing tip of his cigarette. "It is the Sicilian code of silence, fear inspired and honor-bound, that ensures the police can never find a witness to any Mafia crime. But it goes so much further than that."

"But surely there was a witness today," Casey insisted. "Someone was killed in broad daylight in a public thoroughfare."

"Ah, but there will be no witnesses." He looked up and captured her gaze, wanting to make her understand the shadowy ways of his society. "That is the nature of *omertà*. You could question every single citizen in that town, including the ones who were standing within a dozen feet of the victim when it happened, but you would find no witnesses. They will claim the dust got in their eyes, they left their glasses at home or that the police are mistaken, it was really someone *else* who got a good look at the executioner this morning."

"Well, sure, they're afraid. It's like that anywhere. But—"

"And anyone who *did* come forward to offer evidence would risk his own life and his family's—for ever since they assassinated Alberto dalla Chiesa and his young wife, the Mafia do not scruple to murder women and children. He would also almost certainly be shunned by his neighbors for having broken the code of silence." When Rico saw her stunned expression, he added, "Often, even the dead man's own family won't give evidence, Casey. That is how powerful *omertà* is in Sicily."

"I know that the Mafia were all-powerful during Giuliano's time, but surely things are changing," Casey argued, recalling her research.

"There is a great deal of anti-Mafia sentiment sweeping the country," Rico admitted, "and hundreds of *mafiosi* were jailed a couple of years ago, thanks to the maxi-trial in Palermo. But Casey, you cannot erase in a few years something that has existed for centuries. *Omertà* has been our way of life for so long. It is even older than Mafia."

"How old?" she prodded.

He shrugged. "This island has been dominated by foreign conquerors for some twenty-five centuries. Phoenicians and Greeks, Romans, Vandals and Ostrogoths, Byzantines, Arabs and Berbers, the Normans, the Germans, the French, the Spanish, the Austrians and finally, the Italians." He sighed. "Just about everyone except the Japanese, it seems. For the Sicilian, there was never any justice from foreign rulers who only cared about what they could take from his island. And so justice and retribution became entirely personal matters to Sicilian people.

"That's why 'to be a man' is to keep silent, to never tell the authorities anything. If a man's wife and children were murdered before his eyes and he knew perfectly well who had done it, he would still say nothing to the authorities. A man took care of his own business, extracted his own vengeance, and did not share his *vendetta* with outsiders. And the authorities were always outsiders in this country."

Casey brushed her hair away from her shoulders, interested in his convictions, attracted by his passion. "So you're saying that the Mafia arose out of a system that already existed, rather than vice versa?"

"Well, that's *my* theory." He grinned boyishly, stealing her breath. "Some say the word 'mafia' comes from an Arabic word meaning 'sanctuary,' and that the roots of the 'honored association' may have sprouted a thousand years ago."

"Sanctuary from the conquerors and their lack of justice?"

"Presumably. As we know it, Mafia developed in the nineteenth century, after Italian unification. They were essentially agrarian at first, a sort of protection society, developing their power over the estates and peasantry of absentee landlords. Of course, they were very clever and learned to urbanize and organize with the advent of the twentieth century."

"So what is this difference between old and young Mafia that you and your father argue about?"

"Oh, you could fill books with the subject," he assured her. "Even I will admit that the character of the Mafia changed when they moved into the drug trade. Tomasso Buscetta claimed that that's why he betrayed *omertà* and ratted on his fellow *mafiosi* at the maxi-trial. He liked to say he was of the old school—men of respect, men of honor, as my father would say."

"Would *you* honor and respect such men?" she asked curiously.

"They were not philanthropists, Casey, they only wanted to be admired and feared in equal measure. *You* would say they were criminals and extortionists, *they* would say they merely liked doing favors and giving advice and that, unfortunately, certain men sometimes had to be taught a harsh lesson."

"But what would *you* say?" she persisted, aware that he had evaded her question.

"I would say that times have changed irrevocably. Once upon a time, when a local politician would not do the bidding of a *mafioso*, the *mafioso* could nudge the man a few times, and then look around for a replacement when he realized he wasn't getting anywhere. Now, with the drug trade, a recalcitrant politician or determined investigator can cost certain *mafiosi* millions of dollars a day. And so there is only time for a quick, brutal murder."

"With no witnesses," she said huskily.

"That is still usually the case. But the Mafia has finally alienated the people it once claimed to protect. No Sicilian can forgive the killing of women and children. There is now a whole generation of young people that want to be free of the old ways, the shameful past. They protest publicly against the Mafia, while the word could not even be spoken aloud during my father's youth." He smiled again and tiredly rubbed the back of his neck. "But me, I am impatient. I want to see everything change now, not *someday*. But I know it must take time. The tentacles of the octopus still reach into everything."

"The octopus?" She was blank for a moment, then dredged up more information from her memory. "The octopus symbolizes the Mafia, right?"

"Yes. Besides being a very tasty meal," he added.

"A tasty meal?"

Casey's expression of fastidious disgust charmed him. "Truly. Perhaps I will have the opportunity to cook an octopus for you before you leave Sicily."

"Don't feel obliged," she said dryly. "Is the octopus the symbol of the Mafia because of the eight long tentacles?"

"Yes. And if you cut off a tentacle, a new one grows in its place. The octopus squirts a murky black fluid which forms a dark cloud that obscures the vision of its enemies. And some kinds of octopuses can inject a poison that paralyzes their prey."

"Very appropriate," Casey conceded. "Do the tentacles really reach into everything, as you said?"

"At the moment. And so does *omertà*. The adherence to silence in the face of authority has translated into many qualities among Sicilians. All knowledge becomes a valuable commodity not to be given away to strangers for any reason. *Omertà* is the reason an adult will look half-witted and deny knowing where his own next-door neighbors live when asked by a stranger. It is the reason six different people will answer the same question six different ways, and the truth will lie somewhere in the middle of all that."

"That could make things very sticky for a journalist," Casey said.

"Didn't you say you love a challenge?" Rico reminded her with mischief. "Sicilian writers have often shown in their novels how extensively this attitude permeates Sicilian society. I think it was Leonardo Sciascia who referred to the 'low moral latitude' of Sicily. There are so few absolutes. Everything is a compromise here, and truth is the currency of power.'' He scowled and added, ''Yes, things are slowly changing, but it doesn't help us when American journalists and novelists try to romanticize organized crime, extortion and imposed silence in our country.''

Now we come to it, Casey thought. ''I'll keep that in mind.''

He lowered his cigarette and gave her a long, thoughtful stare with those dark, thick-lashed eyes. ''Will you? Giuliano himself was a rigid enforcer of *omertà.* Ask my father about all the informers Giuliano and his bandits killed.''

''Your father killed, too?''

''You will have to ask him that.''

Her eyes locked with the opaque hardness of his gaze. ''So it's more than just a custom or story to you, isn't it? Your own father has killed to protect the silence.''

He looked startled for a moment, then sheepish. ''I can see that you are a very good journalist, Casey McConnell. You've had me talking ever since we came out here, and now I have already given away some of my father's interview to you.''

She smiled, acknowledging the compliment and his desire to back away from a topic she sensed was more than a little uncomfortable for him. He was as loyal to his father as he was critical of *omertà.*

''Questions are my job,'' she admitted, ''but I like talking to you.''

''I like talking to you, too,'' he replied with the open honesty of a child.

There seemed little to say suddenly, and the silence lengthened. He was, she acknowledged with a sudden feeling of self-consciousness, not only the most attractive man she had ever interviewed, but also the most intriguing. When she realized a moment later that she hadn't been *in-*

terviewing him after all, but talking to him, woman to man, because his vibrancy and his inconsistencies fascinated her, she started to feel distinctly uncomfortable.

His eyes grew heavy-lidded. Casey caught her breath, aware that her heartbeat had picked up. The moonlight gleamed off his black hair, and every shrug, gesture, or movement pulled his jeans tightly across his hard thighs, stretched his shirt over his contoured shoulders or pulled the neckline away from the firm, golden-brown column of his throat. Why was she noticing these things? *Everybody's* clothes stretched across their bodies when they moved. Why did it hold such dangerous fascination for her on this occasion?

Without warning, he started walking toward her, a slow, sensual smile teasing around his full lips. Those were lips, she thought, that a woman could really get into kissing. *Stop it.* They had been talking about organized crime only a moment ago, and now she was thinking about kisses in the moonlight. Too much Saharan dust, she decided.

He stopped directly in front of her. She had to tilt her head to hold his gaze. After a tense staring contest, which she apparently lost, he let his gaze rove over her hair, face and neck. She wondered what he thought. *She* was thinking about the long torso in front of her, about the straight line of buttons stretching vertically down the length of his torso, about the way those buttons seemed to suddenly want to be *un*buttoned. Trying not to look, she nevertheless saw the way the seams running down the front of his shirt moved gently in and out with his shallow breaths. Even with her eyes locked resolutely on his face, she could see the snug way his jeans fit his hips, the way they molded his firm thighs and—

"Well, I'm sure glad that wind stopped," she said loudly.

She saw his lips twitch. "I have questions, too, you know. I am very curious about you," he murmured.

"Tall, dark, handsome strangers always say that to me."

He grinned and suddenly plopped down beside her on the edge of the fountain. His mood had apparently taken another unpredictable swing. She didn't know if she was relieved or disappointed.

He took a final puff of his cigarette, stubbed it out and said, "I wonder why you are here."

"To talk to your father, of course."

"I mean, why should you travel thousands of miles to interview a man in a backwater province of another country to learn about events that took place over forty years ago?"

"Because he's still alive," she said simply. "Because it's different and interesting. Because he has never consented to give an interview before, and he will present a new perspective on intriguing events."

"How did you find my father in the first place? What got you interested in doing this story?"

Since he seemed genuinely curious, she decided to tell him. "Well, there was a rather mediocre American novel a few years ago written about Giuliano."

"Yes, I remember it."

"Followed by a dreadful film."

"I remember that, too." His expression made his opinion clear.

"An article caught my eye at about that time. The one thing that stood out in my mind was that the writer kept insisting that the truth itself was so interesting, so fantastically improbable, that it needn't have been so fictionalized." She shrugged. "I guess it was a combination of things that made me look a little further. The physical beauty of Sicily in the photos and films I saw, the paradox of an idealistic bandit on horseback, robbing from the rich and giving to the poor—and all of this in modern Italy."

"But you have had bandits in America. Jesse James, Billy the Kid, Butch Cassidy and the Sundance—"

"Yes, but none of them were so recent. And none of them were apparently so idealistic. I suppose the real fascination of Giuliano's story was the classic element of tragedy. Sicily bred him, nursed him, fostered his career, worshiped him, and then Sicily finally killed him. I mean, it was Gaspare Pisciotta, Giuliano's best friend and co-chieftain, who betrayed and murdered him."

"Yes," Rico agreed. "Though many others tried to claim credit for the kill."

"I know. I've seen microfilms of the newspaper and magazine accounts. Even stories printed simultaneously about Giuliano's death contained wildly conflicting information. I didn't understand it, at the time." She looked thoughtfully at the starlit sky. "Things are very confusing here, aren't they?"

"Another understatement," he said wryly. "So get back to how you found my father."

"Well, when I was considering doing a piece about Giuliano and started researching, I discovered a number of interesting things. The lies, the contradictions, the mystery of Giuliano's death and so on. Concrete information was so hard to find. There's only one biography in English about Giuliano, Gavin Maxwell's *Bandit*—and that's been out of print since before I was born.

"The most interesting thing of all was to learn that there are still people alive who knew Giuliano, who perhaps know some of the answers. But some won't talk at all—code of silence, I suppose—and the others don't seem to know anything new.

"Then I met an old Italian journalist during an assignment. Just out of curiosity, I started pumping him. And he mentioned your father to me. Well, sort of."

"What does that mean?"

"This journalist told me that there was an old man living in western Sicily who had once been one of Giuliano's band of original followers. He said the man had escaped the fate of many of Giuliano's followers by fleeing to America in the late 1940s and that the man had returned to Sicily several years later and has lived quietly ever since."

"And you decided to track him down?"

"Yes. The Italian journalist discouraged me, saying this man had never once consented to give an interview during the past forty years, claiming he knew nothing of Giuliano's life and death. And since the journalist didn't even remember the man's name, it would obviously take me a while to track him down—which it did.''

"You were very determined."

"Yes. I'm always determined when it comes to my work," she told him.

"I admire your tenacity, Casey, but I don't understand it."

"Why not?"

He looked at her with those chocolate-dark eyes, his changeable expression serious and sincere at the moment. "You obviously have abilities, yet you come to a country like this, a country torn by desperate problems, and all you want to write about is something that has been explored and argued and fictionalized to death, something that has been over since before we were born."

Casey shifted uncomfortably and felt her stomach churn. Was the story really so trivial? Surely not. "But there are still a lot of unanswered questions."

"They will remain unanswered."

She looked at him sharply. "Why do you say that?"

He grinned and held his hands up. "Don't look at me that way. *I* don't know what my father's going to tell you. But even a man like him, who still believes in *omertà,* surely cannot have kept secrets this long that are important enough to win you a Pulitzer Prize."

Casey sighed. He had hit a little too close to the mark with that comment. "Never mind the prizes, Rico. I'm just looking for a great story. Listen, I think the problems of modern Sicily are newsworthy, but that's not what I was sent here to write about." She glanced at him from under her lashes. "Anyhow, your father is thrilled about this. Don't you want to see him have his moment in the sun?"

"Of course I do. I'm happy to see him so excited about something again. He has not been the same man since my mother's death. Just don't—" He stopped himself.

"Don't what?" she prodded.

Rico wrestled with his conscience for a moment and finally compromised by saying, "He tires easily, that's all."

"I—"

She was distracted by the crunch of gravel, the low rumble of a motor and the hooting of a horn.

"Paolo's car," Rico confirmed. He took her arm, helped her to her feet and guided her through the dark interior of the house to the entrance hallway.

Moments later, Paolo and Nolan burst through the back door, supporting Totò between them. Nolan and Paolo were loudly singing an old Beatles song, distinctly off-key, while Totò hummed along and occasionally made up a word or two.

"Casey!" Nolan exclaimed once they were inside and had seated Totò comfortably. "You know, I'm going to love it in this country! Friendliest people in the world! By the way, everyone in town knows you're here. Tomorrow may be a little hectic, since Totò has invited them all over to meet you."

Rico said something to Paolo, who responded. Rico said something more urgently, and Paolo pressed his hands together like he was praying and said something very long and involved, all of it very loud. Rico said something else, then Paolo drew his shoulders up around his ears, turned his palms to the sky, and spoke some more, sounding rather desperate this time.

"What's going on?" Casey demanded.

"I asked him if Papa really invited everyone over. He says yes."

"That's all?" Casey said disbelievingly. This had been going on for nearly five minutes.

"We're arguing about who has to tell Daniela."

"Ahh," Casey said wisely. Then she looked at Totò. "It will be difficult to interview you with half the village here."

Totò waved this problem aside. "So we will interview the next day, or the day after that."

"Totò, I have to have everything done before I leave in exactly one week."

Totò smiled. "So if it's not done, you will leave a little later."

"It doesn't work that way," she said, shaking her head.

"Is this a way to live?" Totò said incredulously. "Things must be done by this or that moment? Schedules must rule you? *È pazzo!*" The exclamation was obviously derogatory. "Rico, you talk to her."

"Despite his years in America, my father operates on Sicilian standard time," Rico said wryly. Totò made another comment and then began humming loudly again, chuckling in between notes.

"Were you just saying that he tires easily?" Casey asked dryly.

Rico's eyes met Casey's. Something hot flashed between them with startling speed and recklessness. After a moment Rico became aware of a heavy silence. He looked around the room to see the others staring at the two of them. Confused, he said, "Come into the kitchen, Papa. Daniela will be back late, and she told me to give you your medicine at the proper time."

Rico helped his father out of the *salone*. Paolo went with them, talking a blue streak. Casey plopped into a chair across from Nolan. He regarded her with speculative curiosity.

"Anything interesting happen while I was gone?" he asked.

"No." She caught his disbelieving look. "No. Of course not." When he continued to stare, she added, "I'm on *assignment*, Nolan."

"Just asking," he said with exaggerated innocence.

"Leave the asking to me. You just take the photographs."

She tried to brush away the growing fascination she felt for Rico on a purely personal level, the warm thrumming of her blood that he had set off while discoursing on the ills of his country. It would only interfere with her job, and she wouldn't be here long enough to experience anything except frustration where he was concerned.

She was equally eager to brush away the doubts he had raised within her, but they wouldn't disappear any more willingly than the aura of enchantment tingling along her skin. Though she fully suspected *Sentinel* had been throwing her a sop by sending her to Sicily, she was determined to make this as interesting a story as the one they had denied her. And Rico's assessment of the situation—that it was at best an old man's mildly interesting memories of a well-covered story—set off a chain reaction of fear and determination inside her.

Please, Totò, she begged silently, *don't let me down. I hope you've fooled your son all these years.*

Chapter Four

Totò was right about the rain. It rained relentlessly, dramatically, unceasingly throughout the following day.

Nolan had been right, too. With apparently half the local village tromping into the house to meet Casey, the "very famous American journalist" who had come to interview old Totò Butera, it was impossible to get any work done.

One local family had relatives in America whom they visited every couple of years. Consequently, they spoke enough English to chat pleasantly with Casey. When their children joined them after school, things really got lively, since the kids spoke excellent colloquial English with accents they'd obviously acquired from their cousins in New Jersey.

Old men wearing tweed caps, old women wearing black mourning, plumply pretty young women with babies and young men who stared at Casey with unnervingly obvious passion, cluttered up the house from morning till evening. Daniela took it all in stride, providing an endless supply of cold drinks, *espresso, cappuccino,* sweets and biscuits and ashtrays. Casey wondered wearily if *everyone* in Sicily smoked.

Nolan's work was less inhibited than Casey's, since he got a lot of great shots of Totò chatting with his friends and neighbors, posing in his *salone,* toasting Casey at the dining table and playing with his two grandchildren.

Casey tried to enjoy the experience rather than worry about how much time she was losing. She was unpleasantly aware, however, that not all of her frustration was due to being unable to begin her interviews today.

Rico had left the house first thing that morning, before she had arisen, and he still hadn't returned by the time the last of Totò's guests departed. Rather than craning her neck to see out the front window and jumping at every sound, Casey finally asked Daniela when he was expected back. When she was told he wasn't coming back, Casey's own reaction disturbed her more than the actual news did.

She was here to *work.* She was here to interview an old bandit, not to get acquainted and infatuated with his son. She was *not* going to feel dismayed to learn that Rico didn't live here but had his own apartment in Palermo.

"He stays here when he has work in this area, which is often lately. But certainly not every day."

"Oh. Well, I hope we get to see him again before we leave."

"Of course you will!" Daniela said, and left it at that.

Casey decided not to press her for something more specific. She went to bed that night feeling restless and dissatisfied. A wasted day, she thought bleakly. A day spent chatting in broken English with total strangers and mooning over a man she would never see again after the following weekend. She punched her pillow and vowed to do better tomorrow. Didn't this story mean everything to her right now? Hadn't she promised herself it would be *Sentinel*'s best story of the year?

The rain had let up by the following morning, and the sun burned bright in the dazzlingly blue Mediterranean sky. It was a land, Nolan declared, that was just begging to be photographed, and he disappeared with his cameras for the rest of the day.

Totò was exhausted from all his recent socializing, and Daniela's noisy scolding about it gave Casey a headache. Totò, in turn, insisted that Casey go amuse herself today. He would be feeling better tomorrow, he assured her.

Daniela apologized profusely for not being able to entertain Casey, but she had to take the children to school, then go help her cousins with their wedding preparations, then buy bread and groceries, then prepare lunch.... Casey assured her she didn't mind. She hadn't come to Sicily to be entertained. She had come here to work. She would read some of her research material while Totò rested and gathered strength.

By the time Rico showed up, Casey was going stir-crazy. She heard his car pull up while Daniela was boiling pasta, Totò was napping, the children were telling their mother about their day at school and she herself was taking notes from a battered copy of Gavin Maxwell's *Bandit*.

Casey tidied her flyaway hair and left her room to head down to the kitchen. She found Daniela and the children milling around Rico, who sat at the table, smiling as he leafed through Miss Winnifred Hampton's alphabetical guide to Sicily.

"Hello," Casey said.

Rico looked up at her, momentarily startled by the low, honey-smooth sound of her voice. Their eyes met, and he felt something warm stir inside him. His colleagues in Palermo had been surprised to see him so anxious to leave town early today in order to be on time for lunch with his family. He was *always* late, they had pointed out, so why should today be any different?

"*Ciao*, Casey." Today was different, he acknowledged silently, because she was here. He hadn't liked leaving here yesterday morning without even having a chance to speak to her. And he had been annoyed about not liking it; she was a foreigner, and she would be leaving in a few days. "Have you been having a good time?"

"Well," she said slowly, gliding forward and taking a seat near him at the table, "your family has been wonderfully hospitable and generous, but I'm afraid I haven't gotten any work done."

He tilted his head. "Why not?"

Before Casey could answer him, Daniela started speaking to him in rapid Italian as she bustled around the kitchen. Casey didn't need an interpreter to know that Daniela was telling him how their father had worn himself out with socializing and left "the famous American journalist" at loose ends.

"Ah, now I understand," Rico said with an indulgent smile.

"I'm behind schedule," Casey admitted.

"But this is always the case if you try to operate on an American schedule in a Mediterranean country," Rico chided. Casey rolled her eyes and he grinned. He liked the way she handled herself. He could see she was worried about her work, but trying to adjust to his family's ways without judging or criticizing them. He arched one brow inquisitively and asked, "Is this your guidebook?"

She shook her head. "It's Nolan's."

"It's priceless." He lowered his gaze to the page and read aloud, "'*Wine* comes in many reasonably palatable varieties in Sicily.' Sacrilege," he added. "We have the best wine in the world. '*Wine shops* sell bread, in addition to wine, as well as many other foodstuffs enjoyed by the lower orders.'"

"Winnifred was a bit pompous," Casey conceded.

"So where is Nolan?" When Casey explained he had gone off to photograph and explore and might not be back until much later, Rico said, "So you're really on your own, then? Well, I'll make it up to you this afternoon."

And although that was exactly what she had just decided she wanted, she nevertheless protested, "Please, Rico, I'm not your responsibility."

"But of course you are. I'm the one who told my father he should agree to do the interview with you."

That surprised her. "But... I mean, don't you have to work?"

"Officially, I only work half a day, six days a week."

"But *un*officially he is *always* working," Daniela added.

"Today I won't, though." He leaned an elbow on the table and studied Casey, admiring the soft sheen of her hair, the frank attraction in her expression and the supple swell and curve of her body under her clothes. "Since you apparently met all our neighbors yesterday, perhaps you would enjoy a little sight-seeing today? We are very near Segesta."

He was freshly shaven today, and the olive-skinned smoothness of his jaw invited her touch. She resisted touching him, but said, "If your father still isn't up to working with me today, then I'd love to go, Rico."

"*Bene*—fine. We will see in a moment."

Rico helped Totò downstairs a few minutes later, and one look at the old man told Casey that he wouldn't be up to anything except another nap when they were done eating. The meal was mercifully smaller than it had been the past two days, consisting only of spicy pasta and fresh bread, followed by salad and fresh fruit. Paolo showed up at the last moment, looking tired and muddy. Daniela and the children greeted him with as much exuberant affection as if they hadn't seen him since last week. Casey smiled at the warmth, even as she wondered how oppressive family life could become. She had already noticed that no one scrupled to interfere in anyone else's private business, and she supposed that was one of the disadvantages of being so closely knit.

Conversation was less volatile than usual in the Butera household, since Totò barely had the strength to eat, Paolo was obviously weary and Casey was too pensive to pose questions.

She was aware of the liquid softness of Rico's gaze moving over her features again and again throughout the meal, and it made the hot pepper and garlic she was eating seem bland in comparison to the excitement shooting through her. She knew where his gaze rested at any given moment, because her clothes would burn against her skin in that very spot, the soft jersey of her pale blouse spilling sensuously over her shoulders, then caressing her cleavage a moment later when his gaze slid there.

Her breath quickened in tempo, making her breasts rise and fall in smooth, rapid motion, attracting the scrutiny of those velvet rich eyes. Her bra suddenly felt abrasive against her tender nipples, and they tightened as if touched by his callused fingertips. She shifted, torn between embarrassment and a more pleasant sensation of languid arousal. Did he know?

She met his eyes. Yes. He knew. His eyes grew heavy-lidded, and a slight, enigmatic smile curved his full lips.

Casey swallowed and asked him to pass the olive oil. Without ever taking his thick-lashed gaze from her face, he picked up the bottle of dark, aromatic oil and handed it to her. A shock of sudden, urgent desire jolted them both into momentary stillness when their fingers brushed, and Casey helplessly pictured his muscled arms wrapped around her, pulling her into the human heat of his hard chest, pressing her face against the golden skin of his smooth, strong throat....

"Thanks," she said hoarsely, taking the bottle from him. She closed her eyes for a moment and tried to focus on Daniela's cheerful chatter about their cousin's wedding, vaguely amused at Daniela's assumption that all women were fascinated by wedding plans.

Her eyes locked with Rico's again when Daniela suggested *espresso* for everyone. Then Rico said quickly, "No, thanks, Daniela. We would like to get going."

"But there's plenty of time," Daniela protested.

"Ah, you know how restless these Americans are," Rico advised solemnly. "Rush, rush, rush."

Casey grabbed her big purse from her bedroom and met Rico outside at his red Citroën, eager to edge a little closer to this fascinating, charismatic man, despite knowing that she was playing with fire.

She had forgotten, however, just how recklessly he drove. She realized now that seeing the scene of a Mafia killing in Alcamo had subdued him that first day, for now he showed no regard whatsoever for the bumpy surfaces, narrow roads and blind turns of the rural area through which they traveled. What's more, the few cars they encountered during the siesta hour were all driven by equally deranged Sicilians.

Casey resorted to her former means of defense and squeezed her eyes shut.

After a few minutes, Rico said, "There are fine vineyards in this valley, and if you look... Casey, are you all right?"

She felt the warm, firm touch of his hand on hers as he leaned across the front seat, making her heightened senses tingle in response to his vibrancy. Her eyes snapped open and she saw him studying her with concern. "Don't look at me," she said. "Keep your eyes on the road."

He glanced briefly ahead, swerved deftly to avoid a car that was turning into the road before them with no warning, and then looked back at her. "What's the matter?"

"The road!" Casey insisted, looking at it for him. "Watch out! It's a crossroad!"

He removed his hand from hers and looked straight ahead again. When Casey risked a peek at him, his lips were twitching. "I'm sorry," she apologized quickly. "I'm not usually a back-seat driver. It's just that—"

"My driving makes you nervous?" he asked, apparently amused. "Don't worry. I'm a very good driver." He glanced her way again and then laughed at her blank, disbelieving stare. "Driving here is a little different than driving in America. Trust me."

Casey smiled weakly. "Then you don't mind if I keep my eyes closed, do you?"

"If it makes you feel better," he said generously.

It did, though little involuntary gasps still escaped her when the car swerved without warning or jerked because of Rico's sudden and incautious use of the brakes. For her benefit, he described the scenery she was missing, and occasionally he would coax her into opening her eyes for just a moment to enjoy a peek at the breathtaking countryside. The area around Segesta was mountainous, rugged and verdant from the lush spring rains, with tiny blossoms dotting every vast splash of green.

His voice soothed her, warmed her and made her want to curl up against him. He was tolerant of her lack of faith in his ability as a driver, teasing and amused by turns, and she found herself relaxing despite her very reasonable fear, felt her lips curving and twitching at the jokes he made with his expressive, lightly accented English.

Finally, out of curiosity, she asked, "When were you in America?"

"My father sent me there when I was nineteen to complete my higher education."

Eyes still closed, she said, "Sent you? You make it sound as if you didn't want to go."

"I didn't," he admitted. "Though I later became glad that I went. But at first, I didn't want to leave Sicily."

She tilted her head, thinking of all his comments in the dark courtyard, the real sorrow, frustration and hope he had expressed for his island. "You really love it here, don't you?"

"Of course I do. How else could I live amidst such insanity?"

She heard the smile in his voice. "What did you study in America?"

"Engineering."

"That's right. You said you were a civil engineer." He didn't look like any of the engineering students she remembered from her college days, but then she had already started to realize that he was one of a kind in many ways.

"Yes. I build aqueducts, bridges, dams. I was interested in water supply because it has always been such a problem here." His voice sounded thoughtful and a little weary, but not cynical, when he added, "I wanted to heal the ills."

"Was it hard for you to go alone to America when you were so young?"

"I didn't exactly go alone. A Sicilian doesn't do things alone, Casey, as you may have noticed yesterday."

She smiled and risked a brief glance at him, enjoying the warm intimacy of his gaze but wishing he would keep his eyes on the damn road. "Yes, I noticed." She closed her eyes again. He sighed briefly. "Who did you go with?"

"My cousin Giovanni. We moved into a little apartment over the grocery store of my uncle in Brooklyn. My father's eldest brother," he added. "The same brother my father stayed with in America after he escaped from Sicily in the 1940s. The same little apartment even."

"And you worked in your uncle's grocery store and went to college there?"

"Yes. It was very hard at first. My math was very good, but my English was very poor. But finally," he said cheerfully, "I got an American girlfriend, and she really helped my English. Also my hormones. Ah, yes, I found that American girls knew many things that Sicilian girls had only guessed at."

Casey risked another peak at him and could see a faint reminiscent smile curving his lips. When he flashed her a quick, flirtatious look, she said automatically, "Keep your eyes on the road."

"*Scusa.* Anyhow, my grades suffered a little my first year from my poor English and my exploration of the sexual revolution—"

"*Really,* Rico."

"I was young!" he insisted good-naturedly. "Anyhow, I got into the groove after that, as you Americans say—"

"We don't say that. Trust me."

"I must be out-of-date," he said despondently.

"Your grades picked up after that?" she prodded.

"Yes, and I eventually won a teaching assistantship at a school in upstate New York, where I went to earn my master's degree."

"Did your cousin Giovanni go with you?"

"No. He married a girl from New Jersey and settled down to a new job right after graduation."

"So you were on your own at last," she mused. "Did you enjoy the freedom?"

He appeared to think seriously about her question. After a moment he concluded, "I liked it better than Brooklyn, because I had been raised here, on my father's farm near a small town. But I didn't like being far from my relatives. Or my family in Sicily."

"That's funny. Most American kids long for that chance to move far away from their parents and their authority."

"Yes, but it's a very different culture. In some ways I liked and admired it, but in other ways I felt rather sorry for Americans."

"Really? How?"

"So many Americans seemed very much alone to me. We Sicilians like to live together, or at least near each other, to mingle in each other's life, to care for each other. We think not only of ourselves, but always of our whole family. And in return, we know the family is always concerned for us, is always surrounding and protecting us. We are never alone. We are never isolated. And to be isolated is like slow death to a Sicilian."

Casey was about to pursue that point with him when the car swerved dramatically and came to a sudden, teeth-jarring halt.

"We are here," he announced.

Casey opened her eyes and looked around. "It looks like a parking lot."

"It is. We must walk the rest of the way. As the Greeks used to."

Casey slung her heavy handbag over her shoulder and got out of the car without waiting for Rico to open her door. She tested her legs and figured their wobbly condition was a strong measure of just how much she hated his driving; she usually had a pretty resilient reaction to fear and was not normally given to jelly legs. However, having observed glimpses of the way everyone else in Sicily drove—even worse than Rico, by and large—she was *not* going to offer to drive home.

Once they had left the virtually empty parking lot and Casey got a vantage point on the hillside, she paused to look around. "Oh, this is beautiful!" she said sincerely. "Nolan will be so sorry he missed this."

"We'll get him some postcards," Rico promised.

Ancient, austere hills swelled all around them, rolling proudly down to the sea. In the distance she could see the blue sky dip down to mingle with the azure waters of the Mediterranean at the edge of the island. The hills were sprinkled with craggy boulders, tumbled heaps of rubble left by the people of many centuries and a bold array of wildflowers. Nestled atop one of the lower hills, Casey saw the clean, grand lines of a well-preserved Greek temple.

"Look!" she exclaimed.

"Yes, I know. We'll go there after we see the amphitheater."

Casey turned in a slow circle, letting the wind blow her hair around as she absorbed the natural grandeur of the scene surrounding them, feeling small and lucky to be alive. On impulse she turned to Rico and put her hand on his arm. "Thank you for bringing me here."

He covered her hand with his and pressed it against his arm. He looked down at her, at the wide blue eyes and the hopelessly tangled golden hair, and he felt a surge of longing so strong it made him feel speechless and awed. Why had he never realized until this moment that he was lonely?

"Thank you for coming with me," he managed to say at last, hoping she wouldn't think he was a fool for the huskiness in his voice or the triteness of his words. A thousand Italian men would have said that exact phrase to a lovely blond woman at this moment. But Rico meant it. The day had been simply another ordinary one until he began to share it with her.

"Come," he added, taking her hand in his. "You have yet to see the best part."

He led her up the steep path to the top of the mountain, his fingers wrapped firmly around her soft, slim hand. How much choice did a man have? he wondered vaguely, feeling the current of attraction running through Casey, into her hand linked with his and pouring through him. It was strong and sweet, like the almond wine his sister kept chilled for special occasions. Did a man make the choice, or did something inside of him make it for him, despite what he knew was best? Would there be only foolishness between them, only the awkward mating dance of two people who should know better than to invite pain and frustration?

He glanced back at her lowered head, noticing how carefully she placed her booted feet on the rocky path leading to the crest of the hill. Suddenly aware that he had slowed down, she raised her head to meet his eyes and give him a reassuring smile. And he knew, in that fleeting moment of communication before she again lowered her eyes to the path, that she would leave him with something valuable when she returned to her own country, however brief or limited their time together must be. Whatever they shared, whatever he had to remember her by, he would think fondly of this afternoon, and of any other time they could steal together.

"You are keeping up well," he said as they neared the top of the hill, noting how she maintained a brisk pace even though her face was prettily flushed.

"Aerobics," she said, breathing steadily and deeply. "You must be in great shape. You're not even breathing hard." The hill was very steep.

"I've had to do a lot of hiking and climbing this year," he confessed. "All through the Belice Valley and all around Agrigento in the south. Here we are!"

The ancients had nestled their local theater in the very peak of the mountain, the semicircular stone steps of the amphitheater descending to the grass and stone stage, with its extravagant backdrop of mountains, sky and sea.

The theater was wonderfully preserved, and even the backrests remained on the highest row of seats. Casey plopped down on one of them and declared, "These must be about the best theater seats in the world."

"Not quite," Rico said, sitting down next to her, letting his thigh rest comfortably against hers. "The amphitheater at Taormina in the east is even more dramatic. Mount Etna is the backdrop for that stage."

"Must be quite a show when it's erupting," she commented. "But I don't see how it could be any more beautiful than this."

"This is probably my favorite spot in all of Sicily. You can sit here and realize that it's no wonder that every conquering race has coveted this island since the beginning of time."

"What's that man doing?" Casey pointed to the grassy floor of the amphitheater where an elderly man wearing a *coppola*, the flat tweed cap she had already seen on numerous older Sicilians, was wandering around, occasionally stooping to pick something.

"Gathering bunches of wild oregano to sell to tourists."

Casey fanned herself and squinted at the sky. "After what I went through at the airport, I don't even want to think about what would happen to me if I tried to take a little bag of wild oregano out of the country with me."

Rico chuckled. "Oh, I would come up with a good story."

Casey stretched languidly toward the melting gold of the sun. "I'll bet it's cold and raining in New York right now."

"Most likely," he murmured.

She heard the huskiness in his voice, and she felt his gaze upon her as she lowered her hands and brushed them through her tangled, windblown hair. She lowered her eyes to where their thighs rested together, to where his heat was flowing into her charged senses. She saw the tightening of muscle beneath faded, close-fitting denim as he shifted, and she lifted her face until their eyes met, locked and held.

A man who appeared to be at home in many circumstances, he had never looked more perfectly in his element than he did now: his bronzed skin and jet-black hair gleaming under the Mediterranean sun; his dark, thick-lashed eyes holding all the mystery and exoticism of the mixed Greek, Arabic and European blood of his people; the hard masculinity of his body surrounded by the rugged terrain in which he belonged as irrevocably as the ancient stone upon which the two of them sat, their heartbeats pacing together.

"Do you have a man in America?" he asked quietly.

"Not lately." She was pleased he had asked. "Do you have someone?"

"I am by myself." He smiled sheepishly a moment later and added more honestly, "Most of the time."

That qualification didn't surprise her. The first time she had spotted him at the airport she had guessed that he wouldn't have to look far for female companionship. *She* had come with him readily enough, hadn't she?

"Casey...." He pressed his palm against hers, then laced their fingers together. She felt the tenderness in him, and she wanted more of it. After a moment he smiled softly. "What *does* Casey stand for?"

"Discord and disharmony."

"Cosa?"

"Family problems. I've got a brother about two years older than me, and we figure that his name was about the last thing my parents ever agreed upon. When I was born, my mother wanted to name me Kathleen, but my father insisted I had to be named Catherine, with a *C.*" She sighed. "So their bright idea of a compromise was to name me Kathleen Catherine McConnell. Can you imagine?"

"That's... that's..." He grinned and finally admitted, "That's pretty awful, Casey."

"It's pathetic.

"So your parents—did they get divorced?"

"Eventually. Not soon enough, believe me."

"What do you mean?" He traced his free hand over her knuckles and the small bones of her wrist, distracting her with the touch of his long, sensitive fingers.

"Oh, my old man was a rotten egg," she said dismissively, toughing it out. To ease the feelings, she had developed a quick, well-rehearsed summary that she could deliver with relatively little effort. "Before my mother had the brains to finally throw him out, he got fired for embezzlement, then gambled away my mother's savings on some crazy stock scheme, declared bankruptcy and got another woman pregnant. Not to mention being locked up a couple of times for being drunk and disorderly."

"But that's terrible," Rico said. "To harm the family like that."

"He wasn't like Totò, that's for sure," she said with a touch of envy.

"He sounds very misguided, Casey. We are not strangers to adultery here, or even to divorce, but to think a man could willfully continue to behave in a way that destroys his family is still shocking." He paused and asked, "And the family your father was born to? Did they not help him?"

"No, of course not, Rico. He was a grown man, and they were probably smart enough to figure out he would just waste any money they gave him."

Rico shook his head. "Even aside from money, he needed someone to guide him."

"That's what therapists are for, Rico."

He gave her an exasperated look, but tempered it with a smile. "Why do you prefer to pay strangers for what your family should do for you?"

"Why do you want to trouble your family, when there are professionals who get paid to do these things?" she countered.

He grinned and reached for her, naturally and comfortably, sliding his hand into her loose hair to tug briefly on it, another expression of exasperation. "I have always found the ways of your people very strange."

"This from a man who eats octopus," she said dryly.

"*Pazza, ma bella,*" he said and pressed a soft, affectionate kiss against her lips. He felt the quick breath she drew, felt the tightening in his own belly, and he closed his eyes, resting his forehead lightly against hers while his hand caressed the back of her neck, tangling in the silkiness of her hair.

"What does that mean?" Her voice was breathless, pleasing him.

"Crazy. But beautiful," he murmured.

"I've been called worse," she admitted.

He brushed his lips against her forehead. Soft. She was so soft. And she smelled like the sunshine. "I'm sure you have," he teased. "Being such a famous American journalist and everything."

"Yeah, right."

Her hand crept slowly, exploringly across his thigh, and he swallowed, trying not to beg her to touch him, hold him, wrap her arms around him. He hadn't realized how it would affect him, to be this close to her, to burrow his nose against the curve of her neck and drown in the scent of her skin, to feel the rhythm of her breath against his cheek.

Their hands were slow on each other. Casey had never felt so awed by a man's nearness, had never felt that brushing the edges of his emotions could singe her like this. She turned her lips against his cheek and pressed a tender, affectionate kiss there, intoxicated by his smooth, hard jaw, the coiled tension of his body, the sudden rise and fall of his broad chest.

He raised her hand to his mouth and pressed his lips to her palm. There was nothing gentlemanly about it. The touch of his tongue surprised a whimper from her, a pleading sound to which he responded.

His arms slid surely around her waist, and Casey's eyes fluttered closed when he covered her mouth with his, slowly and softly, but with an intensity that made her shake, that almost made her want to run and hide from him. A man shouldn't know how to make a woman dissolve with just a kiss, she thought vaguely, drowning in the special, swirling feel of his embrace.

His lips were firm, insistent, probing. His gentleness overwhelmed her, because she could feel the power of his passion in the rigid set of his shoulders. Her own excitement flooded her senses, demanding more, forcing her closer to him. When her lips parted, he accepted the invitation without hesitation. His tongue slid easily into her mouth, and made a long, leisurely sweep of its moist interior.

She touched her tongue to his, dying for the taste of him, thrilled to tangle with his agile, teasing invasion. And then his gentleness changed into something darker and stronger, something as rich and heady as the wine that still flavored his hot mouth. His sturdy arms pulled her tightly against the rock-hard, sun-warmed strength of his body, making her feel soft, cherished, desired. His mouth remained on hers, rubbing, teasing, nibbling, caressing, until the tender bud of passion opened and blossomed fully between them, flowering in vibrant color, without shame or hesitation, under the fiercely blue sky.

Could it happen so suddenly? she wondered desperately, incoherently. She had so willingly followed him, perhaps suspecting all along that he was leading her to this precipice, and now she was falling, falling so deep and hard, tumbling away from safety and into a place of terrifying depth....

"Basta." His voice had a gravelly sound as he pulled at her hair and lifted his mouth from hers. "That's enough."

"No, it's not," she said without thinking.

She felt him smile against her cheek as their hot, frantic breaths brushed each other's skin.

"No, it's not," he agreed. "But there's an old man down there picking wild oregano. We can't..."

"Oh." And despite the hunger crying out in protest inside her, she laughed. "No, I guess we really can't."

He kissed her mouth briefly, pulling away reluctantly when her lips clung to his. "You are good to laugh," he murmured. "I want to cry."

She laughed again, then said, "Maybe we should get up and walk around a little." It would help what ailed her.

He shook his head quickly. "Not yet. In a minute."
When her brows rose, he grinned sheepishly. This time they
both laughed, comfortable with each other and ridiculously happy.

"No wonder you want to cry," she commented.

"And you?" he asked.

She knew what he meant. She nodded. Their eyes held
for an honest moment, the kind of moment she didn't think
she had ever shared with any other man. Then she said,
"Rico, this is crazy. I'm leaving after the weekend."

His expressive eyes went sad. "I know."

"I...I didn't come here to have a fling with a handsome Italian."

Those eyes changed again. "So would you settle for an
ugly Sicilian?"

He was such a flirt. "I think you know how handsome
you are, so I'm not going to pump up your ego any more,"
she said severely.

"Okay. And I didn't tell my father to invite you here so
I could seduce a beautiful American journalist."

"And I really don't want to, uh, embarrass your family
by—"

"Nothing human embarrasses my family."

"I don't want to be indiscreet."

He linked his fingers with hers and whispered naughtily,
"So we'll be discreet, then."

"Rico!" But his audacity delighted her, and she knew he
could see it. She shook her head. "I'm on assignment."

"I promise not to tell your editor about your unprofessional behavior a moment ago." He winked.

"It *was* unprofessional." She tried to untangle her hand
from his, but he only wrapped both of his warm hands
around it and held it more firmly.

Now his dark eyes grew serious and sincere. "Listen to
me. I am not a fling."

"No, you're not," she agreed softly. The memory of him
would stay with her longer than men she had known for

years. She knew that already. "You'd be easier to handle if you were."

He drew her hand against him and slid her palm along his chest, playing with fire. "I have been told," he confided, "that I'm very easy to handle. If you want to handle me." When he saw her sudden intake of breath, he grinned slowly. "I think you do."

"For just a few days?" she said skeptically.

Eyes still serious, he agreed, "It's not enough."

"You see?"

"So stay longer, Casey."

That shouldn't be so tempting. She tried to shake off the desire to say, *Yes, let me stay with you until I know why I want to be with you so much, though you're a stranger, a foreigner... even an occasional liar. Let me stay with you.*

She swallowed. She could see in his expression that he knew she was struggling. "I can't. I have to be back at work on—"

"Take a vacation. Tell them you have something important to do."

"But I don't."

"Your personal life is always more important, Casey."

That struck her as an odd thing to say. It broke the spell of magic, leaving only the ache of physical desire. She smiled at him. "I can tell you've been away from America for a long time, Rico."

He sighed. She had escaped him. Oh, well, maybe it was best this way. He must have lost his mind for a few moments there. "Yes, I guess I have. For you, nothing is more important than your career, true?"

"I have obligations. And goals. Just like you," she added.

"Goals and obligations back in America," he said. "But no man."

"So I should stay here with a man and forget my goals and obligations in America?" she said sharply.

"You could send them the story."

"There are other stories waiting for me, Rico. My life is very busy there."

He nodded and lowered his eyes. "Then perhaps..." He shrugged, released her hand and reached into his pocket for a cigarette. "Then perhaps we should be wise."

She almost apologized, then realized he already knew how sorry she was. And why should she apologize anyhow? She was right, after all. But she felt such an ache when he stopped touching her, stopped looking at her.

"Where are you going?" she asked a moment later when he stood up and started walking down the ancient steps to the grassy stage of the amphitheater.

He turned and looked up, slim and muscular, as graceful as a panther, darkly exotic and eternally at home here. "I want to buy some herbs from that old man. He could probably use the money, and Daniela would appreciate the wild oregano."

He descended the rest of the steps quickly, and she bit her tongue not to call out a warning. As remarkably preserved as the amphitheater was, it looked too bumpy for him to simply dash down the steps like that. However, he reached the bottom without mishap and began speaking with the old man.

It was nearly twenty minutes later when he returned to her side. Casey was scribbling in her spiral notebook. "What took you so long?" she asked absently.

He sat down beside her. "It would not be civilized to simply give money for a thing, with no discussion." He peered at the notebook on her lap. "What are you doing?"

"Notes," she explained, remembering how she had cut him off when he had asked once before. "I take notes about everything. All the time. I don't like to trust anything to memory. Better that I should be able to describe this place from my notes than simply hope I can remember it accurately."

"You will write about this place?"

"Maybe." She shrugged. "It's not really part of your father's story, but it's best to be prepared in case I decide to include it. You know, something like, 'Antonio Butera's farm is located near the ancient ruins of Segesta, whose tumbled rocks whisper tales to the wind of centuries of suffering in Sicily.'"

"I like that," he said consideringly.

"You would," she replied. "It's so dramatic."

"You are a good writer. I saw one of your articles in the magazine that Daniela bought after you wrote to my father."

"Is that why you advised him to invite me?" she asked curiously.

"No. I did it because I thought it would be best for him."

She believed that. One had to spend only a very little time with Rico to recognize his unswerving devotion to his family. She finished writing and put the notebook back in her purse.

"Would you like to see the temple now?" he asked.

"Lead on, MacDuff."

"Cosa?"

"I'd love to see the temple now," she amended wryly.

He smiled, just as enchanted by the things she said that he didn't understand as he was by the things she said that he understood only too well.

He transferred his bundle of wild oregano to his left hand and stretched out his right hand toward her. "Come." When she looked at him doubtfully, he promised, "We'll just hold hands."

But he knew just as well as she did how incendiary mere hand-holding was between the two of them.

Chapter Five

"Sometimes the *carabinieri* thought Giuliano's band numbered in the hundreds, or perhaps the thousands. But always, we were only a few."

"How many, Totò?" Casey asked, scribbling in her notebook while Nolan set up lights and other equipment in an alcove at the end of the room.

"Perhaps a dozen, perhaps twenty. Never more than fifty. We were many at the beginning of the Separatists' action against the Italian *carabinieri*. But toward the end," he murmured sadly, "we were very few."

"I'm nearly ready, Casey," Nolan said. He and Casey had decided to add a few formal photos to all the candid shots Nolan had been getting.

"Okay, Nolan. In a few minutes."

After she and Rico had returned from Segesta, two evenings ago, a telephone call had come through from Palermo, taking him away again despite Daniela's objections. Casey had been restless and edgy since then, telling herself that maintaining a sensible adult attitude was the only way to deal with her unexpected and inconvenient attraction to Totò Butera's son.

"Tell me about the regular members of the band, Totò," she urged. "What do you remember?"

"There were two leaders of earlier outlaw bands, Cucchiara and Terranova, who brought their men with them—hard men, tough and ruthless. There was Frank Mannino, who was better educated than the rest of us, but a dangerous man. I remember a musician named di Lorenzo who gave Giuliano guitar lessons." Totò chuckled. "Some woman pretended Giuliano had serenaded her on his guitar, but he was never that good."

Casey wrote down the names, asking Totò how to spell them. Yesterday, Totò had been feeling much better, and Casey had been able to get some valuable work done. Totò's memories were dramatic and fascinating, funny and sorrowful by turns. He had some wonderful anecdotes about Giuliano and the band, as well as a few remarkable stories about *mafiosi* and the *capo di tutti capi*—the boss of all bosses, the most powerful *mafioso*. Unfortunately, however, he hadn't yet given Casey any reason to believe he knew secrets that no one else had ever revealed.

"There was also Castrenze Madonia," Totò continued, "who carved the famous phrase on the butt of Giuliano's gun." When he rattled it off in Italian, Casey asked him for a translation. "It means, 'I can look after my enemies, but God protect me from my friends.' "

"Very appropriate," Casey murmured, "since his best friend, Pisciotta, killed him."

"With help. And for a price." Totò spat contemptuously.

Curiously, Casey asked, "Did you ever think Pisciotta would do such a thing, Totò?"

Totò scowled. "I did not like Pisciotta."

"But he was closest to Giuliano."

"Yes. But I always detested him, and I followed only Giuliano's orders. Pisciotta was cruel and selfish. He had no respect for women. He even insulted Loredana," Totò added vehemently.

Casey had already learned that Loredana was the Sicilian girl with whom Totò had fallen in love during his days as a bandit, the girl he had later returned to Sicily to marry. She was Rico's mother—gone but not forgotten. And Casey could see from the photos Totò had shown her that Rico and Daniela had inherited their high cheekbones and lustrous black hair from their mother, just as they had inherited their father's darkly expressive eyes.

"Why do you suppose Giuliano loved Pisciotta best?" she asked.

"Who can say? I think Pisciotta's illness—he had tuberculosis, you know—inspired pity in Giuliano's great heart. Giuliano trusted him most of all. But the heart is never wise, and we choose our loved ones with our heart."

Casey felt a swelling fondness for the old man whenever he uttered these homilies in his thickly accented English. She asked, "Were you surprised when Pisciotta confessed to killing Giuliano a year after his death?"

"Of course." Totò sighed pensively. "But I had left Sicily in 1947, so ill I wasn't even sure I would survive the journey to America. Since then, I had only occasional news from Sicily, and none from Giuliano. Things changed so much for Giuliano after Portella della Ginestra. One by one, everyone abandoned him—the politicians, the Mafia, the bandits, the peasants. But Pisciotta was certainly the cruelest betrayal of all," he concluded, his voice wistful and sad.

Casey knew that the massacre at Portella della Ginestra on May 1, 1947, remained one of the great mysteries of Giuliano's career. But before following that line of thought to learn how much Totò knew about it, she wanted to return to one of Totò's earlier comments.

"Although you weren't here, Totò, I wonder what you can tell me about the night Giuliano died in 1950. When you say Pisciotta killed him with help and for a price—"

She stopped speaking when she heard a car door slam in the distance. It was late afternoon already, so she permitted herself to hope that the new arrival was Rico. Glancing at her small tape recorder to see if it was still recording, she returned to her question.

"I've read that at his trial, Pisciotta said, 'I have not sold my soul, though I have been offered millions for it.'"

"Yes..." Totò blinked, as if only just realizing Casey was there.

"What do you think he meant when he said that? Who do you think convinced Pisciotta to betray Giuliano?"

"He... There was..."

"Do you think they were the same people who poisoned Pisciotta in his prison cell in 1954?"

"They..."

"What about Giuliano's papers, his memorandum? Who do you think destroyed it? Pisciotta or someone else?"

She frowned after a moment of silence, chastising herself for getting carried away by the unsolved mysteries of another era and asking the old man too many questions at once. Then she noticed how pale and breathless Totò suddenly looked.

"Totò?" She rose from her chair and knelt before him. "Are you all right?"

"Casey, you must understand," he whispered urgently, too low and hoarse for Nolan to hear as he fiddled with his equipment across the room. "You *must* understand. I was young. It was the only way we knew, the only we had ever known. And nothing ever changes here. Not really. Not the way Rico..."

His face crumpled, filling Casey with alarm. "Totò, are you in pain? Do you need your medicine? I'll get Daniela."

"No," he commanded hoarsely. "No. Say nothing to them. Promise me."

She didn't want the responsibility of keeping the old man's illness to herself. "Totò, I can't—"

"You must understand, Casey!"

That was loud enough to make Nolan look across the room at them. Casey only spared him a glance before she looked back into Totò's eyes, so like the eyes of his son, so compelling and complex, so exotic and expressive. He wasn't making any sense.

"I came here to understand, Totò," she said slowly. "You must help me. You must tell me everything."

"Everything?"

His eyes were glassy, his expression so strange she was afraid he might be having another stroke. "Yes. Everything. But only if you're well enough."

He covered her hand with his. His grip was so strong, she almost gasped. She wondered if a man could have such a crushing grip if he were in the middle of some kind of seizure.

"The tentacles of the octopus reach into everything," he said solemnly. "But if you are prepared, then I will break my silence for you."

Does he know something, or is he losing his mind?

"I'm prepared, Totò," she promised him, reminding herself that she would check and double-check her facts before printing the story. She didn't intend to destroy her career over the memories, ramblings and possible imaginings of an old man who just might be losing his hold on reality. *Oh, Totò,* she thought sadly. She felt the pain she knew his children felt for the slow death of such a remarkable, enduring man.

She heard conversation in the kitchen, the musical sound of Italian, and she recognized the deep timbre of Rico's voice as it penetrated straight to something deep inside her and spread warmth through her belly.

Totò heard the voices, too. "You will say nothing of this to my children. *Nothing,*" he whispered urgently. "We cannot speak of this in front of them. Do not ask."

"But I—"

"We will speak of something else," he insisted. "Something simple. Kidnapping!"

"Kidnapping?" she repeated incredulously. Something simple?

"Ah, he is telling you about the good old days," Rico said cheerfully from the wide doorway.

"I . . . um . . ." Casey licked her lips and looked at Rico. "Hi."

He smiled, and the dying sunlight suddenly seemed to fill the room. "Hi."

Their gazes held, his dark, thick-lashed and intimate enough to make her want to squirm. Why did the appearance of a man she hardly knew seem like the long-awaited homecoming of her heart's companion? She should have felt absurd, kneeling awkwardly on the floor near his father, but his eyes offered only flattery and admiration. Above her, Totò said something in a passionate and dramatic voice, sounding so strong and argumentative that Casey almost wondered if she had imagined those strange moments of whispered intensity and physical weakness.

"Yes, I know it's only Friday, Papa," Rico responded prosaically. "But I have to spend part of tomorrow in the valley again, so I decided to come home today." He crossed the room, his long legs brushing very close to Casey—intentionally, she was sure. Then he bent over his father's chair to kiss the old man on both cheeks.

"So have you been getting your work done?" Rico asked, turning to Casey.

"Some." He was wearing a tie today. Her eyes fixed on it.

"But never as fast as you intend." His grin teased her American impatience, and she responded with a smile she couldn't have stopped. Did any other man in the world fill a room with color and warmth the way he did?

"Your father was just about to tell me about—"

"Kidnapping!" Totò interrupted jovially.

"Ah," Rico said. "Then I will sit and learn something, just in case I ever solve the water problem in Sicily and then need to find new work."

"Ha!" Totò said with more energy than he had shown all day. Casey could see that she wasn't the only one vivified by Rico's presence. "Kidnapping is hard work, not something for this lazy generation of college graduates in my family."

Rico smiled and plopped into a chair near Totò's, stretching his legs out lazily before him. Casey wanted to wrap her hand around the smooth, hard bulge of his calf and follow a path up to his thigh.

"My father forces us all to get college degrees, then he calls us lazy for not earning ransom money," Rico said teasingly, his gaze caressing Casey's golden hair and soft eyes. A man could race home to those questioning, yearning eyes every day of his life, he thought. And then he wondered if she yearned for the same thing he did.

"All of you?" She tilted her head, distracted from her interview by personal curiosity. "How many of you are there?"

"Three," Rico answered. "My brother is a lawyer in Verona in the north. And Daniela is a researcher in English at the University of Palermo."

"Then I can see why none of you might take up kidnapping to pay the bills," Casey answered. Rico's skin glowed, as if he had been outdoors today. What did he do when he wasn't here, she wondered, suddenly more interested in that than in the activities of Sicily's most famous bandit.

"So when did you get into kidnapping, Totò?" she asked suddenly, aware she was once again drifting in the direction she had promised herself she wouldn't go.

"It was not an original concept," Rico remarked. "Abducting people for ransom has long been a custom here."

"Yes. From the start," Totò continued, "we realized we would need money, now that we could not have jobs as other men. We needed money to give to our starving families, money to provide ourselves with food, medicine, supplies, ammunition and arms."

"And silence," Rico added.

"Of course. Silence," Totò agreed. "Because we were outlaws, we had to pay farmers, shepherds, doctors and everyone else much more than other men paid them. Sometimes ten times as much. But this was Giuliano's choice, for he knew that the suppliers would not betray us if they knew they could grow rich off us."

"So kidnapping seemed a logical way to establish an income?" Casey asked, enjoying Nolan's incredulous expression as he abandoned his equipment to come sit with the rest of them.

"It was a time-honored profession here, Casey." Rico's voice was amused, and she couldn't tell what he really thought about his father abducting people. "The best kidnappers were the toughest *mafiosi*. They were so efficient, that all they needed to do was send a note before the kidnapping."

His eyes glittered, awaiting her response. Aware that she was rising to the bait, she admitted. "I don't understand. Wouldn't a note warn the intended victim?"

"Exactly," Rico answered. "If the victim paid before the kidnapping, the ransom would be considerably less, because then all the nasty details and added expenses—including the kidnapping itself—would not be necessary." He smiled at her amazed expression.

"Very efficient," she agreed wryly. "And people paid the ransom in advance?"

"If they were smart," Totò said. "But Giuliano was not of the Honored Society, so he was always obliged to kidnap the man and wait for the ransom. He was very patient. I remember that he once waited one hundred eight days."

"That long?" Casey asked. "But what did you do with the victims? Where did you keep them?"

"We kept them with us, in the mountains. We were very civilized and correct. We respected their rank and dignity, we provided whatever food they requested, if we could. One man was so fussy, we had to provide him with clean stockings every day." Totò rolled his eyes and Casey laughed.

"One man had diabetes, and Giuliano made sure we provided him with his . . . his . . ."

"Insulin," Rico supplied.

"Yes. And we entertained them."

"How?" Casey asked.

"Oh, we played cards or talked with them. One man had to be kept locked in the bedroom of an abandoned house for three weeks, so I read to him every day from the window."

"This is incredible," Nolan said. "Giuliano sounds like Errol Flynn."

Rico looked both interested and annoyed as his father talked. Casey speculated again that he was more drawn to the legend of Giuliano and his father's part in the legend than he liked to admit, yet he also disliked the glamorization of ancient codes and lawless ways.

Totò vehemently explained that the band kidnapped only men. Never women, and never, never children. Casey had remained on the floor, between Totò and Rico's chairs, and her knees began to complain. She shifted slowly to one side while Totò began another story. After a moment, she felt a broad hand on her shoulder, unseen by Totò and Nolan, gently easing her closer to the arm of Rico's easy chair.

"Once we made a foolish mistake," Totò admitted cheerfully, "and we kidnapped a relative of a *pezzo di novanta*—a big shot—in San Giuseppe Jato."

Submitting to the subtle pressure of Rico's hand, to the silent message passing between them—*come closer to me, closer*—Casey leaned back against his chair. His fingers tightened briefly on her shoulder, thanking her, encouraging her.

"Naturally, this man of honor was humiliated by our disregard for his position," Totò was saying. "So he went to Giuliano and explained his problem."

"Uh-huh." Casey heard the distraction in her own voice. She drew in a sharp breath when Rico smoothed his hand along her shoulder and gently began kneading the tension in her neck.

"Of course, Giuliano was sympathetic to the man, realizing our mistake. So he released the man's relative, asking only for enough ransom to cover our expenses in the abduction. That was fair," Totò concluded sagely.

"How..." Casey was grateful that Rico ceased his seductive massage long enough for her to utter a coherent question. "How was ransom usually arranged?"

Then he was there again, his fingers finding her private stores of fear and anger and worry, unlocking her secrets with his knowing touch, unwinding her senses with his caress. After a moment, his hand started to wander down her back, still hidden from the others' view by the position of their bodies.

"Certain *mafiosi* would arrange the transaction. This was customary. For their services, they took a small fee. Ten or fifteen percent."

"Sounds like an agent," Nolan muttered.

Casey felt Rico's fingers move down her back to her bra strap, easily discernible through the thin material of her blouse. He traced it slowly, teasingly. She squirmed.

"Are you comfortable on the floor, Casey?" he asked solicitously.

She didn't know whether she wanted to smile or bite his hand. "Yes," she answered shortly. "And the victim's families never thought of notifying the authorities?"

Totò stared at her. "No. Of course not."

"No, of course not," she murmured, remembering her conversation with Rico about *omertà*—fear-inspired and honor-bound.

She could feel his index finger impertinently trailing along the bottom edge of her bra strap. She tried to concentrate, tried not to picture the hot look she knew would be in his eyes.

"Totò, let's go back for a moment to early 1944."

She felt the hand at her back suddenly close firmly over her bra to pull it, and the soft blouse, away from her skin. Then Rico rubbed his knuckles against her back, slowly and enticingly.

"To the days before the Separatists," she added unnecessarily. She hoped her voice didn't betray her excitement when Rico gently released her garments and trailed his fingers down to the waistband of her trousers.

"What, specifically?" Totò asked.

"The first informer Giuliano killed," she answered. She felt the tantalizing exploration at her back cease suddenly. Rico rested his warm palm against her, waiting.

"Giuliano could be ruthless," Totò said.

Casey recognized the truth of that statement when Totò told her the story of how Giuliano shot in cold blood an eighteen-year-old boy whom he suspected of spying on him for the police. It was only the first of many murders he would commit to enforce his own code of silence.

"He would leave a special note on the bodies of informers," Totò said. *"Così muoiono i traditori contro Giuliano."*

"Thus die traitors against Giuliano," Rico translated quietly. He pulled his hand away from Casey. She steeled herself not to turn around and reach for him. She could feel his stillness, so close behind her, could sense his intensity.

"Did you participate?" Casey asked Totò.

"He killed alone that time."

"But there were other times?"

The old man's face grew darker with remembered pain. "There were many other times," he said at last. "And I killed."

"Who was the first?" she asked gently. She could feel Rico's tension behind her. In front of her, she saw Totò stare at his son. Yes, murder and *omertà* were more to this family than stories in the newspaper.

"I helped him kill a postal official," Totò said, so slowly that every word seemed to draw pain. "The man was stealing money sent to people in Montelepre by their relatives in America."

Casey wrote down the postal official's name when he spelled it for her. She realized now that she hadn't been prepared to reconcile this sweet old man, this man who had read stories for three weeks to an unharmed abductee, with the rough justice of Giuliano's legend.

"A year later, I killed a man who had betrayed us to the *carabinieri*," Totò continued, his voice low and heavy. "I...I did not like to kill. I had apprenticed to be a carpenter, to build things, to give shelter. But this is a land where only the strong stay alive and free, where a man must win his respect with raw power. We could not survive traitors."

Unable to prevent herself, Casey asked, "Did you believe in *omertà?* Is that what you were enforcing?"

"Omertà?" Totò shrugged. "We knew of no other way. Here in Sicily, *no one* knew of any other way, so honest people respected us when we executed informers. It was something Sicilians understood."

Judging by the way the villagers of Montelepre and the citizens of most of western Sicily had protected Giuliano's band for years, Casey supposed Totò had a point. In a land where a man supposedly wouldn't have reported his own wife's murder to the hated authorities, why would he tell them where to find a respected bandit, a bandit who had proved his manliness in time-honored ways? A bandit who stole from the rich and gave to the poor, who distributed black-market food to starving villages and kept the authorities running in circles for seven years.

But Giuliano, Casey knew, had also massacred women and children at Portella della Ginestra. He was a bandit who had asked President Truman to annex Sicily to the United States, who had killed a Mafia chief for betraying him, and who was finally killed by the best friend that betrayed him—the friend that was later poisoned when he threatened to break his silence.

"It's so complicated here," Casey said, more intrigued by this story than any other she had ever worked on.

Totò admitted he was not quite sure how many men he had killed during his years as a bandit: The victims of abductions, he assured her, were never killed. That was civilized business. But there were slayings of informants. There were many battles with the *carabinieri,* and sometimes they were very confusing. And there was trouble with the public security police, who eventually shot and nearly killed Totò in 1947.

"That was when I finally accepted that I could never hope for amnesty, for a normal life in Sicily. And after I met Loredana, that was all I wanted. To live quietly, with her, and to raise our children without fear."

There was a melancholy silence before Casey finally said, "I'm sorry, Totò. I've tired you out today."

It was true. She could see weariness in the droop of the old man's shoulders, the drawn expression on his face, the slight tremor in his hands. The memories he was reliving for her would have taxed the strength of a much healthier man. "Do you feel well enough to pose for some photographs?" she asked.

"Of course!"

"Foolish question," Rico said. "My father is always well enough to posture before a camera."

Casey turned to look up at Rico. He smiled fondly as he spoke of his father, but his eyes were troubled and serious. How was it possible, she wondered, that he seemed to get better-looking, more starkly beautiful in a totally masculine way, every time she looked at him?

"Rico, Rico, *vieni qua,*" Totò said. *Come here.*

Rico reluctantly looked away from Casey and saw his father struggling to get to his feet so he could move to the area Nolan had prepared with lighting on the other side of the room. Automatically, without any self-consciousness, Rico pushed himself out of his chair and went to his father's side, gently helping the old man rise and cross the room. Once he had his father settled in the straight-backed chair Nolan had provided, he stepped away from the scene and stood close to Casey in the fading afternoon light.

While Nolan and Totò bantered back and forth and discussed Totò's "best side," Rico quietly folded his hand over Casey's and led her out of the room. Alone in the shadowed hallway, knowing the children were in the kitchen with his sister, he pulled Casey against him and kissed her. He didn't care if it wasn't wise. He had been a fool for lesser things.

She stiffened with surprise for a moment, then responded almost instantly, her body softening against his, her sweet mouth adjusting to his kiss and returning it with warm enthusiasm.

"We fit perfectly together, you and I," he whispered against her lips. He trailed his palm down her spine, smoothing it over her bottom, pressing her hips against his, showing her how blissfully they melded and matched. "You see?"

"Oh, Lord," she said in a bewildered voice that made him smile.

He nuzzled her neck. "I have thought of you all day," he told her, meaning it. "I have thought of how I would enter the room and you would fly into my arms."

"But I didn't," she mumbled.

"So I improvised."

"Rico, I thought we agreed the other day that we would just be friendly."

"I *am* being friendly."

"You know I'm leaving Monday." Her hands squeezed his shoulders caressingly. "I have to go back." Then her arms crept around his neck. "I mean, I *told* you I'm not looking for a hot Italian fling," she continued seriously. Rico felt her fingers tangle in the hair at the nape of his neck. "It would make me feel like that old movie about the silly woman who comes to Italy looking for a Latin lover and a shallow affair." She pressed closer to him, her full breasts flattening against his chest. "So we just shouldn't...shouldn't..." Her eyes fluttered closed as she raised her face for his kiss again.

Her kiss was welcoming and promising, stealing his breath and filling his mind with fantasies that definitely couldn't be realized in the hallway of his father's house. When their lips parted and she kissed his jaw, he murmured, "I think this is what you Americans call a mixed message."

"It's your fault. If you would just stay ten feet away and read my lips, the message would be clearer," she muttered, nuzzling him delightfully.

"When I stand ten feet away, your eyes tell me to come closer." He rested his cheek against her hair and squeezed his eyes shut, trying to absorb the wonderful feel of her as much as he could under the circumstances.

"But they *don't* tell you to put your hands all over me when I'm in the middle of interviewing your father, buster." He suspected she was trying to make her voice sound sharp, but she failed miserably.

"They weren't all over you. Just on parts that nobody could see," he said innocently.

She pulled back enough to search out his features in the dying light. "I'm not going to try to argue with you about it," she said at last. "I don't think I can win."

"It's not the winning," he countered, "but the pleasure of the argument that counts."

"That's so Sicilian," she said, having noticed in only a few days how much everyone she met enjoyed a good argument.

"Everything about me is Sicilian."

"Except that you object to your father's enforcement of *omertà*."

He drew in a sharp breath and stepped back, breaking their bodily contact. "That's the reporter in you," he said ruefully. "Swift, unexpected and a little brutal."

"Do you mind his participating in the killing of informants more than you mind his killing of *carabinieri?*"

"Will this be in your article?"

After a long pause, she said, "No. I just want to know what you think. Personally."

"Personally, I find it hard to think of my father killing anyone. He never even spanked me when I was a child— and believe it or not, there were a few times when I really deserved it."

"I believe it," she said dryly. "And I know what you mean. He's a very gentle man."

She waited, and he found her silence somehow relentless. So he said truthfully, "I don't want to judge my father for what he did in a chaotic, starving, war-torn nation after being unjustly arrested and beaten, Casey."

The forgiveness and love she heard in that sentence moved her heart to her throat for a moment. Finally she said, "Sometimes you seem to judge Giuliano."

He shrugged. "I didn't love Giuliano. He died long before I was born. And if he had never killed his first *carabiniere,* my father would never have been arrested in the first place."

"I think your father loved Giuliano," Casey mused. "And feared him, too. Or at least feared the things Giuliano was capable of."

"Well, you know what that American journalist said about Giuliano after meeting him, don't you? He said that Giuliano was a nice guy, a sincere guy, who had just one small problem—he rather liked killing people."

"That's the mystery of Giuliano's character, isn't it? He was responsible for a couple of hundred deaths, yet he was the bandit who fed whole villages. He earned a great fortune in ransom money, yet he was always poor himself, because he gave so much of it away. He murdered informants, yet he let kidnapping victims go without paying on several occasions because they convinced him that their debts were so overwhelming. He spared the lives of some *carabinieri* when he held them in the palm of his hand, yet he went out of his way to kill others."

"Ah, but that was usually when his mamma was in jail."

"Yes, he was very attached to her, wasn't he?"

"That's also very Sicilian," Rico said dryly.

Casey leaned against the wall. Wanting him to know that her next question was purely personal, she reached out to touch him. "Were you very attached to yours?"

"Yes. I loved her very much." He said it frankly, with no embarrassment or self-consciousness. "I miss her. We all do."

"Rico..." She hesitated over her next question, afraid of causing him pain. Could she really be a little brutal, as he had said?

"What?" he prodded softly, moving his hand to cover hers where it rested lightly on his arm.

"You said your mother was killed by a hit-and-run driver in Palermo last year. Did... Were there any witnesses to her death?"

The hand covering hers pressed harder. He felt pain so suddenly, so thoroughly, she thought.

"There were people there. No one had seen the driver or noticed the license plate. No one could agree on the color of the car. They tried to help my mother, and they called an ambulance immediately. But she was dead on arrival." His voice was flat and dull. Then he sighed and added, "But that is different, Casey. It was an accident. It would be so in your country, too."

"Yes," she admitted. "There are careless murders, accidental deaths and ordinary people who are bewildered at the moment of truth."

There was a poignant silence between them during which their hands clasped and he drew her closer, wanting her warmth and comfort in the memory of his loss. Then he said whimsically, "I like that phrase. *The moment of truth.* There will be that for us."

And before she could ask him if he meant for Sicilians in general or for the two of them specifically, they heard Totò's voice from the *salone*. Though Casey didn't understand the words, she recognized the tone. Rico touched her cheek briefly, then released her hand and went back into the room, bantering good-naturedly with his father's argumentative voice.

Casey followed shortly, wondering if she looked as if she had been kissing and cuddling only moments ago. Trying to appear professional, she joined in the discussion that was going on in a confusing mixture of English, Italian and dialect. Finally, she went into the kitchen at Nolan's request to get Daniela and the children for a formal family portrait. Then Daniela called Paolo in from outside, and soon the *salone* was filled with the Butera family at their noisiest.

Nolan worked well with them, especially with the children. Still generally baffled by the Sicilians' way of speaking, he could at least speak to Franco and Maria with his elegant, limited, college-level Italian. They giggled and squirmed, delighting in the attentions of the photographer, the very important American journalist, their doting grandfather and—perhaps most of all, Casey thought—their teasing uncle.

When the last photo had finally been taken, Paolo went back outside where he had been dealing with some local farmworkers, the children tagged along with him and Daniela went back into the kitchen. It seemed to Casey that Daniela spent an awful lot of time cooking.

Totò complained loudly to Rico that Paolo had invited some colleague of his to dinner that night. Totò asserted that the man was a dreadful bore who would monopolize the conversation. This would be terribly dull for everyone, Totò said apologetically to Casey, but most of all for her, because the man spoke no English and didn't know how to keep his mouth shut.

Rico looked up at Casey. "So let's go out for dinner."

Her heart thumped for just a moment before Nolan said, "Yeah, that sounds great. According to Winnifred, some of the restaurant food in Sicily is reasonably palatable. Or was, in 1913."

After a brief look of regret in Casey's direction, Rico grinned and said, "She was undoubtedly a skinny old maid who disapproved of anything pleasurable. We have the best food in the world."

"Of course you do," Casey said blandly. She was becoming accustomed to the typical Sicilian assertion that everything in Sicily was the best that existed.

"This is a good idea, but where will you take them?" Totò asked.

That simple question precipitated twenty minutes of debate between the two men. Casey began to grow restless, and a little annoyed. When she went upstairs to freshen up and grab her big purse, she wondered why Rico, despite all his affection for his father, didn't simply tell the old man to mind his own business. Rico was a grown man, for God's sake. Casey couldn't imagine her own mother, whom she only saw about once a year anyhow, arguing with her for twenty minutes in front of two guests about where she should take them to dinner. A suggestion or two would be fine, but Totò was acting as if Rico were a teenager who didn't know how to entertain visitors.

She had observed Totò behaving in this way with Paolo and Daniela, but she had also observed enough of the manner in which the frequent visitors to the Butera household all behaved to know that Totò was not at all unusual. Everyone she met in Sicily comfortably mingled, interfered, questioned, criticized, advised—and all of it in this multigenerational atmosphere that made Casey feel strange.

As she came downstairs to find Nolan by the door, Rico came out of the *salone* and asked, "Ready?"

"Yes." She called her goodbye to Totò. She was rewarded by more advice.

"Tell Rico to take the old road, not that new highway. You understand me?"

She sighed. "Yes, Totò."

When she sat next to Rico in his red Citroën, however, she realized that to his way of thinking, nothing unusual had occurred. But when she gave him Totò's advice about the road, he spread his hands in a gesture of impatience and said, "That's crazy! Who does he think the new road is for? Donkeys?"

Chapter Six

Rico took Casey and Nolan to a beautiful seaside restaurant, where they ate a spectacular meal outside, amidst waving palm trees and fluttering bougainvillea, while the reflection of the moon and stars overhead danced on the lapping waters of the Mediterranean Sea.

Casey decided she was glad Nolan had come with them. She had noticed a beautiful little seaside inn next to the restaurant, and if it weren't for Nolan's presence, she had a feeling she would have urged Rico to spend the night with her there and to hell with the consequences.

The warm, glowing light in the black depths of his eyes, the subtle nudge of his knee against hers under the table and the way he sought many small excuses to touch her hand, all assured her that he wouldn't have needed much urging to spend this beautiful night alone in a seaside bedroom with her.

She sighed wistfully and took another sip of her delicious wine. Nolan was busy asking about the Phoenician ruins in Sicily and didn't notice her sigh. Rico noticed, but she saw by his expression that he knew the reason for it and didn't need to ask. His gaze flicked across the terrace to where the inn she had seen was nestled in a rocky cliff, then back to Casey. A thrill shot through her when she realized he was thinking the same thing.

Just as well Nolan's here, she reminded herself.

The conversation turned to the family after a while.

"What does Paolo do?" Nolan asked. "He's always so dusty when he comes home."

"He's an agricultural consultant. But he's only doing that part-time at the moment. Since my father's illness, Paolo has been managing the farm."

"And Daniela?" Casey asked. "Didn't you say she works at the university?"

"Normally," Rico replied. "She and Paolo met there originally. But last year, everything changed quickly. My mother died, and my father had a stroke. Someone needed to take care of him and the farm."

Casey frowned. "So Paolo and Daniela gave up their lives in Palermo?"

"They both took a leave of absence at the university, and Paolo moved most of his consulting work to this area."

"But...I don't mean to pry, Rico, but why didn't they simply sell your father's farm and move him into the city with them?"

Rico gave her a look that said she clearly didn't understand. "It's not my father's farm, Casey. It's the family's farm."

"Well, why didn't they sell the *family's*—"

"This is our home. This is our tradition. We do not sell these things to strangers because one generation grows old. The next takes up the responsibilities. That is natural."

"But Daniela is a university researcher who is reduced to cooking pasta all day and caring for a very sick old man miles from any decent modern medical care." Casey tried to keep her tone even and reasonable since she was speaking so frankly about things that were really none of her business.

Rico tilted his head and studied her. "The family is more important."

"More important than Daniela's work or fulfillment or personal and professional growth?" Casey challenged.

"You do not mention Paolo," he noted.

"At least he still gets to work at his profession, even if only part-time. And that still seems like quite a sacrifice to make for one's father-in-law's farm." She held up a hand. "Sorry, the family's farm."

"He does not make a sacrifice for the farm, Casey. We never questioned that we would keep the farm. But for all of us, Daniela included, the family comes first. She could not be fulfilled, as you say, at the university if we sold the farm and our father were staying at home alone all day in an apartment in Palermo where he has no friends."

"So why is Daniela the one who had to give up her career, even if it's only a leave of absence? Why didn't you?" Before he could answer, she added, "It's because she's a woman, isn't it?"

Rico had no answer to that.

"You can criticize the way we pay strangers to do things for us in America, things that you think the family should do, Rico, but at least a woman has some choice besides cooking, cleaning and caring for others all day."

"Daniela has a choice, Casey," he replied seriously. "She chose to marry, and she chose to have children. I admit, she would have been very unusual here if she had made any other choice, but nevertheless, she chose her way. And when our lives changed last year, she chose to move out to the farm again."

Casey looked down at her empty plate. The calamari had been superb. "It seems oppressive," she said at last.

"And I thought American life seemed very lonely. People seemed adrift there, left alone to cope with their problems."

"But don't you ever find it intrusive? Your father and your family watch and criticize and advise every move, every moment."

He smiled. "And to think, I didn't even live with my parents after I came back to Sicily from America. Here, most adults live with their parents until they are married, you know."

"You're kidding," Nolan interjected with a grimace.

Rico shrugged. "It's our way. I know that Americans value their privacy, but there isn't even a word for it in Italian."

Casey's eyes widened. "No word for privacy?"

"No." He shook his head. "Solitude, but not privacy."

She digested this information, then asked, "Don't you ever mind the lack of autonomy?"

He thought it over for a moment. "Do I mind that my father seeks my advice like an adult, yet scolds me like a little boy? That he constantly provokes me to find a wife and have children? That he spends twenty minutes explaining to me where I should take an American woman for dinner, while she waits impatiently nearby?" His quick smile told her he had noticed. "It can be tiresome, but it's our way. It's normal and comfortable, and I am at least free to express my irritation to my family, because nothing I can say can alienate them."

He paused to drink some of his wine. Casey noticed Nolan's speculative, uneasy expression as he looked at her. He had been unusually quiet for the past few minutes. He was used to her asking many questions, but she knew that he considered these particular questions surprisingly personal. He was evidently wondering just how personal her relationship with Rico had become while he was busy looking through his viewfinder.

"Every way of life has its drawbacks," Rico said. "Within the family, we do not divide up so cleanly and say, 'This is your property, and this is mine,' or 'This is your affair, and this is mine.' For us, it is all part of what matters to us, what belongs to us, what is our affair, for whatever touches our mother, father, sister, brother or children, touches us, too."

Casey could sense the love and belonging, she could see the oppression and burdens and she recognized, above all, the unswerving loyalty and commitment. "It's different," she said mildly at last.

"Different from your ways?" he asked. "You are not close to your family?"

"No."

"You do not spend much time with them?"

"Not much." She shot Nolan a warning look when he opened his mouth to speak. Nolan came from a close family and was usually urging her to forgive her father and grow closer to him. She didn't want him to bring up that old subject.

Nolan cleared his throat and finally said, "My family is close. Not as close as yours, obviously, but close."

Nolan spoke about the weekly phone calls and visits several times a year that kept him in touch with his parents and siblings. Casey finally admitted to Rico's obvious dismay that she only saw her mother and brother about once a year, spoke to her mother about once a month and spoke to her brother far less often. She carefully steered the conversation away from any mention of her errant father.

Their salads arrived, fresh and crispy, seasoned with lemon and pepper and a dark olive oil that even Rico admitted was unusually good.

"So tell me about your work," Casey urged Rico. "You have said there are water shortages, that your work involves a struggle against the Mafia, that you spend a lot of time hiking up and down valleys. I'm curious about all that."

"It's fortunate you ask me this question here instead of at home," Rico admitted with a boyish grin. "They are all sick of hearing me talk about it."

"This is our first time," Nolan said, "so feel free."

"Water has been rationed in Palermo for quite some time now, as well as in many parts of western Sicily. Some towns in the interior may get water only once every five or ten days."

"How do they survive?" Casey asked, pulling out her notebook despite having eaten only half of her salad. She had a feeling she was about to be drawn into the web of Sicily again, and she found herself feeling more willing every time.

"Well, some go to public fountains and collect whatever water trickles out, though no one feels comfortable about drinking it. Most have no choice but to buy water, either from private wells in the country or from trucks that bring it into the towns."

"And I can guess who's selling that water," Casey said cynically.

Rico nodded, his eyes darkening. "A couple of years ago, there were strikes. People protested that they were without water for many days, while the lush orange groves outside of Palermo were damp and green, and certain olive groves near Agrigento had sprinklers watering them."

"How can water be available to some people but not others?" Nolan wondered.

"Because the Mafia control the major wells and springs that tap the subterranean water layers, and they are very clever at manipulating government and property. They are also ruthless. When change began coming to Sicily after World War II, it was not unknown for them to have dams blown up that threatened their monopoly on the water supply."

"So you mean whole towns go dry because the water supply is controlled by these guys?" Nolan demanded. Casey was scribbling furiously in her notebook.

Rico smiled mildly at Nolan's question. "Actually they are not the sole problem. The water shortage in Sicily is very complex. The greatest frustration is that there is, in reality, enough water."

"What are the other factors?" Casey asked.

"In Palermo, the water system is such a confused maze of modern connections to ancient conduits built by the Bourbon conquerors that the water authorities hardly know how water gets from one place to another, much less how to ensure equitable distribution. The pipes are so old and rotting, that we estimate at least one third of the water, probably more, leaks out before it reaches its destination.''

''That must be sickening to think about if you haven't had tap water for five days,'' Casey commented.

''Political corruption is another problem. Some government officials simply let *mafiosi* have their way, because it has always been so and is only slowly changing. Others are hand in glove with the Mafia. Two years ago, three of the officials responsible for Palermo's water supply came under investigation for fraud and association with the Mafia.

''Then there are also the age-old problems of political patronage and general chaos. I am working as part of a newly appointed commission to deal with the water supply in western Sicily, which has been managed—or rather mismanaged—until now by a collection of various local agencies all under the control of various political parties, none of them talking to each other or cooperating in anything, and all of them interested mainly in providing jobs to their friends.''

He sighed heavily and took a long drink of wine. ''And I'm spending so much time in the Belice Valley right now, hiking up and down like some Boy Scout, because, once again, water is disappearing, not getting where it is supposed to go. And I have to find out why.''

''You think there's been some sabotage to the water lines?'' Casey asked.

He nodded, looking suddenly weary. ''It's what we suspect. I want to build dams, reservoirs and aqueducts, to give water where there has never been enough. But before we do that, we must know the extent of the problem. And trying to push sensible recommendations through such a complicated bureaucracy, and then trying to get funding from Rome and the E.E.C. when so much of their money has already disappeared with no results in Sicily...'' He shook his head, overwhelmed for a moment. Then his dark eyes glittered as they met Casey's. ''But we will do it, somehow. And when *I* have grandchildren, they will have water every day of the week, no matter what part of Sicily they inhabit.''

She lowered her notebook and let him see her admiration. For a moment she was just a woman, not a skeptical journalist, and she believed in him, believed in his strength and his ability, relished his commitment and his passion.

''I've heard of the Belice Valley before,'' Nolan said. ''Why is that?''

''More sad stories of Sicily,'' Rico said. ''There was a terrible earthquake there in 1968. It destroyed five whole towns and many farms. And funding for rebuilding has disappeared into certain pockets many times since then. Many parts of the Belice Valley are still a wasteland, and many people either live in tents and metal shacks, still awaiting the promised reconstruction, or else they have left the valley forever.''

''How do you stand it?'' Casey asked suddenly, wondering at the pain he must feel for every scar borne by this island he loved.

''By remembering and taking pleasure in everything that's good here, by hanging on to everything that makes me love Sicily, that makes it impossible for me to leave.''

''*Is* it impossible for you to leave?'' she asked curiously.

''Impossible.'' He touched her again, careless of what Nolan might think. ''It was good for me to live in America, to learn other ways, to get a fine education. But I could only enjoy it because I knew that I would eventually come home for good. I belong here.''

Casey supposed she had recognized that all along. His roots here were as deep as those of the olive trees planted by the Greeks some twenty-five centuries ago.

''I guess we should consider ourselves lucky that there's been enough water at your father's farm while we've been here,'' Nolan said. ''Casey, if you're not going to finish your salad . . .''

She pushed her salad in Nolan's direction while Rico said, ''We always have enough water at the farm now.''

"Why?" Casey asked.

"I have seen to it."

She stared at him. "How?"

"I know the right people," he said simply. He poured some more wine into all of their glasses, looking quite untroubled by this remarkable statement.

"You mean you use the system—this system about which you have told me so many woeful tales—to your advantage?" she demanded.

Rico's eyes flickered up to her face. He looked faintly surprised at her tone. "Yes." When she continued to stare, he added, "I know the world I want, Casey, but I also know the one I live in."

"Apparently it's one without principles," she said quietly. Nolan's eyes bulged.

Rico's eyes narrowed. Not with anger, Casey realized. He simply didn't see how she could fail to understand. "Should I let my family go without water, when I can make sure it is provided?" he asked. The question was so obviously rhetorical that Casey remained silent. "Should I let their garden grow thirsty when I can prevent it?"

"It's a difficult question, Rico," she said at last, "but it seems to be that by participating, you're perpetuating and supporting a way of life that you keep saying you want to see disappear."

He leaned forward, resting his elbows on the table, and she realized wryly that far from being dismayed by her challenge, he was prepared to relish a new argument. "The most important thing about our way of life here—and one I would never want to change—is that we care for each other. How could I neglect the people I love?"

"Couldn't you find an official way to make sure your family gets water?" she countered.

He smiled. "You mean, a way you approve of?"

"Don't heap this on my plate," she chided. "*You're* the one who's been complaining to me about protectionism and double-dealing ever since I got here."

"Then let me put it this way. If I did not use my con-
tacts—whatever their nature—to help my family, no one in
all of Sicily would understand that. Myself included."

"I find the inconsistencies hard to understand," she said.

He fixed his gaze upon her, a look that spoke of all the
mutual fascination they had felt for each other since her
arrival in Sicily. "But you like to explore them."

I'd like to explore you.

The thought echoed through Casey so strongly that, for
a moment, she was afraid she had spoken it aloud. A fur-
tive glance at Nolan, however, assured her that it had been
only a thought. But she saw in Rico's eyes that he had heard
it. The silence of their longing was deafening between them.

The waiter came to their table, and Rico asked for the
check after Casey and Nolan assured him they didn't want
anything else.

"What about your brother?" she asked after the waiter
had disappeared again. "You said he lives in the north.
Obviously, it wasn't impossible for him to leave Sicily."

"No, but he misses it terribly sometimes."

"Why did he leave?"

Rico shifted in his chair. Casey could tell immediately
that the subject was a sad one to him. "He's a lawyer. Like
me, he believed we could change things. He worked in Palermo, investigating and prosecuting cases against the Mafia in the early days of the maxi-trial."

"What happened?" Casey asked, afraid she already
knew.

"He was scared, of course," Rico continued, "after
several of his colleagues were killed, but he persisted. When
his wife and daughter were threatened, however, he quit.
And he was so bitter about the defeat that he couldn't bear
to remain in Sicily. He finally came to believe that nothing
would ever change here." Rico shrugged. "His wife is a
northerner who had never really wanted to live here anyhow, so they moved to her native city of Verona. We only
see him a few times a year, and that is a source of great
sorrow to my father."

"I'm so sorry," Casey said.

"That's a hard story," Nolan said, pensively. "Do you stay because you think things can change?"

Rico nodded. "I believe it. But some days," he admitted with wry sadness, "it's harder to believe than other days."

No longer caring what Nolan might say to her later, Casey reached for Rico's hand and laced her fingers with his on top of the white tablecloth. "The battlefield looks largest to the one fighting in the middle of it." It sounded like something Totò might say.

Rico's expression softened with pleasure, or maybe gratitude, and he lifted her hand to his mouth for a tender, gallant kiss. Something about the gesture squeezed Casey's insides.

Their mood changed a moment later, however, when the waiter brought the check over and Casey tried to pay for it. "Look, I appreciate your generosity, Rico, but your family has already done so much for us," Casey said. "At least let *Sentinel* pick up the tab for dinner."

"No. You are my guests."

That obviously seemed to settle the question in his mind, but Casey wasn't satisfied. She cast Nolan a pleading look, so he said, "Come on, Rico, hand it over. I've got to show *something* on my expense account when I go back to New York."

Rico looked at Nolan and hesitated. "I don't . . ."

"Be a sport and give me the check," Nolan urged.

Seeing Rico's indecision, Casey became incensed. "Wait a minute, wait a *minute*." Both men looked at her. "When *I* asked for the check, it was clearly out of the question. Now that Nolan's asking for it, you're considering it. Why is that, Rico?"

He gave her another of those infuriating stares that said she didn't understand something very simple and obvious.

"It's because I'm a woman, isn't it?" she demanded.

"Casey, I don't let women pay for me."

"All right, that *does* it." She threw her napkin on the table and pointed a stern forefinger at him. "I've had it with your machismo, Rico!"

"*Machismo* is a Spanish—"

"It doesn't matter!" She interrupted him. "When I first got here, you talked about me like I wasn't there, telling Nolan to go everywhere with me like I was some kind of helpless child."

"Women here do not—"

"Then you tried to *order* me to stay in the car when we got to Alcamo and you realized there'd been a killing."

"I did not *order*—"

"*Then* you kept trying to haul me back to the car with your 'this isn't fit for the eyes of a woman' routine."

"Casey, I think you're exagger—"

"And *now* you're refusing to let *me* pick up the tab with my company card, but it's okay if Nolan picks it up." She took a deep breath, her eyes daring him to contradict her, then continued, "I am an experienced, responsible, capable, self-supporting, professional adult, Rico, and I insist upon being treated as such. I am not accustomed to being protected, ordered around, spoken about as if I weren't present or treated like a silly blonde who can't handle myself. Is that clear?"

"Yes, Casey," he said placatingly.

The fact that he failed to look suitably chagrined only added to her annoyance. "I am paying for tonight. Is that also clear?"

He held his palms up in that now-familiar gesture of acquiescence. "Of course, Casey. Pay it."

The notion that she had enchanted him more than she had impressed him made her continue speaking as she handed the waiter her credit card and waited for him to return with the credit slip. "I used to be a crime reporter for a daily paper, you know. I saw all kinds of things, Rico, under all sorts of circumstances. I'm not some fragile flower in need of protection."

''No, I have seen that you are not.'' His gaze was fond and admiring. ''But it is my nature to try to shield you. I was taught that by my father and my culture. A woman walks through the door first, sits first, doesn't go out alone, and,'' he added with a grin as the waiter placed the credit slip before him, ''a woman is never allowed to pay.''

''Well, you'll just have to make an exception in my case,'' she said crisply, reaching for the bill and signing the credit slip.

''I'll let you pay tonight,'' he conceded. That was all he conceded.

He teased her on the trip home about the way she still kept her eyes closed when he was driving. He had noticed it on the way to the restaurant, too. He wasn't offended. It was one of those quirky things about Casey, like her boundless curiosity and the sudden challenge of her arguments, that he found so enchanting, so intriguing, so special. It was just another one of those things, he acknowledged silently, that made it impossible for him to stop thinking about her.

It was late by the time they reached the Butera farm. Totò, Franco and Maria had all gone to bed already, and Paolo and Daniela went upstairs right after asking Casey and Nolan about their evening.

''Well, I guess I'll hit the sack, too,'' Nolan said, rising from his chair in the kitchen. ''I was up and out by dawn again today with my cameras. God, you have a beautiful island, Rico.''

''Yes, we do,'' Rico agreed with quiet pride. ''If you like, perhaps we will have time to see some of Giuliano's country. The hills and caves where he and my father lived as bandits.''

''Hey, that would be terrific!'' Nolan exclaimed. ''Wouldn't that be a nice visual touch for the article, Casey?''

Casey agreed it would be. She knew that the archivist at *Sentinel* had already found a few old shots of Salvatore Giuliano, handsome and proud. Photos of Sagana Mountain, Monte D'Oro and the Grotto Bianco would help the readers visualize those days of yore. It was such a shame, she thought, that no photos existed of Totò during those days. As an outlaw, he had uncharacteristically but wisely avoided cameras.

"Well," Nolan said, "have a good night, you two." He paused. "I mean, I'll see you both in the morning." He cleared his throat and said, "I mean, we'll all three see each other in the morning." He grinned at Casey's incredulous expression and finally finished, "What I mean is, I'm going to bed and minding my own business."

Casey remained sitting silently beside Rico as Nolan exited the room and tromped upstairs. When she heard his footsteps fade, she finally said, "I guess it's noticeable."

He knew what she meant. "I guess it is."

Their gazes met in silent communication. She loved his eyes, she thought suddenly. They were so filled with complex and continually changing combinations of laughter and anger, kindness and impatience, excitement and resignation. "You're a complicated man," she murmured.

"But you love a challenge."

She felt sad. "My challenges are thousands of miles from here, Rico."

He looked away from her. She regretted having spoiled the moment with the truth, even though it was her way. Looking to change the subject, to bring cheer back into the room, she said, "What's that wonderful smell? I've noticed it before, especially first thing in the morning."

He sniffed the air and smiled again, ready to be happy for the moment. "I'm so used to it, I hardly ever notice it. It's my mother's window box." He stood up and parted the curtains over the long, low window on the eastern wall of the house. Casey followed him and peered through the open window. "It's been there since before I was born. My father built it for her."

Perched outside the window was a large window box, over a foot wide and three feet long. An abundant collection of fresh spices and herbs grew there.

"Your parents have been here since before you were born?"

Rico nodded. "This was my mother's family's farm. She had one brother who died in the war, one sister who emigrated to America with her husband and another sister who didn't survive childhood, so my mother inherited the farm." His eyes sparkled as he added, "My father built the window box for her long before they were married, while he was still a bandit. It was sort of a courtship gesture."

"Totò must have been a fine carpenter. That thing is sturdy."

"It has strong supports. You can see them, if you look at it from the outside."

She hadn't explored the east side of the house yet. She probably wouldn't have time to, either. "It's nice to have fresh spices in all your food." And then, as if she couldn't stop herself, she added, "I'll miss Daniela's cooking when I go back to New York."

"Is that all you'll miss?"

"No, of course not." The admission came out of her throat with husky honesty. "Rico..."

He heard the sadness in her voice and pulled her into his arms without thinking, aware only of the need to comfort and be comforted. He buried his face in her soft blond hair, smiling because her hair was always a little messy, and kissed her neck, her earlobe, her shoulder. He ran his hands over her back and round bottom, soaking in the pleasure of holding her.

"Before," he said wistfully, "I always thought of a Sicilian woman, a woman whose ways were the same as mine, a woman who wanted to fix my meals, care for my children, wait for me to come home." He sighed and kissed her hair. "Now I think only of you."

"That's a switch," she muttered.

"It is," he agreed wryly. "I am more Americanized than I thought."

"We live thousands of miles apart."

"It would place a strain on courtship," he admitted. Then he whispered fiercely, "I don't want you to go."

To be held by him was to be healed, she thought. Healed of loneliness and weariness. "I don't want to leave now," she answered, "but...Rico, it's also very important for me to get back to New York on time."

"I know. Americans are so punctual."

"It's more than that."

He drew away and looked down into her smooth face with its creamy skin and exotically foreign features. He brushed her hair off her forehead and touched her cheek with all the tenderness welling up inside him, feelings so strong he felt stunned by them. "Tell me."

She pulled slowly out of his arms, ending the embrace. She circled the table and looked out the other window, into the dark rural night. "I kind of left unfinished business there."

"A story you have to complete?"

"No. It's harder to explain than that." She sighed and turned to face him. "I've always been very ambitious, Rico."

"I believe that." It didn't take much insight to see that she was one of those Americans whose work came before all other things—family, friends and lovers. He only needed insight to understand why such a woman was able to touch his soul.

She looked around, as if seeking hints to her own complex character. "I grew up in tough circumstances, seeing my mom scrape and scrounge after my father lost everything and split on us. I guess I felt a lot of humiliation while I was growing up."

Alienation, he thought, but kept silent. Her father sounded like an abandoned man to Rico, so how could he have known not to abandon his own family? It was wrong, certainly, but the wrong began with the family who had failed to guide Casey's father.

"And I always felt the need to prove myself, academically, socially, professionally." She shrugged. "And I like excitement. I...I'm not capable of being that kind of woman you described. You know, they also serve who stand and wait. That's not me."

"No." She liked to be at the center of the action. He had already seen that.

"I'm a good journalist, and I love my work. And certainly there's something to be said for human-interest stories and personal interviews. But it's not really enough for me."

"Then why did you leave being a crime reporter?"

"Well, it was very limiting," she said. "Of course, it was interesting. But essentially, I would just go to scenes of crimes day after day, keep up with the police department on the latest developments—that kind of thing. I grew dissatisfied after a few years because there was no in-depth work, no chance to really explore things."

"So you went to *Sentinel,* where you have more scope."

"Yes. I still work at a ridiculous pace—I was finishing another story right up until the moment I hailed a cab for the airport, and did half of my research about *this* story in the plane on the way here—but that's the nature of journalism. I accept that. At least I get to explore a topic thoroughly, do an article every couple of weeks instead of every day, do different kinds of topics."

"So what is your dissatisfaction now?" he said, hearing it in her voice despite her positive comments.

"I had more than one job offer when I accepted the job with *Sentinel.* One of the reasons I wanted to work for them was that I thought they offered me the best chance of fulfilling my particular ambition."

"Which is?"

"I want to be a war correspondent. I always have." She saw his slightly surprised look, and rushed on, "It's not because I think that's the way to a Pulitzer Prize or anything arrogant like that. It's just where I really believe all of my personal and professional talents would finally be used to their fullest. It's what I see as the greatest challenge, and...I love a challenge.

"I remember when that famous Italian journalist was reporting in Vietnam, when I was a kid. I've read all her accounts in translation, and I wanted to learn for myself if I would be as brave as she was, if I would contribute the quality of work that she did under such circumstances."

"I believe you would," he said honestly.

"But I want to *know*." She came forward and sat across from him at the table again. "*Sentinel* made all kinds of vague promises when they hired me three years ago. I've put in my time, honed my skills, proved myself in a variety of situations. I put together a proposal on a story about rebel troops and training in a South American civil war. The editorial staff got so interested that they decided to do a series on it.

"I was so excited. I kept working on all my other stories, naturally, but I just knew they were going to send me to the front lines at last. I speak Spanish, I had made the proposal, I had put in my time. I was ready. I was the obvious choice."

"Oh, Casey... They didn't choose you?"

She shook her head. "No. They didn't." She couldn't dispute the bitterness in her voice. "I listened to their reasons, all very weak and vague. I really tried to examine their comments honestly, to see if they had a point. But they didn't. They didn't send me, Rico, because I'm a woman, and nobody really likes to send women to the middle of a war zone. Particularly *that* one, where everything is so unstable and confusing."

"So they sent a man," Rico concluded.

"Yes. And there's nothing wrong with the guy they sent. He's good at his job. But *I* would have been better, and that story was *mine*."

"I find it ironic that they sent you to Sicily, Casey. This *is* a war zone."

She hardly thought so, but she didn't want to argue about it. "They sent me here to placate me. Until all of this happened, the magazine had been relatively skeptical about the merit of this story on your father. It all took place more than forty years ago, as you keep reminding me, and I didn't know how much Totò could really tell us. But they gave me the story to make up for the one they'd taken away. And then," she added in remembered irritation, "my editor was worried about my staying here with a retired bandit. That's why I've had it up to *here* with people worrying about this helpless little woman, Rico."

"Yes, I can understand that," he conceded.

"Everything happened very fast after that. They more or less gave me the go-ahead on this story so I wouldn't quit, but I'm still not sure whether or not I want to quit. I definitely want a straight answer about what kind of future I can expect at *Sentinel,* because if I'm always going to have the same problem with them, I'm looking for a new job the day after I get back." She sighed. "And if this story is good enough, it... Well, it'll help me out a lot, either as leverage with *Sentinel* or as an added credential while I'm looking for the kind of job I want."

"Will it be good enough?" he questioned.

If you are prepared, then I will break my silence for you. Totò's voice floated through her mind, agonized and breathless, serious and desperate.

What did Totò know? Was it something important to him alone, or was it something that everyone wanted to know, the answer to one of Giuliano's many mysteries? Or, she wondered bleakly, had his strange behavior this afternoon merely been the dizzy spell of a sick old man?

"Casey?" Rico prompted.

"What? Oh. I don't know yet." She smiled. "The interview's not over yet."

"Yes. Something about a fat lady singing comes to mind?" Rico rose one dark brow, his eyes heavy-lidded and playful.

She grinned, brushing aside her thoughts. Totò had made it clear that whatever his secret might be, it was for her alone. "You picked up a lot in America."

"Yes," he agreed. "Slang, habits, fashion...women." He wiggled both brows.

She laughed at him. "What...habits?"

"Orange juice with breakfast every day. Fast food. Southern jazz music. Baseball. Old gangster movies—they have a certain charm when they're so far removed from the source," he added wryly. "Blue jeans."

"Yes, I notice you're always wearing jeans when you come home from work. Do your employers approve?"

"Not really," he admitted. "But they need me too much to make a fuss about what I wear on my legs."

"But you went formal today." She reached across the table and touched the knot of his necktie.

"I had to deliver a speech to a lot of self-proclaimed very important persons today."

"On what?"

"The chronic water shortage, what else?"

"And tomorrow you have to hike around the Belice Valley looking for the source of drainage on a particular system?"

He shrugged. "I've been doing it so much this season I'm starting to think I should form my own hiking club." He folded his hand around hers and pulled it against his chest. "I wish you could come with me."

"So do I," she admitted softly.

"There are some lonely spots out there." He glanced above their heads for a moment, to where half a dozen other people slept on the second floor of the house. "And it seems as if you and I shall never be alone."

"Perhaps it's just as well."

"No." He shook his head as he raised her hand and pressed his lips warmly against her palm. He kissed each of her fingers in turn as he spoke. "Even if you and I shall never meet again, we should enjoy whatever we can have together now. For there will never be another time like this."

When she felt his tongue, moist and velvet soft, tracing teasingly between her fingers, she made a little sound of longing and squeezed her eyes shut. Maybe he was right, she thought suddenly. To be with him only once and never again probably wouldn't be as bad as never having shared even a single night with him.

She watched him rub his cheek against her knuckles, his eyes closed with concentration, his jaw raspy with the shadow of his dark beard. "You never come to New York?" she asked bleakly.

He kept his eyes closed as he answered her, massaging her hand with gentle, knowing fingers. "For you I would come. But Casey, would you want me to? Once a year? Maybe twice if things go well and I can get away?"

"Oh, Rico..." No, there was no life in that. She couldn't have a relationship with someone she only saw once or twice a year, and knowing those visits were imminent would add guilt to any normal relationship either of them tried to develop in their own countries in the meantime.

Accepting that there was no future with him, she made a sudden decision to relish every moment of this special time. "How can we be alone?" she whispered.

His eyes opened at that, slowly, their dark glittering depths still partially hidden by his lashes. Nevertheless, his expression set her heart to thudding heavily. "Do you want to?"

"Yes."

He reached forward and took her other hand, cradling both of hers between both of his. His brow furrowed as he thought. "Tomorrow night," he said slowly.

"Yes," she whispered again, excited now, realizing it was really going to happen.

"I will tell my father that you have expressed a wish to see Erice, a mountain town not very far from here. But far away in another sense, Casey," he added. "You can tell Nolan whatever you wish. He will realize the truth, anyhow."

"Will your father? And your sister?"

He shrugged. "Probably. But they will still be respectful of you."

She smiled, finding him endearingly quaint sometimes. "I was thinking more in terms of whether or not they'd be embarrassed about us going away together for a night. Or offended at my disappearing, since I'm their guest.''

"You are also my guest," he pointed out. "Let me handle them.''

"All right." She paused, thinking. "I want to spend the morning interviewing your father, but he tires so easily that—''

"No, I'm afraid we'll have to leave much later. My father's planning a surprise for you tomorrow morning."

"Oh?" she said uneasily.

"I've promised him that I'll take the morning off and do my work in the afternoon so we can all take you into the village for Saturday morning. You can see the market, sit with my father in the piazza…. Meet more of his friends," he added wickedly.

Casey groaned. "I can see it's going to be a long day."

"Yes. And a long night," he promised her.

She smiled at him, feeling both eager and strangely shy. He kissed both of her hands, then turned them over to kiss the palms. Casey sighed, wishing the next twenty-four hours would just disappear. He held her gaze for one long, hot moment.

Then he grinned and said, "You had better go upstairs now, before we disgrace my mother's kitchen table."

"What about you?"

"I will finish locking up the house and sleep on the couch in the study."

"All right." She rose from the table. At the doorway she paused and said, "Good night, Rico."

"Good night, Casey."

Both of them were glowingly aware that come tomorrow, they wouldn't have to say good-night. By this time tomorrow, they would be wrapped around each other.

Chapter Seven

Their pleasant breakfast of hot rolls and *cappuccino* the next morning was followed by a panicked hour during which Daniela tried to organize her two children for a morning in the village, while Rico helped his father prepare for the adventure and Paolo chatted with Casey. Although Casey had learned a dozen or so phrases of Italian over the course of the week, she still had no idea what Paolo was saying. However, she had developed a fondness for this friendly, generous man, and she enjoyed his earnest efforts to communicate with the foreign strangers in his home. Nolan was occupied with showering, having already been reminded by Rico to disconnect the hot-water heater before he turned on the water—it was not unknown for people to be electrocuted by their hot-water system in Sicily, Rico explained cheerfully.

Nolan, Paolo, Daniela and Totò departed in Rico's red Citroën. Rico, Casey and the children followed behind them in Daniela's little Fiat 500. Casey had never seen such a tiny car and commented that it was a good thing Maria and Franco were so small or they'd have to ride on the roof. Rico translated this comment for his niece and nephew, and they repeated it often, obviously thinking Casey was a great wit.

The western Sicilian village to which the family brought Casey that morning was a typical rural marketing center of the region, Rico told her. It was evident as soon as they arrived that old Totò Butera knew many people, for Casey spent nearly another hour being introduced to local people who had heard all about her but had not yet had the opportunity to meet her. She also noticed more distant acquaintances, people to whom Totò waved without stopping for conversation or introductions.

Every time Casey encountered people whom she had already met, she was greeted with great enthusiasm. Several of them even gave her the traditional greeting she had noticed among the Buteras and other Sicilians—a kiss on each cheek, perhaps accompanied by a firm clasp of hands.

The Butera cousins who were planning a wedding showed up while Casey was sitting in an outdoor café with Totò, enjoying a drink called *latte di mandorla*. Rico had told her that the words meant "almond milk," and that sounded so exotic she insisted he refrain from saying anything prosaic about the ingredients. Rico was obliged to kiss all of his cousins in greeting, and Casey admired the ease with which Sicilian men embraced each other, for all their annoying machismo.

When Totò introduced Casey to his sister, she immediately pulled out her notebook and began asking the woman questions about Giuliano's era. Although the woman knew a little English, it was far too rudimentary for an interview. Consequently, Rico was pressed into service as an interpreter.

As the slow but enjoyable interview progressed, with all the comments passing from English to Italian and back again, Casey began to realize that most of the staff and patrons of the café, not to mention a considerable number of pedestrians strolling by, were paying rapt attention to the whole process.

When Casey was done interviewing Totò's sister, she herself became the object of dozens of questions from the spectators who had grown so interested in her interview. With that friendly group joviality that Casey was learning to enjoy among Sicilians, a total stranger ambled over and asked Casey about her work, his interest being echoed soundly by the people around them. She in turn asked the stranger about his background, using Rico as her translator.

This process was repeated many times, and Rico was forced to ask Casey, more than once and phrased in a variety of ways, why her mamma had let her come so far from home all by herself, and which man she belonged to. Her repeated answer that she didn't need her mamma's permission to do anything and that she had no man to look after her provoked varying reactions. Some obviously felt sorry for her, some thought those Americans were strange people and some expressed envy or admiration.

Finally, another stranger asked her about her notebook. He had noticed, Rico explained, that no matter whom she spoke to or what they discussed, she wrote something in her notebook. Casey explained her use of the notebook to him, then gratefully smiled at Rico when he suggested they walk around a bit.

"I was starting to feel like a sideshow," she told Rico as they walked away, leaving the family and a few dozen people behind them to mutter about the strange habits of the foreign woman.

"Yes, I could tell," Rico said wryly.

They had made plans with the family to meet at a *trattoria* when it was time for the midday meal. Until then, Rico would show Casey around the market, Nolan would accompany Paolo, Daniela would shop with her cousins and the children would remain in the piazza with Totò and his sister.

Rico led Casey through the maze of the village, the colorful, narrow streets lined by old stone houses, each with balconies brightened by flowers. The outskirts of the town, Casey had noticed, were modern and desolate, composed of characterless gray concrete towers and drab parking lots.

"The only comforting thing about those structures," Rico had told her, "is that they were not built to last. Although that may not be comforting to the poor families living inside them."

But here in the heart of the town was the heart of Sicily: the cheerful, dramatic music of men and women bargaining with each other; the bright banners of laundry fluttering overhead from a dozen different clotheslines in every street; the vegetable-laden donkey carts and the more numerous motorized vehicles from which brawny young men unloaded fresh, sun-warmed produce while older men in tweed caps urged them to be careful or argued with each other about anything that occurred to them; the young mothers with their energetic, dark-haired children; the older mothers, whose teenage sons and daughters cast eager glances at one another; the occasional priest or nun and the omnipresence of old-world Catholicism in religious jewelry, plaques, shop decorations and the carefully tended shrines Casey noticed in a few old streets.

But Casey had also quickly discovered, as she strolled along with Rico, that putting away her notebook and leaving the café had not made her any less an object of curiosity in this village.

Tired of it all, she asked Rico if her face had turned green or her hair had caught fire. When he assured her that she looked absolutely beautiful and quite normal, she demanded, "Then why is everyone staring at me?"

It was the truth, she made him admit, and not just some form of paranoia. As they strolled through the twisting streets, wandering in and out of the sprawling, meandering open-air market, virtually everyone they encountered stared intently at Casey while she examined their wares.

A car full of young men had stopped in the middle of the main street and blocked traffic so they could scrutinize Casey, calling cheerfully to her until Rico had intervened. Two children playing in the shadows of one steep, narrow, ancient street had stopped their frolicking upon seeing Casey and regarded her with a mixture of awe and fear that made her want to look in a mirror to see if something disfiguring had happened to her without her realizing it.

A group of slightly bolder children followed Casey and Rico around for nearly half an hour, quite openly watching her and talking about her, trailing after her into shops and whispering in fascination every time she looked at or expressed an interest in something for sale. When she finally gave Rico a pleading glance, he good-naturedly chased away the *bambini*.

"You are different, so they stare," Rico said simply.

"It's not as if I stepped out of a spaceship, Rico."

"Search this whole village," he invited, "and tell me if you find one other tall, blond, blue-eyed woman."

"But a lot of foreign tourists come to Sicily now."

"Not that many, and the majority of them stay safely within the boundaries of resort towns like Taormina and Cefalù."

"I've looked at the local papers," she persisted doggedly. "More than half the films showing are imported from America and England, not to mention all the American television shows I've noticed Franco and Maria watching. They're all dubbed in Italian, sure, but they're full of women who look like me. Give or take a few pounds."

He grinned at that last comment, for she had confided to him that she feared the consequences of consuming vast portions of Daniela's cooking while missing her aerobics classes for a solid week. Standing so that no one else could see, he gave her bottom a teasing, affectionate caress. "I think your thighs are perhaps the sexiest thing about you," he insisted.

Her eyes sparkled as she tore her gaze away from a display of ceramics and looked up at him. "You're just saying that to get me into bed."

They laughed together, both thinking about tonight, both excited. "Before we left the house this morning, I called a hotel in Erice and made our reservation."

She gave him a playfully suspicious look. "That was awfully efficient. Do you take women there often?"

He grimaced. "No. I was there with two dreary officials from the ministry in Rome last year." He kissed her cheek, touching her more freely now that they had made their decision. "I hope you will be more fun than they were."

"I'll do my best," she said dryly.

When they came to some fishmongers' displays, Casey was fascinated by the way the small fish being sold had been tied so that their tails curled gaily into the air. She made a face at the disgusting display of raw octopuses, and she elbowed Rico sharply when he teasingly promised to have Daniela make some for supper the following night. The threatening snouts of half a dozen swordfish stood straight up, looking almost like weapons, while someone skillfully cut fillets off their meaty carcasses and people crowded around to demand the best cuts and reject the worst.

He led her into a pharmacy after that. Unlike the American drugstores to which she was accustomed, there were no goods on display in this shop. It was a small, dim cubbyhole with many closed cupboards. An attractive young woman dressed in an official-looking white cotton coat waited on them from behind a wide glass counter.

"Self-service is still uncommon in Sicily. Here you must ask the pharmacist for your goods," Rico explained after the female pharmacist had disappeared to the back room to get whatever Rico had requested.

"Even ordinary things? Like cough syrup and antacids?"

"Yes. Even ordinary things like this," he answered, taking a small cardboard box that the pharmacist handed him. Rico responded absently to some comment the young woman made, then held the box out to Casey.

The expression on his face, half tender, half teasing, made her regard him suspiciously. She took the box from him and examined it. A moment later her eyes flashed up to his face again. She didn't understand the writing on the box, but the illustrations were probably the same the world over.

"Do you like this kind?" Rico asked innocently.

Casey glanced at the girl, who returned her look with undisguised curiosity. "Gee, I don't know, Rico. I've never had occasion to use Italian ones." She handed the box back to him. "I'll have to trust your judgment."

He grinned at that and placed the box on the counter, telling the girl he'd take it. Then he was serious for a moment. "They are necessary, aren't they?"

"Yes," she admitted. She added somewhat awkwardly, "I didn't bring... I mean, I wasn't expecting to..." She shrugged. He knew what she meant.

He took her hand and pressed a kiss against her palm. "Neither did I," he admitted, "and Sicilian stores don't keep American hours. If I don't buy them this morning, there won't be another opportunity before tonight."

She smiled and squeezed his hand to show him she didn't mind. Better that they should buy some form of protection together in front of this gaping shop girl—who was watching them avidly even as she wrapped their purchase in gray paper and rang it up on her cash register—than that Rico should just ignore the issue and blame her tonight for her lack of foresight, as many men might have done.

Rico stuck the bag into her purse as they left the shop, and the incident drew her closer to him, making her surer than ever that she really wanted to go ahead with this crazy plan to spend one night in Sicily with a man she might never see again. How could she not want to be with this man who so obviously wanted to take good care of her?

Notwithstanding their interesting morning in the colorful market, the real entertainment actually began just after noon, when Casey found a few things she wanted to buy, including a large ceramic platter with an octopus painted on it. Not only was it beautiful, it would also always remind her of the many things she had learned in Sicily, and of the man who had taught them to her.

When the merchant told her the price, she thought it was quite reasonable and started to reach into her purse for her wallet. Rico's hand on her arm stilled her.

"Don't do that," he admonished. "He's asking you too much."

"It's not so much."

Rico rolled his eyes. "Let me handle this, okay?"

"But I—" As soon as she saw that familiar look, she closed her mouth and nodded.

It all reminded her a lot of the scene at the airport. Rico and the merchant argued for nearly ten minutes, sometimes sounding soft and sympathetic, sometimes loud and irreconcilable. The merchant made a number of those familiar gestures, placing his palms together as if he was praying, making a circle in the air with his fingertips, drawing his shoulders up around his ears and spreading his palms wide. Something about his demeanor suggested that Rico was the single most unreasonable man he had ever met. And just when Casey figured that Rico had really offended the man and she might as well kiss her ceramic platter goodbye, the two men grinned, shook hands and settled on a price.

The merchant wrapped the platter up in some newspaper, then he and the other merchants in the little alley made a project out of finding a suitable carrying bag for Casey when she admitted she hadn't brought one. Rico paid for the platter, over Casey's objections, insisting she let it be his gift to her.

Realizing he wouldn't relent, she finally gave in. As they walked away, she said teasingly, "Well, if I had known *you* were paying, I would have gotten that really expensive one."

"Would you rather have that one?" he asked seriously, looking quite prepared to go back and go through the whole ritual again.

"Oh, Rico." Casey smiled and kissed his cheek. Then she slipped her arm through his and suggested it might be time to meet the rest of the family for lunch.

Rico pressed his lips to her hair briefly before asking, "Have you had a good morning?"

"Oh, yes, it's been wonderful." She squeezed his arm. "I can see why you belong here. You fit in perfectly."

He shrugged. "It's my home. But I fit in well when I was in America, too."

"Yes, I'm sure you did."

"We belong where we want to belong. But my heart is always in Sicily."

And sometimes his heart got wounded, she thought. But he was a strong man, and so he was always ready to try again. "I spoke to Nolan. He told me to have a good time and bring him some postcards from Erice. Have you talked to your father?"

"Yes, he knows we're going away tonight. I pretended you were dying to see Erice, and because he respects you, he pretended to believe me."

"He couldn't respect me and accept that I want to spend the night with his son?"

Rico smiled. "Well, old ways die hard, but he is more liberal than many Sicilians his age. He and my mother were in love for years without benefit of marriage, since he was a bandit. I have never asked, because a good Sicilian boy does not ask such things about his mother, but I have always thought that they probably...weren't saints."

"He loved her very much, didn't he?"

"Very much. Has he spoken to you about her?"

"Not about losing her. He told me about how he met her while giving money to her father, on Giuliano's orders. How they fell in love, suddenly, powerfully and irrevocably. How he risked capture so many times just to be with her, which infuriated Giuliano, who was apparently chaste throughout his life as an outlaw.''

"So they say," Rico murmured. "I suppose Giuliano loved the image too much to tarnish it."

"Give Giuliano credit, Rico. He was clever enough to know how much more vulnerable a woman could make him, so he never got involved with one. Ironically though, far from making your father vulnerable, your mother saved his life. Totò told me that he was shot by the public security police in the spring of 1947, and although he managed to escape, he was so badly wounded he thought he would die. Your mother hid him, nursed him, dressed his wounds and pressured Giuliano to speed up negotiations with the Mafia to smuggle your father to America, where he would be safe."

He nudged her. "She hated them, but she knew the world she lived in, too, Casey."

"She sounds like a remarkable woman," Casey said. "Brave, intelligent, devoted, determined, generous, gentle, but tough when it was needed."

"Yes, she was all that and more. I've always told my father that I haven't married yet because I've never met a woman who can measure up to my mother." He grinned. "It's the one explanation that always satisfies him. Of course," he added with a touch of sadness, "I haven't said it since she died."

"When his pain fades a little," she said softly.

"Yes."

"I'm surprised that she didn't leave Sicily with him."

"Too dangerous, I suppose."

"Yes. But why didn't she follow him afterward?"

"She couldn't leave the family or the farm. Her parents were sick, and she was the only remaining child. Anyhow, she's like me—like him, too, though he had no choice. She didn't want to leave Sicily."

"So he came back for her, even knowing he could be killed or jailed when he returned," Casey mused, still puzzled by that part of the story. Totò and Loredana had been smart enough to know he had to leave if he wanted to stay alive. Though times had changed by the mid-fifties when Totò returned to Sicily, there was still plenty of violence associated with Giuliano. Many of Giuliano's supporters, including his cochieftain Pisciotta, were murdered then. In fact, Pietro Scaglione, the justice official who heard Pisciotta's last confession before he died, was murdered in Palermo as late as 1971, more than twenty years after Giuliano. So why had Totò been able to return openly to Sicily and live quietly ever since then?

The answer came to her so suddenly and sharply that she halted in her tracks, shocked by the implications.

Totò has been under someone's protection all these years.

"Casey?"

She looked up at Rico.

Does Rico know? Has he ever suspected?

"Casey, is something wrong?" He started to look concerned.

She lowered her eyes, trying to hide her racing thoughts from him. Could she be right about this? And if so, why would the "friends of the friends" have chosen to protect a carpenter-turned-bandit? The ramifications roared through her brain, almost shutting out reality for a moment.

Was this what Totò wanted to tell her? Was this his story?

"Casey, are you all right?"

She looked up again, forcing herself to sublimate her suspicions. She smiled weakly. "Sorry, I just had a rush of dizziness there."

"You should have something to eat," he said instantly.

Food, the Sicilian remedy to so many ills, she thought wryly. She would have to handle Rico carefully or he would soon make her as fat as a hippopotamus. Then she realized sadly that in two days she would be on a plane to New York, and Rico would be a part of her past. Feeling already bereft, she pulled herself closer to him, enjoying his suddenly protective attitude as he guided her through the

maze of streets to the *trattoria* where his family awaited
them.

They found the family, including Totò's sister and
brother-in-law, already seated at a large table, talking and
laughing. Casey chose a seat between Rico and Nolan, who
immediately began a long lecture about how Casey mustn't
order some seafood dish called *neonati* or she would wreck
Sicily's ecological system. Then she had to wave away the
family's concern about her dizzy spell, telling them she
probably only felt faint because Rico had made her look at
dead octopuses this morning.

The meal of spicy pasta, roast swordfish and seasoned
salad was so delicious that Casey was finally obliged to admit to her hosts that Sicily did indeed have the best food in
the world.

Much to Casey's surprise, their waiter had already heard
all about her from the local people. Was she really a reporter from America who had come here to ask Totò Butera all about Giuliano? Did she really have a notebook in
which she wrote everything and drew little sketches of all
she saw? Was she really a famous international journalist,
the winner of many awards?

Casey had to deny that last rumor, but confirmed the
first two. The conversation grew more serious when Totò's brother-in-law suggested that Casey and Totò ought to
be more discreet. Totò disagreed, but his argument was
milder than usual. Rico gave Casey a condensed translation of everything the two men were saying.

"My uncle says that many who knew Giuliano were si-
lenced by death. The ones who have survived remain only
because they know how to keep their mouths shut."

Casey glanced uneasily at the two old men at the end of
the table. "Is your uncle telling Totò he shouldn't finish our
interview?"

"No," Rico assured her. Sensing her worry, he squeezed
her hand comfortingly. "He's saying that nothing has really
changed, and that my father should not be so foolish that
he tells everyone in western Sicily that he's talking to a

journalist about the old days. It was a long time ago, but certain people would still like to keep aspects of those days a secret. He says that certain people might look the other way if my father is discreet about the interview. But if he is indiscreet and makes such a show of it, certain people might be forced to set an example."

Casey looked at Rico's uncle, a small, wizened man with shrewd, hooded eyes. Eyes that knew the secrets that only Sicilians knew, Casey thought. "Rico, ask your uncle why anyone would still care about Giuliano's secrets forty years later."

Rico did. They had the attention of the whole table now and, Casey suspected, several neighboring tables, as well. When the old man had finished speaking, Rico said, "He says, *you* are interested, aren't you? If journalists—and perhaps government investigators—would like to know, then certain people would naturally like Giuliano's secrets *not* to be known. It is logical."

"But aren't those people all dead?" Casey asked, speaking directly to the old man. "Isn't it already history?"

Rico translated for her. She could see by expressions around the table that her comment was regarded as naive. She could even see, out of the corner of her eye, that a middle-aged woman at the next table was shaking her head sadly at Casey's foolishness.

Fortunately, she didn't suffer from false pride. She had come here to learn. She asked questions to learn. Her boundless curiosity was a natural result of her acknowledgment that she didn't know enough, could never know enough about anything.

"The game doesn't become history just because the players are dead," Rico said, translating for his uncle. "The families and clans of certain people are still operating. The political parties of certain other people could still be harmed by too many revelations."

Casey didn't need to ask who *certain people* were. Being an old Sicilian, steeped in old traditions, she suspected that Rico's uncle never said the word Mafia aloud anyhow.

Finally, Casey asked the really important question. "Does your uncle think I'm putting Totò in danger?"

When Rico responded negatively, trying to reassure her, she interrupted him and insisted he ask his uncle. The response was, predictably enough, "The tentacles of the octopus are long and reach everywhere." The old man nodded sagely and added a phrase which Rico translated as, "They know you are here."

Casey almost choked on her wine. That somehow struck her as ominous. *They know you are here.* She looked around the room, meeting many curious stares. Yes, she realized. The Mafia were not some distant criminal organization. They lived amidst all levels of Sicilian society, in many forms. Everyone in the village knew Casey was asking Totò about Giuliano and the old days; consequently, there was no doubt that some minor *mafiosi* knew it, too. She was chagrined that she hadn't already thought of that.

She only wondered if any of them had found the information interesting enough to pass along to any *pezzi di novanta*—big shots. She picked absently at her food for a few moments, pondering the issue, wondering if anyone feared what Totò Butera, silent for forty years, might say to her.

When she felt a warm, broad hand squeeze her thigh briefly and then linger there, new and exciting yet oddly familiar, she looked up into Rico's eyes. They told her to stop worrying, to relax and enjoy the day. And to think about tonight.

Casey felt sudden heat seep straight down from her face and neck to some dark, secret place in the core of her body. She wanted him. She wanted a thousand days and nights with him. But there would only be this one, and they would have to make the most of it. She let her eyes tell him so and saw his own grow heavy-lidded and dark.

Daniela turned the conversation back to the imminent wedding, a subject of great interest to the whole family.

Although they tried to accommodate their guests, they nevertheless lapsed into Italian so often that Casey finally insisted they all stop worrying about her. Nolan's linguistic ability had improved slightly, and he could converse simply in Italian with one person at a time, but he told Casey that he had no idea what the family was laughing about now. They were all speaking dialect except for Daniela and Paolo, who both spoke Italian too quickly for Nolan to understand them.

Casey learned from Rico, as he translated bits and pieces for her, that everyone was once again advising him to get married and stop breaking his poor father's heart. Everyone except for Totò, surprisingly. When Casey looked at Rico's father, she felt faintly embarrassed by the knowing, speculative look in those eyes that were so much like Rico's. Then the old man winked at her.

She laughed and turned away, suddenly shy about her passion for Totò's son, but grateful to an aging bandit who could understand the desire of a man and a woman to be alone together, far from prying eyes.

They finished their meal with the strong cups of heavily sugared *espresso* that Casey had learned to expect. She wondered why everyone loaded their systems with sugar and caffeine and then lay down for a siesta, and she and Rico argued cheerfully about this inconsistency while Totò and his brother-in-law argued about who would pay the bill. Casey had made one sincere effort to have *Sentinel* pay for the meal and had been shouted down by everyone present.

"Sicilians do not let their guests pay," Rico said innocently. Casey suspected he was trying not to smirk.

They left the *trattoria* and strolled out to where they had parked their cars. The village had grown terribly quiet. People here were inflexible about their hours, Casey thought. There was a time for shopping, a time for eating and a time for resting. She had already grown tired of dealing with the Buteras' disapproval about the way she habitually worked on her notes throughout the siesta hour, so for the past two days, she rested as they did after *il pranzo,* the large midday meal. Nolan had told her he thought it was the most civilized custom in the world. She was becoming inclined to agree with him.

Consequently, she wasn't at all surprised when Rico's family and relatives all objected when he announced that he would leave alone in the tiny Fiat 500 in which he and Casey had arrived together, because he had to spend part of the afternoon working in the Belice Valley. Several minutes of loud, earnest discussion ensued, all of it incomprehensible to Casey. She thought Rico's aunt was acting as if he was going off to donate both his kidneys to medical science before dinner.

When this merry argument was over, Rico obviously having won, it was time for everyone to say goodbye. The fervor with which everyone hugged, kissed and clasped would have led an outsider to believe that these people wouldn't see each other again for months, Casey thought wryly. She happened to know they were all getting together again next week.

Rico's aunt clasped Casey's hand, pinched her cheek and started speaking, imperiously indicating to Rico that he should translate.

He grinned at Casey and said, "She's telling you a lot of the usual stuff. You're a nice girl, and very pretty, but you should be married." He listened some more and added, "You probably don't want a word-for-word translation of this, Casey. She's . . . talking about your biological clock."

"Well, just as long as she's not getting too personal," Casey said dryly.

"Now she's saying that you shouldn't go out alone. You should also guard your purse carefully, because there are many purse snatchers."

This sort of thing might have gone on forever had Rico not intervened, taking his aunt by the shoulders and steering her into her family's car. He waved them off, smiling with Casey as his aunt leaned out the window to shout more advice as they drove away.

"She means well," Rico said, with one of those tolerant shrugs.

The Buteras were piling into the red Citroën. Casey saw Nolan motioning to her to get in first, since his long legs would be harder to accommodate in the overcrowded car. "I've got to go. When will you be back?"

He glanced at his watch. "This should only take a few hours. I'll be back before dark. We can leave almost right away and have a late dinner in Erice."

She put a hand over her stomach. "Rico, I never want to eat again."

"Ah, you will feel differently by this evening."

"Casey!" little Franco called. *"Andiamo!"* Let's go!

She looked at Rico, suddenly wanting to touch him, to kiss him, to have the right to hold him just because they would be separated for a few hours. "I'll see you later, then."

"Yes." He shifted restlessly. His gaze flicked over her hair and shoulders, then zeroed in on her mouth. "If we were not being watched by my entire family..."

"I know," she said huskily.

"Tonight," he whispered. Then he turned away and slid into the absurdly small car with a grace born of long practice.

Chapter Eight

"You look tired," Casey said as she and Rico drove away from the farm that evening, into the fading darkness and toward the place where their destinies would mingle and intertwine, if only for the length of one night.

"You look frustrated," he countered. He had handled his sister's concerned questions about his intentions toward Casey, and his father's smug, all-knowing glances a lot easier this evening than he could handle the weight of the discovery he had made today in the Belice Valley. Could he ever really make a difference, or was his father right in his oft-repeated insistence that nothing ever really changed here? "Didn't your interview with my father go well this afternoon?"

"Oh, okay," Casey said vaguely. "He was kind of tired. Too much socializing, Daniela said."

Casey *was* frustrated. And bewildered. Totò had freely reminisced about his days as a Separatist soldier, but he had skillfully evaded her more probing questions about his strange behavior the other day. She couldn't decide if those moments of whispered desperation—*I will break my silence for you*—were only the confused ravings of a very ill old man, or if he had something important to tell her but had changed his mind again after today's conversation in the restaurant. She wished she had paid more attention to his reaction to his brother-in-law's cryptic warnings. She couldn't remember any real distress on his part, but then again, she had scarcely looked at him until after the subject had been changed.

"What did you talk about?" Rico asked, trying to push aside his own worries. Tonight, he wanted to think only of her. The ills of his country would still be there on Monday, waiting for him like a faithful wife after his exotic foreign lover had flown away. The day after tomorrow, he thought with a painful sensation in his throat.

"About how the Separatists approached Giuliano in 1945, offering him the rank of colonel in the independence army and inviting him to fight under the movement's yellow and red flag. Giuliano was cynical about their offer. He knew that they needed him only because he controlled that region and they could do nothing there without his help. However, he accepted, since he was genuinely committed to the Separatist cause. Of course," she added, "even Totò thought Giuliano's plan to have Sicily annexed to the United States was a little bizarre."

"Yes, it certainly was a unique idea. And I guess he was quite serious about it."

"The Separatists promised him a pardon if the movement succeeded. Amnesty, legitimacy. They even suggested that they might make him the chief of police in the new government." She looked out the window, suddenly sad for the handsome young man who had died long before she was born. "Of course they sacrificed him and saved themselves when it all came to nothing. Rome put a halt to the whole thing when it granted autonomy to Sicily. Everyone was pardoned for their actions except Giuliano and his bandits. Many of the Separatists even found their way into the mainstream of Italian politics and became powerful. But they never helped Giuliano, who had fought longer, more diligently, and more successfully for their cause than anyone else.''

"From then until his death, he wanted amnesty more than anything else," Rico said, in recollection. "But he never got it."

"Surely there was no chance of amnesty ever again after Portella della Ginestra." Giuliano and his band had been blamed for firing on a Communist rally on May Day, 1947. Many civilians were wounded or killed, including women and children.

"You know, don't you, that investigators for many years—and Pisciotta himself—claimed that politicians had ordered that massacre?" Rico said.

"Yes, and that those politicians must have been in collusion with the Mafia. Every important Mafia chief had an immediate, indisputable alibi for that day, and they had all ensured that any left-wing friends or relatives of theirs didn't attend."

"Even more than forty years later," Rico mused, "it would be something to be the one who discovered who ordered the massacre—which politicians or which political party was so close to the Mafia and so willing to slaughter the innocent."

"Everyone had their suspicions. I've read various allegations, even specific names in my research, Rico."

"Ah, but to *prove* it. Now that would be something. Perhaps my father has already told you, Giuliano had an inconvenient habit of writing down everything that happened."

"No, your father hasn't mentioned it, but I know about it. Giuliano's memorandum was probably the most frequent subject of the numerous trials after his death. Even though they say he made several copies, none has ever been found. Everyone made claims and counterclaims at Pisciotta's trial about what happened to the brown folder containing Giuliano's papers. Having read various accounts, I'd say they were *all* lying—bandits, police, lawyers, politicians. But the end result is the same—Giuliano's papers disappeared forever when he died."

"It's intriguing to think about, isn't it?" Rico said. "Those papers contained all the secrets that biographers, novelists, filmmakers, judges, lawyers, police, investigators and even *mafiosi* and crooked politicians have wondered about for forty years. It was said that Giuliano's memorandum could topple the government in Rome and expose the entire Mafia network of western Sicily. There is no doubt that the memorandum existed, yet no one can trace any of the copies or verify the rumors about them. One copy was said to have been smuggled across the sea into Tunisia, another to have been sent to America with Giuliano's brother-in-law.... Some men would still give anything to see those papers."

"And according to your uncle, some men would still kill to keep them a secret." When Rico shrugged, Casey smiled and leaned over to touch his cheek. "You're such a liar," she teased. "You like to pretend that it all happened so long ago and is of no importance, but you're as caught up in the myth and mystery as any of us."

Rico grinned and turned his head to press a kiss into her palm.

"Keep your eyes on the road," she said automatically.

"Come closer and I will."

The stick shift in the Citroën made intimacy extremely difficult, but Casey got as close to Rico as she could and leaned her head against his shoulder. Each of them forgot all about the bandit Giuliano for the time being and tuned in to the unique rhythms of the other's breath and heartbeat, speaking softly together about inconsequential things.

After about twenty minutes, Rico said, "Your eyes are closed again, I can tell."

It was dark, but his driving still terrified her. "Learn to drive like a sane person and I might change my habits."

They passed through a few towns, then Rico finally steered the car onto the road that began the long, scenic ascent to the mountaintop village of Erice. The road, he said apologetically, would be more interesting by day, since Casey would be able to see the bay of Bonagìa on one side and the luxuriant green of the pine forests on the other. He tried to point out to her some lights in the distance, but relented when she put her hands over her eyes and begged him to pay attention to the road.

The road to Erice was a terrifying, twisting, turning, corkscrew path that climbed steeply up the mountainside, circling around hairpin turns that made Casey sway from side to side in her seat as she braced her feet against the dashboard and kept her hands over her eyes.

"I didn't know you were afraid of heights," Rico said in concern.

"I'm not," she said, gritting her teeth. "If you had warned me what this road was like, I would have insisted on doing the driving."

He spent five minutes trying to convince her to trust him, since he had driven safely up this road more times than he could count. In the end, he sighed and gave up. Sometimes Americans were just too hard to understand. He was one of the best drivers he knew, after all.

When he parked the car near the best hotel in Erice, he leaned across the seat and stroked her hair. "You can open your eyes now. We're here."

"Thank God," she said with great feeling. "I feel like I should say one of those prayers Daniela's always mumbling."

He smiled and shook his head, then got out of the car and walked around to her door to open it for her, sad that she wouldn't stay in Sicily long enough to get over this inexplicable fear of the way he drove, the way *everyone* here drove. But then he brushed aside his sadness. They were together tonight, and tonight was all that existed for him.

They had brought only two small overnight bags, since they would have to leave the following morning. The hotel Rico had selected was simple, dignified and homey. Casey smiled her approval to him as he unlocked the door of their room and showed her inside a few minutes after registering.

"It's a clear night," Rico said, "but the manager thinks there will be fog in the morning." He closed the door behind him and leaned against it, watching her as she crossed the room and opened the glass doors leading out to the balcony.

"I like it here," she said enthusiastically.

He smiled and stalked forward, joining her at the railing as she stood under the stars and looked into the distance. "The hotel? Or Erice?"

"Sicily." She brushed her tangled hair away from her cheek when the wind caught and played with it, then she turned to face him. He looked romantic and slightly dangerous against the night sky, with the breeze stirring the dark locks of his hair and the shadow of a beard darkening his jaw.

"You are smiling mysteriously," he told her, his dark eyes sparkling.

"Nothing here goes the way I thought it would."

"Oh?"

"I thought I'd get here with you... a man I've known only a few days, and I'd feel embarrassed or uncomfortable. I thought we'd walk into this room and feel like strangers, awkward and not knowing what to say, what to do, how to begin."

He arched one dark brow. "And?"

She smiled and stepped closer to him, slipping her arms around his neck. "I've never felt so sure in my life that I'm in exactly the right place at the right time, with exactly the right person."

He slid his hands up and down her rib cage. "Let's postpone dinner," he suggested huskily.

She nodded her agreement and let him draw her closer. "Not even Sicilian food could tempt me away right now," she whispered.

He rested his forehead against hers and savored the moment. He could feel the slim suppleness of her waist, then the firm strength of her ribs as he moved his hands up and down, slowly, luxuriantly, enjoying the way her breathing suddenly increased in speed and intensity.

He felt his heart start to pound with heavy, hot excitement, with the joy of holding her so close and knowing he wouldn't have to let go again, not until morning.

It's not enough, something inside him raged. He smothered it ruthlessly. It's all I can have, he thought, so it must be enough. We will make it enough.

He rubbed his brow against hers, then kissed her eyelids as they fluttered shut, so soft and delicate, so vulnerable. He nuzzled her hair, inhaling its clean, sunny fragrance, murmuring with pleasure at the way it felt against his jaw.

She molded to him, willingly, eagerly, perfectly, her long, elegant neck tilting to accommodate his caresses, her hips pressing forward to cradle his hard thighs, her arms sliding comfortably around him.

She lifted her face for a moment to look at him, and in the dark romance of the Mediterranean night he could see happiness, tenderness, and welcome in her eyes, those wide, sky-blue, foreign eyes which were so unlike any others he had ever seen, even in the gold-paved streets of America. He smiled, too, and touched her petal-soft skin, her cheek, her chin, her lips, awed by how much he wanted to give to her, uncertain if his body could express all that his heart felt tonight.

"I feel . . . too much," he said unsteadily, regretting for the first time that they could only speak together in her unmusical, passionless language.

Casey brushed her fingers along the strong, smooth, bronzed column of his throat and she swallowed. "So do I," she whispered, a mixture of emotions flooding through her, overwhelming her with a bewildering combination of greed and generosity, courage and fear, tender longing and erotic heat.

"Casey, this is more to me than just tonight," he said, sliding his hands down her back and pulling her hips even closer.

She knew what he meant. What happened between them tonight would live inside each of them for a long time, interfering in their separate lives, awakening longings that they would be unable to satisfy. But not to share at least this much would be unendurable, so she committed herself to insanity, as did he.

"Then make every moment count," Casey answered him, her sweet breath fanning his cheeks.

He kissed her, their lips moist and ready, their tongues bold and seeking. He had never before known so instinctively, so unerringly, how to please, how to excite. It was as if the stars had told him this woman's secrets and her own flesh had confessed its desires to his hands.

He nibbled on her full lower lip, brushed it with his tongue, then spread hot kisses across her face and down the length of her throat, feeling her body melt bonelessly against him and her hands rub encouragingly over his shoulders. Then he slid his hand over her lush bottom and between her legs, pressing boldly, knowingly into the warm juncture. When she opened her mouth on a soft moan, he kissed her deeply again, plunging his tongue inside to stroke, to promise, to possess.

Her hands moved into his hair, her fingers tugging, her little moans pleading, her legs shifting restlessly as he massaged that part of her he had never before touched.

He should not have waited so long, he thought vaguely. He should have touched her this way, this intimate and shameless way, on that first tentative evening in the courtyard and shown her that this, *this* was how they belonged together.

To touch, to taste, to treasure, to share the timeless rhythm of man and woman joining, loving, chasing away the dark shadows of their lives in ecstatic intimacy—this was why destiny had brought this woman to his weary, beautiful island. And the absolute sense of rightness he felt, as Casey tugged his shirt out of his jeans and rubbed her palms over the warm skin of his back, assured him that no amount of wisdom or foresight could have kept them apart. This had always been meant to happen between them.

Nothing would ever make him regret this stolen night with her—not the strict teachings of his conservative society that demanded penance for a night of unwed pleasure, nor the aimless longing that he already knew would follow her departure. This was too honest, too necessary, for him to ever feel anything but joy.

"Yes," he urged huskily when she started unbuttoning his shirt with hasty, trembling fingers. "Yes. Undress me."

He kissed her again, excited by the way she rubbed against him, showing him her need, trusting him with it.

Surrendering completely to the drugging, relentless pleasure of his kiss, Casey worked clumsily at the buttons of his shirt, then pushed it off his shoulders and let it fall into a careless heap. He was incredibly beautiful, with hard, heavy muscles and broad shoulders. His olive skin gleamed with good health and the kiss of last summer's sun. Black hair, shiny and springy, covered his chest, and finally tapered down to a thin trail leading the way to the waistband of his jeans. She reached for his belt.

He gave a stifled puff of laughter and grabbed both her hands, pulling them against his chest. "Inside," he urged, tugging her into the darkened room. "There is no privacy on the balcony."

"Oh, Lord." Casey laughed, too, leaning against him as he half closed the curtained glass doors to the balcony. "You make me lose my head," she whispered, doing things with her tongue that made him quiver.

"Good," he growled. He wanted to give her what she gave him—this hot rush of elation, this hungry throbbing, this burning need that obliterated everything else. Long accustomed to being considered attractive by a variety of women, he had never before felt this humble gratitude for being desired by one, this fiercely proud satisfaction about his capacity to impassion one.

He turned her in his arms so that her back rested against his chest and her hair spilled over his shoulder, tumbled and tangled from the play of his hands. He pressed his hips into her bottom, letting her feel his arousal. She gasped and pressed against him reflexively, reaching behind her to stroke his jean-clad thighs, to tell him she still wanted more, much more of him.

He slid one hand over her belly and caressed her breasts with the other, stroking her nipples into tight, tantalizing buds with the flat of his palm, exploring the soft, heavy globes with massaging, greedy fingers. He whispered to her in Italian, knowing that she would understand his admiration, his exultation, from his tone if not from his words.

He stripped off her blouse, kissing her neck and hair and shoulder, whispering to her of how he had fantasized about her since her arrival, how he had known her skin would taste like fresh milk and strawberry wine, how he had dreamed she would scorch his senses like the Mediterranean sun and heat his blood like the winds from the African desert.

As he unhooked her bra and let it slide from her silken skin, he murmured, *"Ti voglio bene,"* that perfectly vague phrase that could mean I want you or I love you, or both. He wasn't sure what he meant; his senses were too tangled in desire. He only knew that the words were the right ones.

Casey couldn't understand his words, only his tone, which admired her as his hands were admiring her. His touch was warm and possessive on her breasts, his fingers teasing her sensitized nipples until she whimpered and her breath burned her lungs in harsh gasps. Still murmuring to her, his language musical and erotic, rhythmic in the heat of her imagination, he unzipped her practical trousers and peeled them down her hips, underwear and all, to pool on the floor.

His hands slid immediately, shamelessly across the white skin of her bare stomach and into the tangle of hair between her thighs. She sagged back toward him, panting, leaning against the broad wall of his chest, feeling its curly hair tickle her skin as his warmth surrounded, supported and reassured her.

He made a soft, drawn-out groaning sound as his fingers explored her damp heat intimately, stroking with infinite delicacy, caressing her teasingly, dipping inside her with shattering boldness.

He shifted slightly, supporting her with one hand while the other continued to devastate her senses. A moment later Casey felt his tongue on her back, licking down her spine with long, leisurely strokes. How did he know every secret fantasy, she wondered, her heart hammering against her rib cage as he moved lower and lower.

She felt his tongue against the backs of her knees, agile, velvety, creative, and she moved with a grace he must have willed when he gently, wordlessly urged her to turn toward him. She threaded her fingers through his gleaming black hair, and he pressed an open-mouthed kiss against her abdomen, then rested his cheek there as his arms slid around her thighs.

"Casey, Casey." He whispered her name and added many other words, all of them mysterious and achingly tender. She caressed his shoulders, his hair, his face, adoring him, moved beyond expression as he knelt before her with his head resting against her in natural, uninhibited intimacy.

She sank to her knees and met his soul-deep kiss, their lips wet and clinging. Wanting to give as he gave, she lowered her head to his lap and kissed him, rubbing her cheek and mouth against the hard bulge of his manhood, hot with need even through the thick denim of his jeans. She heard his heavy groan, felt the involuntary jerk of his body, sensed the way he struggled to maintain control as his trembling hands stroked her hair.

She rubbed his thighs, stroking him with increasing fervor, wanting him to know he was cherished. When he finally drew her up by her shoulders, too excited to realize how rough his grip was, she met his embrace with a wildness that equalled his own, rolling with him on the soft, old Tunisian throw rug beneath them as the night air caressed their frantically intertwining bodies.

She struggled to slide her hands between them, smiling as the rolling music of his language changed into incoherent sounds that were part of the universal language of lovers. She found his zipper and worked it down while he stopped touching her long enough to unfasten his belt.

As soon as she found him with her hands, she made a sobbing sound and rolled against him.

"No," he said between kisses, speaking in English this time. "All the way off. Not like this."

Breathing as if she had run twenty miles, she sat up and watched him stand to slide his jeans off and kick them away. When she reached her arms out to him, he hauled her off the floor, crossed the moon-streaked room, tossed her onto the waiting bed and followed her down into the sun-bleached sheets, all in one smoothly fluid act of predatory strength.

Settling heavily, restlessly on top of her, he parted her thighs. "I don't want to be rough," he growled, burning her throat with his hungry kisses.

"Never mind. Be rough," she said in a choked voice, touching him everywhere she could reach.

He lowered his head to her breast, kissed a burgeoning nipple, then licked it. Suddenly his whole body went rigid. "*Porca miseria!* Where did we put them?"

"What?" She forced her eyes open.

He sat up suddenly and ran his hands through his tousled hair. "Where's my bag?"

Casey groaned. Rico slid off the bed and crossed the room. He found his bag where he had left it, sitting on top of the antique bureau. Muttering to himself and making impatient gestures, he rifled through it. Casey smiled fondly as she stared at his lean, well-muscled backside. Her mercurial Sicilian lover, she thought. All fiery passion one moment, drowning her in his hot seduction, then tearing across the room in the next, cursing and gesticulating the way he did when he bargained in the marketplace.

A moment later he found the little package they had bought together that morning. He tore open the box and returned to her, prize in hand.

His dark eyes looked woeful and sheepish as he stood at the foot of the bed. "I'm sorry, Casey," he said apologetically.

She scooted to the edge of the bed and knelt before him. Her eyes teased him. "You've totally destroyed my image of smooth Latin lovers."

He grimaced. His expression changed again, and she knew he was laughing at himself. "I wanted everything to be perfect."

"It's still perfect, Rico," she assured him, sincere and grateful now. He was more of a man than any man she had ever known. She reached for the flimsy object in his hand and, with increasing tenderness, gently eased it over his sex. A moment later she met his gaze and placed her hands on his hard, washboard stomach, feeling it move in and out rapidly with his excited breath. "Now come back to bed."

His eyes grew heavy-lidded as he let her draw him onto the mattress again. They stretched out together, their long, languid, amorous caresses growing frantic again within short minutes. Her thighs cushioned him, as he had dreamed they would, and the cheeks of her bottom were smooth, soft and voluptuous in his hands.

He pressed deeply into her, one long, sweet, enduring thrust, watching the changes in her face and body as she accepted him, her eyes squeezed shut, her lips parted, her pale breasts heaving enticingly, her smooth arms skimming restlessly over his back. She tilted her hips and pushed strongly upward, pulling him deeper inside her as she wrapped her legs around him. His name on her lips, whispered, murmured, sighed, was the most heart-stopping, soul-splintering thing he had ever heard—until he heard the sharp catch of her breath and the soft moans that followed it.

They moved naturally together, finding their rhythm easily, as if their bodies had waited and planned for this moment all their lives. He wanted it to last, as he wanted the night to last, so he pulled back from the edge again and again, soothing her with his kisses and his hands when she begged him not to stop, not to wait any longer, not to shred her senses this way.

Their sweat-slick bodies thrashed and writhed together, danced with frantic, plunging haste, only to cease their frenzied undulation each time they reached that breathless, near-dying moment. Then Rico would change his pace to a slowly pulsing cadence that made Casey sob as she smothered in the dark honey of his passion, pleading with him to go on, and on and on.

And when he finally reached that crest of passion from which he couldn't turn back, he drove into her roughly, recklessly, wanting to disappear forever in the rapture of her body, in the bliss of her embrace. He felt her release—the unmistakable violent shuddering of her wonderfully feminine body—and he exulted in the raw moans that escaped her throat in an endless, breathless wave of profound pleasure. The sound and feel of her at that moment carried him over the edge, and he flowed with it willingly, ready to drown in the flood of love he felt. It seemed to last forever, hot and burning, warm and glowing, engulfing him from within and without, scalding him with its intensity.

When the thunder was gone, she was still there, sighing softly beneath him. Even the pleasure remained after the storm, changing into something deeper and richer and strangely more satisfying. It was new and unfamiliar to him. He lay with his eyes closed and his cheek resting on the beginning swell of her breast, savoring this unexpected sensation. His right hand groped blindly until it touched hers. He pressed his palm to hers and laced their fingers together, his head reeling, his body basking in the afterglow.

Yes, she was there, and so was the pleasure—even now. And so, he realized without the surprise he would have expected, was the love.

Perhaps it had been ignited by his passion, but he knew with the age-old wisdom of his people that now that it was there, it would not go away. Not today, not tomorrow, not the day after, perhaps not even when the ancient pillars of Segesta had crumbled into dust and the hills had been covered by the sea.

And that's when he knew that tonight would never be enough for him.

Casey opened her eyes and, after a moment of confusion, realized she must have dozed for a while. Rico had lit a candle on the bureau, and its reflection in the mirror cast a golden glow around the room. She was alone in the wide bed with a crumpled sheet carefully tucked around her. She heard soft voices at the door.

She sat up when Rico closed the door and came back into the dimly lit room, barefoot and shirtless, wearing his jeans slung low on his narrow hips. He noticed she was awake, smiled and came over to her. He was carrying a rustic basket whose contents were concealed by the linen napkins draped across the top. He put it on the floor, sat on the edge of the bed and kissed her soundly. She answered with enthusiasm.

"Did I sleep long?" she asked, stretching her arms over her head.

He gave a helping hand to the sheet as it slid down her body, then regarded her breasts with frank, intent interest. "Almost an hour." He leaned over again and kissed one nipple, then the other. Then, not wanting to seem partial, he kissed her shoulder, her neck, her ear, her nose and her mouth. He lingered at this last stop, teasing her with the languid caress of his tongue.

"Wow," Casey said with feeling, slinging an arm around his neck.

He grinned and pushed her back into the pillows, stretching out beside her. "You have given me many wonderful surprises since you came to Sicily, but tonight was the most wonderful of all."

She brushed the dark stubble on his jaw that made him look so alluringly disreputable. "If I had known you were here, I would have come to Sicily years ago."

"Really?" He immediately regretted the eagerness in his voice. She hadn't meant that she would *stay* for years.

Casey shifted restlessly. Mentioning the past they didn't have together was suddenly a painful reminder of the future they didn't have together. So she asked, "What's in the basket?"

"Ah." He sat up, wanting to push away any reminder that morning would come at the end of this night, as it came at the end of every night. "I thought you might get hungry after all, so I bribed the boy downstairs to find us some food." Rico smiled again. "I thought he'd go to some local *trattoria,* but instead he went home and got his mother to pack us a basket."

"I'm starved," Casey admitted. "What did she give us?"

There was fresh crusty bread, creamy ricotta cheese and saltier pecorino, sweet black olives and green ones soaked in garlic, paper-thin slices of prosciutto and hard pieces of salami, sun-ripened tomatoes and crispy cucumbers, juicy apricots and some smaller sweet fruit that Casey didn't recognize and whose name Rico didn't know in English. The Sicilian woman who had packed their late-night meal had also naturally included a bottle of local wine, as well as a few rich sweets made with almond paste.

"When you bribed this boy," Casey said as Rico laid the food out, "did you tell him we needed enough for a week?"

He kissed her and tugged teasingly on her hair. "You should know after spending a week in my family's home that no self-respecting Sicilian would give you less than three times what you can eat."

"Why aren't you fat?" she demanded.

"I work hard." He shrugged. "Or maybe I just have what you Americans call a good metabolism. Anyhow, it is not so fattening as American food, really. We eat mostly pasta, salad, fruit and fish."

"Oh, yeah? Those *cannoli* that Daniela bakes must have five thousand calories apiece."

He pulled the sheet away from her legs and kissed one thigh. "You don't look like you've ever taken a single bite," he assured her.

She smiled and curled up against him as he plumped some pillows against the headboard and leaned back. "You're very good for my ego."

"You wreak havoc on my hormones," he countered. Then he gave her a quick kiss. "But I like it."

They relaxed against the pillows, sampling slowly from the enormous spread of food, sometimes feeding each other and sharing the bottle of wine. Their conversation was light and easy, their eyes bold, their hands unashamed and their mutual responses uninhibited. It was a honeymoon night, Casey thought whimsically, without the wedding beforehand or the marriage afterward. She pushed the thought aside and ordered herself to be grateful for this perfect slice of sheer happiness. She tried to think of this week with Rico as something that had been given to her by fate, rather than as something that would be taken away by circumstance.

When they had finally packed away the remainder of their feast and placed the basket outside the door, Casey boldly peeled Rico's jeans down his body and he carried her back to the bed. They made love again, intending to be less urgent and more patient than the first time. It didn't quite work out that way, but it didn't matter.

When Casey lay curled against him, all of her physical appetites sated for the moment, her natural curiosity reasserted itself. "What happened today to upset you?"

He pulled away a bit to look at her in surprise, his dark brows arched in silent question.

"I noticed," she said. "Of *course* I noticed. But you didn't want to talk about it on the way here."

He smiled sadly and brushed her hair away from her smooth cheek. "I am always surprised by how clever you are."

She was more than clever where he was concerned. She was attuned to him, more so than was comfortable. "Can you tell me about it?"

He sighed. "I didn't want to spoil tonight with sad things."

"You can't spoil this by sharing your pain with me. I want you to be able to talk to me."

He held her gaze and saw that it was true. She was the comfort he needed, she was the well at which he could replenish his optimism and strength. *Stay with me,* he wanted to say. Instead he said, "I found the source of the water drainage today. In the Belice Valley as I suspected."

"It's *mafiosi,*" she ventured, "and there's nothing you can do."

"No, that's not it." He rolled away from her to reach for his cigarettes. He sat up and lit one, the first he had wanted since they had driven here together. She sat facing him, the sheet bunched in her lap, her beautiful breasts naked to his gaze, and waited for his explanation.

"The Belice Valley is still so poor, Casey. Some parts of it are like a ghost land—empty crumbled towns, devastated farms. It's a symbol for misery, poverty and corruption throughout Italy." He shrugged. "So some poor farmers there, who don't have enough water and can't afford to buy it from 'certain people' anymore, have started secretly draining the government pipelines to the southern coastal towns."

He took a deep drag on his cigarette and studied the glowing tip. "If I don't report them, then it continues, and not enough water gets to those towns. And there are women and children in those towns, just as there are in the Belice Valley. However, if I do report them, not only do they lose this water they desperately need, but they will then owe heavy fines to the government for breaking the law. In which case, they will go bankrupt and lose their farms. And of course, even if they manage to survive that, their farms will go dry."

She scooted closer to lean against his legs and rest her hands on his bent knees. She wanted to comfort him, but the problem was so complicated and his pain ran so deep. "What will you do?"

He shrugged. "I don't know. What can I do? I cannot fail my duty to make sure the water gets where it's supposed to go, but I also cannot turn in these farmers and ruin their lives."

"But . . . I mean, Rico, don't you have to?"

His look said once again that she didn't understand, but this time it was wearily sad, rather than exasperated or teasing. "This is Sicily. Of course I don't *have* to turn someone in to the authorities."

"But those are old ways, Rico. And you have real responsibilities you cannot ignore to people who are obeying the law and waiting for the water that's due to them."

He gestured impatiently at her, looking suddenly very Sicilian. "And what is due to those farmers in the valley, Casey? What are their choices? To go without water because it is badly managed by us and wrongly controlled by others? To go bankrupt buying water which should be their right to have? To put money into the pockets of the same men who are keeping water out of their fields?" He shook his head. "Tell me if you can that those farmers deserve to be punished."

"Then plead their case for them with the water authorities. After all," she added flatly, "you told me that you have all the right connections."

"No," he said. "I will not tell anyone else about them."

His sudden decision surprised her. "Then what will you do? Just let it continue?"

"No, I can't do that, either." He took another puff of his cigarette. "I will bargain with the farmers. They must stop now, in exchange for my silence. And I will do what I can to help them get the water they need." He sighed. "That is the best I can do."

Casey shifted uncomfortably. "I see."

He looked at her sharply in the warm, golden light of their room. "You do not approve?"

She shrugged. "I'm not sure, Rico. I'm...ambivalent about it. I think..." She let her breath out in a rush and nodded. "I think that you belong here. Irrevocably."

He tilted her chin up and forced her to meet his gaze when she would have looked away. "I don't think that was a compliment," he said quietly.

She wrapped her fingers around his and squeezed. "I don't mean it as an insult, either. I believe in right and wrong, truth and lies, the real and the imagined." She shrugged. "And it just never seems to apply here. It's all so complicated. I know you hate *omertà*, but now you will let these farmers buy your silence with their cooperation. I know you hate the whole Mafia mentality, but you use that same mentality to protect your family."

"And I would use it to protect you, too," he confirmed, guessing the direction of her thoughts.

"Because you know the world you live in, as well as the one you want." Her voice was soft, pensive.

"And I am bound to both." He stubbed out his cigarette. "Like every man here who has even given it any thought, I both love and hate Sicily."

"Yes." She moved up until she rested beside him against the headboard. "I guess I'm starting to feel that way, too."

"You would have to be here a long time to understand this country, to understand me." He nodded. "Even a woman as clever as you, Casey, would have to suffer with us to truly understand."

She rubbed her hand across his warm chest, her heart aching with the need to understand him. Finally she said, "No, I don't really understand, but I've learned so much from you, Rico."

He said wryly, "Like what? Water shortages, political corruption, secret societies and long-dead bandits?"

"Generosity," she said seriously. "Forgiveness. Courage." She kissed him and added, "I have learned valuable things."

"I have learned a lot from you, too, Casey. And the most important thing..."

"Yes?" she asked, hearing that familiar note of teasing creep back into his voice.

"That I'm not as old as I thought I was." He pulled her down into the rumpled sheets and proved his point.

Mount Erice was actually not such a large mountain, Rico explained to Casey the next morning as they strolled around town. It was roughly three quarters of a kilometer high, but its position, all alone at the edge of the sea, gave it an impression of greater height. And the thick fog that descended upon them as they walked, so unlike the brassy Sicilian sunshine Casey had come to love, gave the stony town of Erice an aura of mystery, like Brigadoon, Camelot or Avalon.

Although they were so near to the rest of Sicily, the people who lived here behaved in such a different manner that Casey was fascinated by the contrast. The Sicilians who lived high atop Mount Erice kept to themselves and lived quietly behind the sedate walls of their houses, aloof from the seething, passionate, noisy, hot, dusty, vivacious way of life that went on roughly half a mile below them. The streets were among the cleanest and tidiest Casey had ever seen and, amazingly enough, none of the very few people she saw stared at her as she meandered along, her arm tucked through Rico's.

As they passed a lookout point, distinguishable mostly because of the thick white intensity of the fog that hung beyond the low stone wall, Rico regretfully explained that on a clear day she could have seen Africa from this mountaintop, as well as the jagged edge of the Sicilian coastline leading out to the ancient coastal salt flats with their windmills, the tiny island of Mozia, once a thriving Punic port and now an archaeological site, and the Aegade Islands of Levanzo, Marittimo and Favignana.

"You'd like the Aegades," Rico added mischievously. "No cars."

"We should have made our reservation there," Casey replied. She shivered a moment later.

"Cold?"

She nodded. The altitude and the fog had made it rather chilly in Erice. She had dressed for the hot, sunny climate of the plains below. When Rico put his arm around her, she burrowed against him for warmth. He kissed her hair, and her heart started pounding. Three times, she thought, you would think three times in one night would be enough for a grown woman.

But she said, "Let's go back to the hotel."

He looked down at her through thick-lashed eyes. "I was right and you were wrong," he said smugly.

He had booked the room for another night, just in case they wanted to make one last stop there after touring Erice and before heading home. Casey had insisted that it was a needless extravagance, and very arrogant on his part, anyhow, since he wasn't eighteen anymore.

"You were right and I was wrong," she admitted. "I want to make love again. If you think you're up to it," she added impertinently.

He grinned. "You'll pay for that. Come."

They chased each other back to the hotel, where they spent the next two hours locked together, letting their joy in each other war with their inevitable sadness. The night was over, and the day would demand its toll.

Rico left a generous tip in the room to make up for the way they had decimated the bed that morning, and he and Casey climbed into the car after a brief argument about who would drive. She only relented and let him drive in the end because, as he pointed out, he was more accustomed than she to the steep, twisting road and the *other* crazy Sicilian drivers.

She sat as close to him as she could on the way back, touching him often with her hands and her lips, affectionately, tenderly, a little desperately perhaps. They had lingered later in Erice than they had intended, and so they stopped for lunch at a small *trattoria* on the road, knowing they wouldn't make it home in time to break bread with the family. They sat close together at their linen-covered table, touching often, talking about many things, as if this were the beginning rather than the end.

By the time they pulled into the bumpy driveway of the Butera farm, Casey was trying very hard to pull together her wits and her professional determination. They had intended to return earlier because she still had more work to do with Totò. Rico had promised to take Nolan to some of Giuliano's old stomping grounds in the afternoon and Casey would have her last interview with the old man.

As she got out of the car and looked across its roof at Rico, who returned her gaze wistfully, she tried to remind herself how important this interview was to her. She tried to call up that competitive hunger that had made her want this story to be her best. She tried to summon that fierce desire to learn Totò's secrets.

None of it seemed able to make a dent in her consciousness as she gazed into the fathomless depths of her lover's eyes. Taking a shaky breath, she turned and headed into the house.

Chapter Nine

"When it was announced that there would be amnesty for the Separatists, we rejoiced. But soon after that," Totò added, "we became bitter, for we learned that the amnesty did not include us, Giuliano's bandits."

Casey and Totò were sitting in the *salone,* and they had been alone since Rico and Nolan had driven away together to visit the hills and caves of Giuliano's territory. Paolo had taken the children somewhere, and Daniela was chatting in the kitchen with one of her friends. It was a peaceful, sunny, late afternoon in the country—Sicily at its most seductive.

They had begun today's interview by talking about Totò's years in America. Giuliano had paid an enormous sum of money to certain *mafiosi* to have Totò smuggled out of Sicily and into the United States. It was not the first or last time he would do such a thing for one of his men.

Totò told Casey of how he had spent his first few weeks in America hiding out in his brother's Brooklyn home, fighting death as the infection from his bullet wound grew worse.

Eventually he recovered and moved into the little apartment above his brother's store. Throughout that first year, he worked in the store by day and stayed indoors at night, afraid that he was being hunted by the authorities.

He finally relaxed, however, and began plying his trade as a carpenter in the neighborhood, learning English through practical experience and with the help of his American-born nieces and nephews. He was able to save a good deal of money, but he never stopped longing for Loredana and Sicily. Finally, heartsick for home, he returned to his native island after seven years of exile.

Now, at Casey's request, they had returned to discussing Totò's final months as a bandit.

"The Mafia chief that Giuliano killed—that was after you had left Sicily, wasn't it?" she asked.

"*Sì.* But I know why he did it. The man betrayed Giuliano. He began to inform the authorities of his movements and plans."

"So Giuliano enforced *omertà?*"

"Yes, he killed the *sbirro.*" At her questioning look, Totò explained, "In most of Italy, the word *sbirro* means 'cop,' and there is no insult intended. But in Sicily it means 'traitor' or 'spy.'"

"Most definitely an insult," Casey said, having learned something during the past week.

"The man had to be killed, obviously, for Giuliano to survive. But to kill a *mafioso* is a dangerous thing. It isolated Giuliano. And in Sicily, isolation is like slow death."

The words sounded vaguely familiar to Casey, and she remembered that Rico had said something similar when explaining the closeness of Sicilian families. Everything was interwoven here, she realized, each thread part of the tragic, vivid, improbable, wildly colorful tapestry that made up Sicily.

She pulled her thoughts back to her next question. "You were still in Sicily, however, during the massacre at Portella della Ginestra, weren't you?"

Totò's face clouded. "Yes, I was here."

"Tell me what you remember."

He sighed and his gaze focused on some distant memory. "I wanted to go straight, as they say in America, but the government would not forget my crimes. Giuliano wanted to help me escape to America, but I couldn't bear to leave Loredana and Sicily any more than I could bear to remain a bandit. I was lost and unhappy.

"I knew that there was talk of the Communist rally at Portella della Ginestra on May Day, and that Giuliano would somehow be involved with his most trusted men, but that was all I knew. Perhaps he was losing faith in me, as I had lost faith in myself. Only Loredana had the strength to keep believing in me."

Casey's heart contracted painfully, and for some reason she thought of Rico. Yes, she believed in him. He was a good man, a strong man who tried to act with honor in a confusing and changing society.

I want to stay.

The thought came out of nowhere, assaulting her with its power. She frowned and tried to concentrate, suddenly as heartsick as Totò had once been.

You would have to be here a long time to understand this country, to understand me. Rico's voice echoed in her head.

Casey's longing clawed at her insides. The memory of last night and this morning burned through her skin so hotly, she wondered why her clothes didn't go up in smoke.

Listen to the old man, she chided herself.

"Then one day in late April, 1947," Totò continued, "I was with Giuliano and three other men just outside of Montelepre when Giuliano's brother-in-law delivered a letter to him. They spoke quietly together for a moment, standing where we could not hear them. Then Giuliano read and burned the letter."

"He burned it?" Casey asked, wanting Totò to be sure.

"Yes, I remember it well. That was how I knew the letter was from someone important rather than a friend or relative. Then, after his brother-in-law had left, Giuliano told us that the hour of our liberation had come. We were going to fire on the Communists at Portella della Ginestra."

"So you believe that the letter contained the order to do it?"

Totò nodded. "I was shocked. I argued with Giuliano, telling him that there would be many women and children there. He insisted we would not hurt them. I told him this was crazy, but he would not listen. He said that we had finally been promised amnesty if we did this thing."

Amnesty—Giuliano's obsession since the failure of the Separatist cause. Casey's eyes widened. "So whoever wrote that letter was someone who had the power to grant amnesty?"

"This is what Giuliano said. Me, I thought the letter lied. Even if there was a man or group of men so powerful they could grant amnesty to Giuliano and his bandits, I didn't believe for a moment that they would do it just because we killed a few people at a political rally."

"But you weren't able to convince Giuliano?"

"No. He believed that this time we would get amnesty. And he also hated the Communists enough to relish the plan." Totò sighed heavily. "My protests made the others lose the last of their trust in me. Then, two days later, I was discovered and shot by the public-security police. I . . . I think I was betrayed, Casey."

"By Giuliano?"

"No!" Totò shook his head vehemently. "He would never do something so dishonorable. But there were others who would." Casey refrained from commenting on the honor of the bandit king who had fired on unarmed civilians at a political rally, and Totò continued, "And although I escaped the ambush alive, I was badly wounded and losing too much blood."

He told her about how he had contacted Loredana, who bravely smuggled him past a roadblock and hid him in a cave deep in the western hills. On May Day, while Giuliano was firing on the crowd at Portella della Ginestra, Totò was tossing and turning in delirium while Loredana struggled to keep him alive. It wasn't until nearly a week later that she was able to contact Giuliano. He came as soon as he could to their cave, bringing food, medicine, bandages, blankets, money and a rifle.

Heartbroken and sobbing like a forsaken child, and his body burning with infection, Totò begged Giuliano to deny the news about Portella della Ginestra that Loredana had heard. Angry and ashamed, torn by guilt and grief, Giuliano couldn't deny that the bandits had wounded and killed women and children at the rally.

"Did he tell you who had ordered the massacre?" Casey asked breathlessly.

"No. I begged him to tell me. I wanted to buy my freedom with their names. But I think Giuliano guessed this, for he refused to tell me. He told me instead that I would be leaving for America the following night and that I should put all this misery behind me and save my strength for the journey. He gave instructions to Loredana, who took me to the meeting point the following night." Totò shook his head. "That was the last time I ever saw Salvatore Giuliano."

They shared a long, pensive silence. Some three years later, abandoned and betrayed by almost everyone except his family, Giuliano's bullet-ridden body had been dumped in a courtyard in Castelvetrano. Dead at twenty-seven, so many of his secrets had died with him, lost in the murky silence of Sicily.

"As I grew older," Totò said, "I preferred to remember the early days, before the Separatists, before the massacre. I preferred to remember how we fought for our freedom in such an unjust world, how we gave food, money and medicine to starving villages, how Giuliano, a handsome peasant boy, performed such feats of daring. Yes," Totò concluded with misty eyes, "I prefer to remember the great days when Giuliano was king of the mountain and made the earth tremble."

Casey swallowed, moved as much by the old man's frank inconsistencies as she was by his sadness. Yes, Giuliano had diverted wagons of food to feed the poor—and often as not, the food he stole had been intended for equally poor villages, which then went hungry. But she recognized that in this country, the real human truth lay somewhere in the midst of all the ironic inconsistencies and conflicting versions of a story, somewhere in the midst of the mingled myth and fantasy that comprised truth for the generous, imaginative, suspicious, secretive, loving, courageous, long-suffering inhabitants of this island.

She knew that Totò's personal account of the events surrounding the massacre would make an important, moving addition to the article she would write about him. There was only one other subject she wanted to cover with him. It was perhaps the most important subject of all.

"Totò, you once told me that you were prepared to break your silence for me," she said carefully. Totò's dark, expressive eyes grew wary, but Casey willed herself to be tough. "Are you still willing to do that?"

"I . . ." He lowered his head and muttered, almost to himself, "I brought you here to tell all. But it is dangerous, Casey, so very dangerous."

"I can handle it," she said confidently. She could feel excitement coiling inside her. Totò *did* know something else. "What haven't you told me yet?"

Her question was met by heavy silence. Totò eluded her direct, insistent gaze. She leaned forward, studying him intently. "Did you want to tell me that you've been under protection all these years?"

His head shot up and he looked at her with wide, surprised eyes, his expression suggesting that she must be some kind of sorceress. "How did you know?" he whispered.

"I figured it out."

"You are very clever," he said hoarsely.

"What I *haven't* figured out, Totò, is *why* they decided to protect you. Everyone else was either dead or in jail by the time you returned to Sicily. They helped Pisciotta kill Giuliano, then they poisoned Pisciotta in his jail cell at the Ucciardone Prison. They killed everyone after that whom they feared could expose them." She stared intensely at him for a moment before saying, "Yet you returned here unharmed and have lived quietly ever since in the heart of western Sicily."

The old man's breathing started to grow harsh. He fiddled nervously with the hem of his sweater, undecided, afraid to make the leap. Casey leaned forward and covered one of his gnarled hands with her own. "Why, Totò? What made them do it? What's special about you?"

"Casey..."

Sensing that she nearly had him, she urged, "Please, Totò. You must tell me. You brought me all the way here to tell me. How can I leave without knowing?"

His eyes tormented and sad, his breath thick and rasping, his voice low and gravelly, old Totò Butera finally told Casey what made him so special, special enough to have earned the protection of the dark powers that shadowed his sunny land.

"I know where the memorandum is," he confessed. "I know where Giuliano's papers are hidden."

Two hours later, Casey was sitting with Daniela in a barren, noisy waiting room at a hospital in Alcamo. As she held Daniela's clammy, restless hand in hers, murmuring soothing words and giving her comforting little pats, Casey wrestled with her own conscience, her own grief.

Had she caused Totò's sudden collapse?

He had told her everything he knew about Giuliano's papers in the minutes that had followed his startling revelation. Everything, that is, except where the papers were located. And in her eagerness to know, in her hungry excitement over uncovering one of the greatest stories *Sentinel* would ever print, she had failed to notice the warning signs. Totò's glazed eyes, rapid breath, physical tremors and emotional agitation had gone virtually unobserved until that awful, terrifying moment when he had doubled over in pain and passed out.

Now sitting here with his daughter, waiting to learn from the doctors if Totò would live or die, Casey was wracked by guilt and self-doubt. And she despised the tiny, insensitive voice at the back of her brain that demanded, *Where are the papers?* It was a loathsome thing to learn that the ambition and hungry determination she had cultivated all her life couldn't be turned off like a hot-water faucet. She wanted Totò to live because she loved the old man, but the reporter in her wanted him to pull through so he could tell her where he had kept Giuliano's memorandum hidden for forty years.

She swallowed her self-disgust and squeezed Daniela's shoulders comfortingly, wishing another member of the family had been there when it had happened. Daniela had handled the crisis bravely on her own, but she clearly needed her husband or brother right now.

Casey felt overwhelming relief when Rico finally came tearing through the hospital entrance with Nolan hot on his heels. She was surprised to discover what an enormous effort it was to keep from flinging herself into Rico's arms, to let Daniela have the sole benefit of his broad chest, strong arms and comforting presence.

Rico and Daniela carried on an urgent conversation in Italian, clutching each other for courage. As they spoke, Nolan came over to Casey, his sun-reddened face drawn with anxiety.

"We got home and found a scrawled note saying you'd had to rush Totò to the hospital. Rico nearly broke the sound barrier driving here. What happened?"

"We were talking. I . . . I kept him going too long without a break, then I got him on a subject that excited him, and he . . . he . . ."

"Now, now, come on," Nolan said, giving her a hug. "Don't blame yourself, Casey. He knew he was sick when he invited you here. He told me that your visit gave him the strength to keep living."

"It doesn't look that way right now," she said brokenly.

Rico led his sister back to the bank of chairs along the wall and met Casey's eyes when she pulled away from Nolan. His pain was so plain to see in his expression, his posture, his gestures. It was so apparent in his voice when he said to her, "Please. Come sit by me."

She did as he asked, wanting to comfort him in any way she could, wanting to take comfort from his warmth and strength. She sat down and leaned against him as he slid his free arm around her shoulders. He pressed a kiss against her forehead, then buried his face in her hair, holding her for a long, intense moment.

Daniela, who sat huddled on his other side, her arm linked with his, said something to him. A moment later he told Casey, "She's telling me that she doesn't know what she would have done if you hadn't been there. She says you were very clearheaded, and that you have been her strength since the nurses took Papa away."

Casey shook her head and closed her eyes. "Your sister's a rock, Rico." She let out a long breath, trying to release some of her tension and added, "And your father is one tough old man. He'll make it."

Nolan sat on Casey's other side, and Paolo joined them about an hour later, having dropped off the children at the house of one of their many relatives. The five of them maintained their desperate vigil for hours—Rico releasing Casey only long enough to light up the many cigarettes he smoked in rapid succession—until a doctor finally came and spoke to them after midnight.

Casey sensed relief amidst the family, even before Rico explained to her, "My father is still in critical condition, but the doctor believes he will survive the night."

It took considerable urging on Rico's part, but he finally convinced Daniela to go home and get some rest. He would stay at the hospital all night, and she could relieve him in the morning.

"I'll stay with Rico," Casey said, overriding everyone's halfhearted objections. Just before the others left, Casey added to Nolan, "We'll need to talk in the morning. We were supposed to leave tomorrow."

He nodded, "Right. The flight's not till noon. We'll have time to change our plans if... We'll have time," he finished saying lamely.

Casey watched Rico give Daniela one last heartening hug before she left, leaning against her attentive husband who had, as usual, offered Casey a long speech that she couldn't understand. She didn't need Rico's translation, however, to know that Paolo was thanking her for helping Daniela until he could get there.

Casey sat down again with Rico, who slung one arm around her shoulders and laced the fingers of his free hand with hers. After a long silence, she said softly, "I wish I knew what to say to help you."

He squeezed her shoulders. "You help me by being here."

She rubbed her forehead against his jaw like a cat, silently expressing all the affection that blossomed inside her. She wanted it to be that way, wanted to be the one who could comfort him without words. She wanted to be the woman he needed on a dark night like this.

"You were with him when he collapsed?" Rico asked after a while.

"Yes." Then, unable to stop herself, wondering if this remarkably forgiving man could extend his generosity to her, she said, "I got him too excited. I should have seen, should have noticed how he was breathing too hard, trembling, clutching the arms of his chair. But I was so interested, so damned intent on the story that I—"

"Shh, Casey, shh." He put his fingers to her lips to stem the flood of anguished words. "It's not your fault. He is very sick. This could have happened at any time."

"No," she said adamantly. "It happened because I caused it with my—"

"Now you are God, who chooses when a man will live or die?" Rico chided. "My father still smokes, drinks, argues, socializes, stays up too late, eats heavy foods. He always says, 'So I will die a day sooner. So what?'

"I don't want him to die tonight, Casey, but if he did, at least he would have spent his last day on earth telling his life story to a beautiful foreign journalist after having eaten a big Sunday dinner and played with his grandchildren." He smiled wistfully. "How many other of Giuliano's bandits could say the same?"

He stroked her hair soothingly, continuing to assure her that Totò wouldn't want her to feel guilty, that she mustn't blame herself because the old man had gotten too excited during the interview. "He *always* gets too excited," Rico explained. "That's why we feared something like this was imminent."

They stayed like that all night, holding on to each other tightly, drawing strength and courage from each other, sometimes talking softly, sometimes sitting in silence, occasionally dozing off.

By morning, Totò's condition had improved marginally. Only the immediate family were allowed to see him. The doctors refused to predict when Totò would be able to talk, let alone go home, but it seemed certain that he would survive this visit to the hospital.

When Daniela arrived to relieve Rico, she broke down and cried over the encouraging news, then rushed off to see her father in his hospital bed. Bleary-eyed and stiff, Rico drove Casey back to the farm where Nolan awaited them alone. After a brief greeting, Rico went into the kitchen to phone various friends, neighbors and relatives, leaving Casey and Nolan in the *salone*.

"How does Totò look?" Nolan asked Casey when she had finished telling him that Totò was expected to live.

"I wasn't allowed in to see him. Rico says he looks small and pale."

"I hate hospitals," Nolan said with feeling. "What do you think you and I should do?"

"I can't give you any details, Nolan, but as soon as Totò can talk, he has something very important to tell me. It was what he was trying to tell me when he collapsed. I can't leave yet."

Nolan didn't want to leave while Totò was so ill, without even having the chance to say goodbye, but he also recognized that there was nothing he could do for him. What's more, he'd probably only be in the way. The family, he admitted to Casey, would almost certainly rather not have a foreign photographer hanging around while they maintained their grim vigil at the hospital. Nolan didn't need to add that Casey had obviously become more than a visiting foreign journalist, at least to Rico who very clearly wanted her with him during this traumatic time.

Her decision made, Casey went into the kitchen to tell Rico. He hung up the phone just as she entered the room, having reported the latest news about his father to one of his many relatives.

He looked at Casey, sensing by the way she stood in the doorway and twisted her hands that she had something to tell him. "Yes?" He heard the hoarseness in his voice, caused by a sleepless night and too many cigarettes.

She stepped forward slowly. "I'm supposed to leave today...." she began.

He didn't want to hear it. He rubbed his tired eyes, unspeakably depressed.

"Nolan's going back, but if it's okay with you...I'd like to stay."

His head shot up and he stared at her for a moment, heart pounding gladly for this reprieve. Being Sicilian, he didn't ask why or how long or where she wanted to stay. Being in love, he simply vaulted out of his chair with surprising strength for such an exhausted man and wrapped his arms around her.

Their kiss was long, deep, committed, intimate. When she could draw air, Casey said softly, "I take it that means you don't mind?"

He pinched her bottom teasingly, then caressed it, pulling her into the hard strength of his thighs. "It was meant to be this way," was all he said. He wanted to say more, but he could hear Nolan's footsteps in the hallway. He took his hand off Casey's bottom but kept his arms around her. When Nolan appeared in the doorway, he said to him, "My father will be sorry he was unable to say goodbye to you, Nolan. But he has enjoyed your visit, and I know he would urge you to return to us again someday, for pleasure rather than business."

Rico saw the friendly, sincere American man, red-faced from the hot sun, smile in response. "Thanks, Rico. This has been just about the best assignment I've ever had, thanks to you and your family. I'll remember Sicilian generosity as long as I live."

Rico shrugged and released Casey. "You don't need to remember it—you can come back whenever you want." He glanced at his watch and added, "Perhaps we should leave for the airport."

They loaded Nolan's luggage into the Citroën and drove toward the airport outside of Palermo. Casey, naturally, kept her eyes closed most of the way, sadly aware that Rico was too tired and worried to tease her about it.

Nolan checked in at the ticket counter, needing Rico's help with the chaotic and confusing processes that governed this airport. Before he went through customs, Casey gave him her ticket.

"I have a feeling," she told him, "that it will be easier for them to change the departure date back in New York and send it to me than it would be for me to get it changed here." She told him to tell her editor she would call tomorrow and explain why she was remaining in Sicily for the time being.

"Here, I don't need this anymore. Why don't you keep it?" Nolan said suddenly, digging into his carry-on bag and producing his tattered copy of Winnifred Hampton's guide to Sicily. "It's always good for a laugh."

Casey accepted Nolan's offering with a smile, then gave him a quick hug. "Have a safe trip."

Rico said goodbye, too, respecting Nolan's American sensibilities by merely shaking his hand, rather than going for a full-blown Italian farewell. They watched Nolan make his way through passport control, then they left the airport.

On the drive back to the farm, Casey leaned her head against Rico's shoulder, suddenly glad beyond measure that she was returning home with him rather than flying away from him forever. Yes, he was right, through some strange twist of fate, everything had been meant to happen exactly this way.

They spoke very little on the ride back, each torn emotionally—between feelings of relief that they were still together after all, worry over the old man who battled for his life in an Alcamo hospital room and a strange, seemingly inappropriate feeling of contentment.

"I've got to make a few more calls," Rico said as he pulled the car to a stop outside the Butera house. "Why don't you go right upstairs and get some sleep?"

"You should lie down, too," she insisted, getting out of the car.

"I will. I must call the hospital to check on Papa, then I must call in at work to let them know where I am." He smiled wearily. "I admit it's a chaotic office, but surely they have noticed by now that I'm not there."

"You'll come up and sleep in my room with me?" she asked hesitantly. She wasn't sure how he would feel about curling up next to her in his father's house. She needn't have worried, she realized a moment later.

He kissed her hand and murmured, "Of course. In a few minutes."

When Rico went back into the kitchen to use the phone, Casey went to the study where Rico had left his overnight bag the day before, upon their return from Erice. It had his shaving equipment inside, which he badly needed, as well as a few other things Casey hoped they would need while they were alone this afternoon. She carried it upstairs to her room.

While Rico was using the telephone downstairs, Casey had time to shower—remembering to unplug the hot-water heater first, of course. She put on her robe and generally cleaned up her appearance, then when Rico came upstairs, she took his hand and led him into her bedroom.

"How's your father?" she asked, pushing him gently so that he sat on the edge of her bed.

Rico's eyes caressed her. "A little better. He woke up for a short while and recognized Daniela. She sounded very calm. Paolo has decided to stay with her for the rest of the day, though. He doesn't want her to be there alone in case something happens."

Casey knelt before him and pulled off his worn boots. Then she reached up and touched his cheek, her smooth, warm palm awakening senses he had thought were deadened with exhaustion. "You need a shave," she told him.

"You told me the other night that I look sexy when I don't shave," he countered.

She smiled ruefully at him. "I have a feeling that you remember every compliment that every woman has ever paid you."

"Oh, I don't know," he said innocently. "There have been so many—compliments, I mean."

He started to wake up a little more when she pulled off his socks and began unbuttoning his shirt, her fingers agile, quick and gentle. He felt a rush of gratitude to the Fates that had brought her to him, and a rush of love for this woman who had comforted him throughout the brutal night, who could now relax him when he was knotted with tension and energize him when he wanted to drop dead in his tracks.

"I can survive all this because you are here," he told her as she slipped his cotton shirt off his shoulders and down his arms.

Casey let his shirt drop to the floor and met his gaze. "You survive because you're as strong as an oak."

He smiled and brushed her unruly hair away from her cheek. "Then you take away the pain of being a lonely oak tree."

Moved beyond words by his open admission of vulnerability and need, Casey rose to her feet to stand between his legs. She ran her fingers through the thick black silk of his hair, sighing when he buried his face against her midriff and wrapped his arms around her waist.

Stay with me forever, he urged silently, wrapped in her warmth and feminine scent, pulsingly aware of the pale, responsive body that was hidden by the worn fabric of her robe. He reveled in the comfort she gave at the very same moment she was arousing other, darker, stronger instincts within him. Memory and expectation mingled inside him, rendering the anticipation of making love with her even sweeter and headier than it had been the first time.

Let me stay forever, Casey begged in silence, not sure whether she withheld the plea from Rico or from whatever mysterious force had brought her here in the first place.

She stroked Rico's hair, absorbing his pain, fear and sadness, glowing with a fulfillment she had never known before, the deep-seated joy that came from giving love so tenderly, sincerely, unconditionally. She would have walked across hot coals or cut off her right arm at that moment if it could have helped ease his weary anguish. She smiled softly. Judging by the way he pressed a kiss against her stomach, rubbed his forehead suggestively against her body and slowly started pulling up the hemline of her robe, she figured she could ease his pain in a thoroughly enjoyable way that didn't involve a single element of sacrifice on her part.

Her eyes soft and rich with love, Casey drew Rico's face up for a long, eloquent kiss, then untied her robe for him and invited his hands inside.

His gaze never leaving hers, he slid his hands over her body in long, leisurely, exploratory caresses, massaging, comforting, soothing, stimulating, exciting, until, impatient with his patience, she slipped out of her robe and pushed him backward on the bed.

They rolled over and entwined their limbs gracefully, their breath a little rushed, their kisses languid and deep. Casey left him for a moment to rummage around in the bag she had left by the foot of the bed. Returning to him, she straddled him, unzipped his jeans and carefully covered him with the protection they had bought together such a seemingly long time ago.

Rico arched his back and stretched out on the bed, his hair tousled, his eyes heavy-lidded, his strong hands guiding her hips as she pressed down upon him, holding him deep inside her where she most wanted him to be. Looking down at him, Casey felt a rush of emotion she didn't know how to express—stronger than desire, more enduring than passion, more painful than affection. She rubbed her hands across his chest, her fingers tangling in the coarse black hair, and whispered his name, aching with a need that went beyond the luscious throbbing she felt in her loins.

He murmured to her, thick, musical words that hummed inside her and made her skin flush, even though she didn't understand them. His hands caressed her thighs with urgent, bold, possessive strokes that made her feel cherished, desirable, daringly sexual.

She moved her hips in a small circular motion, loving the way it made him sigh even more than she loved the way it made heat shoot through her veins.

Bracing himself on one arm, he pulled her lower so that his mouth could reach her breasts, nibbling on the pale curves, wetly teasing her nipples, suckling with gentle, erotic intensity.

Something wild tore through her, and she started to move her hips more violently against his, concentrating on that special male hardness that penetrated her body so beautifully, filling her with his heat, his energy, his life, thrusting in and out of her with such fluid, graceful rhythm, such spiraling, earthy magic.

"*Ohh...* Rico...Rico..." she moaned, wanting to tell him, wanting him to know that he filled her with wonder. Losing strength everywhere except in that part of her that continued to welcome him with increasing fervor, she sank against him, her breasts brushing his chest in cadence with their frantic rocking, her tongue dueling with his as he kissed her again and again.

His breath was harsh in her ears, hot against her cheeks, sweet in her mouth. His hands, grasping, pulling, urging, excited her even more, telling her how lost he was in his senses, in her, in their joining.

She distantly heard the low, desperate sound of her own moans as pleasure melted through her, obliterating everything, washing over her with hot, dizzying waves of liquid flame that seemed to go on and on, all generated by the man who plunged inside her again and again, pushing her further and further into the flood of delight. Finally, weak, exhausted and whimpering with aftershocks of ecstasy, she felt him go rigid beneath her for a heart-stopping moment before he drove deeply into her one last time, then quivered and groaned with relief.

She lay atop him for a long time, panting and making incoherent sounds of pleasure, their damp bodies conforming to each other in perfect harmony. She felt his hands moving soothingly up and down her back, his mouth moving tenderly against her cheek and hair, his chest heaving as he tried to steady his breath. She listened to the hammering of his heart beneath her ear, bathed in the scalding heat of his skin against hers, savored the treasured, lingering warmth of him resting inside her.

She sighed and shifted slightly to touch her lips to the smooth, bronzed column of his throat, her hands clutching involuntarily at him. She was awed by what they had shared, awed enough to feel shock and shyness mingle with the happiness and drowsy contentment of afterglow.

This was intimacy as she had never imagined, she thought vaguely. No place to hide, no secrets, no inhibitions. This had gone further than she could have possibly foreseen on that night she first decided she wanted him to be her lover.

Rico had touched her in ways and places that no one in her life had ever reached. And she didn't have a single idea what she was supposed to do about it now.

She felt his knuckles against her cheek, tilting her face up for his inspection. She glanced up and saw so many complex messages in those dark eyes. Pleasure, contentment, gratitude, lingering sorrow, exhaustion and rueful teasing.

"I thought you invited me up here to rest," he chided lazily. "Five more minutes with you, and I may need a bed next to my father's at the hospital."

"Yeah, your cries of protest nearly broke my heart."

He kissed her and then frowned in concern a moment later. "Look what I've done to your face."

"What?"

"It's all red." He shook his head. "I should have shaved first. I'm sorry, Casey."

"I didn't even notice," she admitted and snuggled against him again.

They rested together for a few more moments before Rico reluctantly rose to answer the phone. The caller was another relative wanting to know the details of Totò's condition. After hanging up, Rico showered and shaved. Finally, seeking comfort and completion, he slid back into bed with Casey, taking care not to wake her as he drew her close.

She had crossed that barrier, he thought with relief, stroking her hair and staring at the ceiling. She had let something matter more to her than rushing back to New York and turning in her story on time. He was glad she had been able to change her mind and stay because of a sick old man. He hoped she had stayed for him, too.

His mother had always said that everything happened just when it was meant to happen. Casey had come to him at the right time, just when he was ready for her and, he believed, just when she was ready for him.

Would she stay? Could he ask her to? Could she want to?

He closed his eyes. His mother also used to say that God took with one hand and gave with the other. It remained to be seen what Rico would have to lose in order to keep this woman.

Chapter Ten

Paolo and the children returned to the house in time for dinner. Casey could have kissed Paolo's dusty shoes when he carried four flat boxes into the kitchen which, she discovered, contained carryout pizzas. She couldn't remember when she and Rico had last eaten.

The children's high spirits were refreshing after two days of tumultuous emotions. They understood that their *nonno* was sick in the hospital but would soon be better. That information digested, they quickly got back to the business of daily life, full of games, teasing, complaints and demands. They swarmed over Rico, whom they complained hadn't played with them in such a long time. Then they whined about Nolan's having left without saying goodbye to them.

They showed Casey, the golden-haired stranger who had brought such excitement into their home, all of their drawings from art class, their history homework and their math problems. Casey had a quick ear, but she had only picked up enough Italian this past week to understand about one

word out of every fifty that the children uttered. They
didn't seem to mind her lack of verbal comprehension,
however, as they showed her all the goodies their relatives
were showering upon them while they stayed with them.

Casey was surprised to learn that the children wouldn't
be staying at home tonight. In fact, Paolo planned to help
them pack as many things as they would need for a week or
so at their relatives' house.

"Daniela will spend a lot of time at the hospital until
Papa comes home," Rico explained over dinner when Casey asked him about this.

"Why? I mean, once Totò starts feeling better, there's no
need for Daniela to sit there—"

"I'm afraid there is, Casey," he answered. "We don't
have very extensive nursing care in hospitals here. Once my
father's condition improves, the family will be responsible
for feeding him, helping him change, assisting him to the
bathroom, ev—"

"The family?" Casey repeated incredulously. "The
hospital staff doesn't—"

"No," Rico said. "So we will try to lighten the burden
at home."

"And Daniela will have to take care of your father all by
herself?" Casey demanded, incensed by the apparent notion that this, too, was "women's work."

"No, of course not," Rico said. "Surely you noticed that
I've talked to nearly two dozen relatives today. Except for
my brother in the north and our relatives in America, all the
others live around here. They will all help. Our cousins
volunteered to take the children for a week so that Daniela
would be able to rest when she comes home."

The children interrupted their conversation at this point,
demanding something else. They liked their mother's
homegrown spices sprinkled on their pizza, Rico explained, rising to search the cupboards for the carefully
dried and chopped spices Daniela had grown in her mother's window box.

Casey bit into her delicious, aromatic pizza and pondered the infinite availability of family in Sicily. She was distracted from these weighty thoughts, however, by the alluring way denim stretched over Rico's narrow hips while he bent over to search a cabinet below the window. A moment later he came back to the table, sprinkled a pinch of spices over the children's slices of pizza, then offered some to Casey. Since Paolo had already insisted she put hot peppers, olive oil and parmesan cheese on her slice, she decided not to risk it.

Casey and Rico had only been awake and dressed for a few minutes when Paolo and the children had arrived, so she had had no opportunity yet to talk privately with Rico. Since Paolo brought good news from the hospital, Casey felt it was imperative she explain the situation to Rico tonight. He would see to it, she felt sure, that she got to speak with Totò as soon as the old man was strong enough.

Paolo conferred with Rico for about half an hour after dinner while Casey voluntarily cleaned up the kitchen. Then, after a frenzied hour of helping the children pack, Rico and Casey waved goodbye to them in the driveway and headed back into the house as darkness engulfed the Butera farm.

"Rico, I need to talk to you about something important," Casey said, taking his hand and leading him into the *salone.*

He raised one brow in silent query, looking darkly handsome and alert again thanks to his afternoon sleep. Casey felt her expression soften and her mind wander as their eyes locked, then she shook her head. "Don't distract me," she chided.

That made him smile. "I could say the same thing. Very well, what is this thing you want to discuss?" He stretched out on the sofa and regarded her with curiosity. She looked so serious, he thought.

"I want to tell you what your father told me before he collapsed. I...I'm so sorry, Rico." She started pacing.

"When I tell this to you, you may get angry with me and think that I did cause his attack after all."

"Casey, no—" he began, but stopped when she held up a hand.

"You don't know what we were talking about," she said.

"The old days." He could see from her expression that she believed it was more than that, and he sighed. "All right. Tell me what you were talking about."

She stared at him for a moment, then picked up her notebook from the table near Totò's chair. She sat down in a straight-backed chair opposite Rico, opened her notebook, and, occasionally referring to her notes, began telling him the one part of his father's story that the old man had never before told anyone.

"When your father lay wounded and ill in a cave where your mother was hiding and nursing him, Giuliano came to see him."

"Yes, I know. It was the last time Papa ever saw Giuliano."

"They talked about Portella della Ginestra, and then Giuliano told your father about the arrangements he had made to smuggle him out of Sicily and into America."

"Giuliano paid *mafiosi* a huge sum to do it, but my father insists on believing he was aided by 'men of honor,'" Rico concluded, some of his usual impatience flaring up.

"That wasn't all they talked about that night," Casey said.

Rico shrugged, his blank look expressing his basic lack of interest in a conversation between his father and a bandit that had taken place over forty years ago.

"Rico... Giuliano showed him the brown folder containing his memorandum. He said that the answers to all Totò's questions about Portella della Ginestra were inside that folder. The answers to many other questions, too."

Rico's eyes narrowed speculatively and he took a deep breath, absorbing this surprising information. "So Papa saw the memorandum. Did he read it?"

Casey shook her head. "No. Giuliano told him to forget about all this and go start a new life in America. I don't think he really trusted your father anymore."

"So that will be in your story, I suppose. That my father saw the memorandum, that it really existed."

"There's never been any doubt that it really existed," Casey said. "No, there's more. I don't know about the extra copies that Giuliano supposedly made, whether they existed, got smuggled to safety or ever survived. But I know what happened to that brown folder."

Rico sat up. "Now *that's* interesting," he admitted. "No one has ever known. Italian magistrates, lawyers and investigators probably spent thousands of hours trying to figure it out." He stopped suddenly as the realization dawned. "My father knows what happened to it?" he whispered.

Casey nodded. She glanced at her notes, her hand gripping the notebook tightly. "Your father left the country and your mother remained. They had only sporadic contact, because she was afraid her correspondence would lead the authorities to him. Giuliano was very impressed with Loredana, despite his habitual disinterest in any woman besides his mother. He admired her strength and respected the way she had kept Totò alive after he'd been shot."

Rico glared at her. "Are you suggesting that Giuliano and my mother—"

"No, of course not." She gave him an exasperated look, wishing he could be a little less Sicilian on occasion. "The point is, he grew to trust her. He saw her only once or twice after Totò's departure, but she remained under his protection until he died."

Rico shrugged. "No wonder Mamma always spoke well of Giuliano."

"You already know that one of the primary subjects of interest in the trials after Giuliano's death was the sudden disappearance of the brown folder containing his memorandum. Pisciotta and the police and everyone else involved gave conflicting statements about when it had disappeared. Someone was even accused of destroying it the night of Giuliano's death, but that couldn't be proven conclusively.''

"So what really happened to it?" Rico asked with genuine interest.

Casey fixed him with a hard stare, hoping he would believe her. "A day or two before his death, knowing that he couldn't trust anyone around him, not even Pisciotta, Giuliano came here and gave the memorandum to your mother.''

Rico vaulted out of his chair. He stood there silently—tall, tense, looking ready to defend himself against physical attack. After a long moment, he whispered, *"What?"*

Casey nodded encouragingly, her own voice hurting her throat as she answered, "Yes. Giuliano gave his memorandum to your mother, right here, over forty years ago. She hid it for him, not realizing he was about to die. No one knew she had it." Casey swallowed. "She kept it, even after his body was found in Castelvetrano. Rico... *It still exists.*''

He blinked rapidly, several times in succession. His breath was shallow and fast as he stared at her. He tried to speak several times, but couldn't figure out what the hell he wanted to say. What did you say to something like that?

"Casey that's impossible.''

"It's true.''

"It can't be," he denied. "Those are some of the most sought-after papers in Sicilian history. Nobody knew where they were.''

"Your mother did.''

"Really? Then why didn't she turn them over to the authorities?''

Casey stared at him in surprise. Surely the answer was obvious. *"Omertà.''*

He looked as if she had slapped him. "I can't...'' He paced the room, needing some outlet for the whirlwind Casey had unleashed inside him. He kept shaking his head, unable to accept the enormity of what she was telling him.

She continued speaking, her voice mirroring her excitement.

"Your mother kept silent for a long time, not sure what she should do. Her father had died, and her mother couldn't have advised her with any level of sophistication. This was too complicated. Finally, she realized that the papers were her ticket for bringing Totò home."

Rico whirled to look at her again, sure he was going to hate what he was about to hear.

"Your mother knew from your father that Giuliano had often dealt with the most powerful *mafioso* in western Sicily."

"The *capo di tutti capi*," Rico said flatly.

Casey nodded. "The boss of all bosses. She knew he could probably make the others agree to something he decided, and he had many politicians in his pocket. She contacted the man through ... intermediaries and went to see him."

"*Madonna*," Rico muttered in horror, "she went alone to speak to *him?*"

"You know who he was?"

"Of course. Everyone knows. But he's dead, Casey." He licked his lips and turned his back on her. "What did they speak about?"

"She risked her life to tell him she had the memorandum hidden in a safe place. She had never read it, she was too afraid. But she knew how important it was. She knew that powerful men from many walks of life, the exalted as well as the infamous, would do anything to make sure the memorandum was never found. By the time Giuliano gave it to her, he had probably even implicated the men involved not only in his own death, but in Pisciotta's murder four years later. Not to mention all the other deaths."

"She could have been killed," Rico said hoarsely.

"She wanted your father back. That was her bargain with them, Rico. In exchange for her silence, they would ensure that your father could return to Sicily, unmolested by anyone on *either* side of the law, and live a normal life here. Her insurance policy against their betrayal was that she kept the memorandum for the rest of her life, rather than giving it to them.''

Casey shrugged and continued, ''I suppose as the years rolled by and those men got old and died, their successors took up the responsibility. Totò lived quietly, never gave interviews and never again broke the law. And, of course, Giuliano had become such a popular folk legend—movies, novels, biographies—that it became very unlikely someone would lock up one of his aging bandits as time passed.''

''Don't be too sure about that,'' Rico said. ''Some of those bandits got life imprisonment after the Viterbo trials.''

''And did you never once wonder,'' she asked quietly, ''why your father has been able to live openly all these years?''

Rico's breath rushed out of his lungs, leaving a burning sensation in his chest. He lowered his head, shocked, confused and ashamed. He sank into a chair, feeling as if she had just kicked his legs out from under him. ''I...never wondered,'' he admitted, his voice low and rough. ''Maybe I knew, somewhere deep inside me, that if I wondered, I would know.... I would have to ask my father...''

Rico choked back the grief of loss. She had just stolen the last of his innocence, taken it as brutally as any conquering marauder might have raped Sicily a thousand years ago. ''To think we have been protected by...'' His breath was harsh in his throat. ''To think of my mother, bargaining with killers...'' He shook his head, unable to continue that line of thought. ''So this is what my father brought you here to learn?''

''Yes, Rico.'' Her eyes filled with tears she didn't want to shed, afraid he would mistake them for pity. She was only a player in this game. She had to keep reminding herself that she had only told Rico the truth, had only told him what he had to know. She wasn't responsible for the betrayal she knew he felt right now.

"Well," he said, his voice strained, "I can understand why he collapsed. I am half his age, and I would like to collapse now."

No wonder the old man's behavior had been so erratic since Casey's arrival, Rico thought dazedly. To break his silence, to betray his protectors, to risk what might happen now.... *Why, Papa, why?*

"As soon as he's better, I must speak with him, Rico."

"Why?"

"Well..." She gestured to her notes, surprised at his question. "So he can tell me where it is."

His heart nearly stopped beating. "You mean he knows where the memorandum is?"

"Yes. Of course. Your mother told him when he came back to Sicily, Rico. But he passed out before he could tell me."

Rico pushed himself out of his chair and stalked forward. He leaned over Casey's chair, his gaze boring into hers. "My God, that's why you stayed. You want the memorandum."

"Of course I want it," she said, baffled by the accusing fire in his eyes.

He nodded, his voice bitter when he said, "Yes, this will be your war story, won't it? This will be your triumph after having been passed over. My father will make you famous."

"Stop it!" She pushed roughly at his chest and stood up, angry at the condemnation in his tone, his words, his expression. She confronted him toe-to-toe, unwilling to be made the guilty party in this scenario. "Your father brought me here to tell me these things. He wants to make the memorandum public before he dies."

"Why? My father would never break his word to the Mafia. Not only does he still believe in *omertà*, he's also not that stupid. They don't overlook little things like giving secret papers to American journalists."

"I don't know why Totò's decided to break his silence now!" she snapped. "He didn't have time to tell me. Just like he didn't have time to tell me where he and your mother have kept the papers hidden all your life!''

Rico took a deep breath. He didn't want to keep shouting at her. She was right. His father had brought her here to learn these things, to take the memorandum home with her. It wasn't her fault that Rico felt sick with shame and betrayal right now. It wasn't her fault that he had fallen in love with her, that he wanted to lash out at her for being merely what she was, what she had always admitted she was—an ambitious woman.

He closed his eyes and lowered his head. "I'm sorry," he said huskily. "I...should not take out my anger on you."

"Rico..." She had learned forgiveness from him, and now she forgave when he was too wounded to. She slid her arms around his shoulders, cradling his head, and murmured, "I know this is a terrible shock to you. I'm sorry. I didn't know how else to tell you, and you had to know."

"Yes." He wrapped his arms around her, trying to hold on to the only comfort he could find in a world that had suddenly gone insane around him: his mother in cahoots with the Mafia to protect his outlaw father; his parents the guardians of secret papers written by a bandit whose life was so bloodstained that no amount of romanticized fiction could ever wash it clean; the woman he loved hungry to prove herself by risking her life over the same papers that had been linked to so many deaths.

"Oh, God," he muttered against Casey's neck, forsaking his smooth Italian for the guttural sounds of his childhood dialect. "Help me, God. Help me forgive, help me understand." He clutched Casey tighter, treasuring her even as he hated her for betraying him, too, with her ambition. "Help me protect her," he begged.

She hadn't stayed for him, he thought brokenly. She had stayed for the memorandum, for her career, for victory. She had stayed without understanding how dangerous it could be, despite everything he had told her.

Casey stroked his hair, wanting to comfort, needing to be needed, confused by the conflicting passions running through him. Only a strong man could suffer so much, she thought, letting a tear escape her eye to roll down her cheek.

What a painful thing love is, she thought, holding him and sharing his anguish. She soothed him until he pulled away, his eyes red, his face drawn, his breathing harsh. He broke her heart by turning away from her. He walked to a window and stared out into the dark night. Determined to help him whether he wanted her to or not, Casey followed him. She laced her fingers through his and pressed a kiss against his hand.

"Where do you suppose it is?" Rico asked quietly.

She shook her head. "Who knows? Maybe buried somewhere on Mount Sagana or Monte D'Oro. Hidden in any one of a hundred caves. Deep in the Cammarata Mountains. Only Totò can tell us." She squeezed his hand. "You'll take me to him as soon as he's well enough?"

Rico nodded, his heart heavy like lead. "As soon as he can talk, I'll take you to him."

She snuggled against him, touching him in ways she already knew he liked. She wanted to make love. He could tell. And he knew how generous she could be. He was torn, wanting to give, wanting to receive, knowing she had never pretended to be anything other than what she was, believing she truly cared for him—but wounded by his own foolish belief that there was more than that between them, unable to shrug off his humiliation. Had he really believed, days ago, that he could comfortably treasure whatever passed between them without regrets?

He sighed heavily, thinking what a fool he could be sometimes. Had love taken his parents this way, with such painful, sharp, demanding, consuming urgency? Had it shredded their souls and torn out their hearts as it was doing to him? Was that why his mother, who hated the slavery of Sicily, had been driven to make a pact of silence with the enslavers?

Casey rose on her toes. Giving in, he lowered his head and met her kiss. *Yes,* he thought, his struggle ending for the moment, *yes*. This much she could give him, and he could feel in her a need to give. She could begin to heal him. She could ease his pain, even though she was part of the source. Who could understand life, he wondered, when the woman who brought a man to his knees was the only one who could help him up again?

He lost himself in her kiss, in the soft touch of her hands, in the heady scent of her skin. He would sort through it all later and come to terms with it. For now, he just wanted to bury himself inside her. He picked her up in his arms, intent on carrying her to the couch, when the chilling ring of the phone stopped them.

Flushed and excited, they stared regretfully at each other for a moment.

"I have to get it," he said.

"I know."

He let her feet slide to the floor and left the room, making his way to the kitchen. He lifted the receiver a moment later and said, *"Pronto."*

"Rico, this is Daniela. Papa's awake. He says he must speak to you immediately. Can you come right away?"

Chapter Eleven

Rico strolled outside the main doors of the hospital very late that night and lit a cigarette. He found a bench near a dying pomegranate tree and sat down, feeling older and more weary than he had ever thought possible. He had sent Daniela home in his car hours ago, insisting he would stay with their father during the night in case the old man needed anything.

He let out the tobacco-scented smoke on a long sigh and looked up at the distant, indifferent stars. Suddenly, without warning, his throat filled and a hot tear rolled down his cheek.

God gives with one hand and takes with the other, he thought. Tonight, He had given Totò the promise of life, and He had stolen Rico's peace of mind forever. The weight in Rico's chest was painful, but the weight on his conscience was unbearable.

He knew where the memorandum was. It was the first thing Totò had told him when Daniela and the nurses had left them alone. Upon reflection, the hiding place didn't surprise Rico at all. How like Mamma, he thought, with a twisting sensation of anguish followed by a swift flood of remorse.

Now he knew, he thought bleakly, why his father had fallen so suddenly, devastatingly ill after his mother's death. Now he understood why Totò had brought an American reporter here to learn the greatest secret he carried, and why, having brought her here, he had agonized and hesitated before giving it to her.

"Papa, are you sure Mamma's death was a Mafia hit?"

"They knew, they must have known, that I had offered the memorandum to the authorities."

"Why, Papa, why? You and Mamma kept the memorandum hidden for forty years. What made you change your minds?"

Rico's face crumpled as a breeze from the sea brushed his hair off his forehead. He bent over and held his head in his hands, consumed by a pain greater than he had ever known in his life. *My fault, my fault.*

He was responsible for his mother's death, and he was responsible for the danger that Casey now faced. He had advised Totò to invite her here. If Rico had disapproved, if he had advised against it, Totò would have let the matter drop forever. He was sure of it. But he had believed it was the best thing for his father, so he had told him to give the American an interview, never suspecting the demons he would let loose.

By dawn, he knew what he must do. He had unwittingly helped them kill his mother. He wouldn't let them have Casey, too.

By the time Daniela arrived the following day, Rico was able to tell her that their father was considerably improved. Totò flirted shamelessly with his female doctor, argued vivaciously with his son and fell gladly upon the food Daniela had brought for him. He still tired too easily, however, and was asleep by the time Rico left the hospital.

Daniela told him that Casey wouldn't be waiting for him at the farm. She had asked Daniela to drop her off at the local village where she would meet Rico for lunch. He drove there and found her waiting for him at his family's favorite *trattoria*. He nearly keeled over when he heard her asking one of the few old villagers who spoke English if he believed that any copies of Giuliano's memorandum might have survived.

"Casey!" Rico lowered his voice when half the patrons looked curiously at him. "What are you doing?"

"Hi, Rico!" she said cheerfully. "How's Totò?"

Rico looked at the old villager chatting with Casey. He had met him once or twice. The man had retired to his native village after thirty years of working in America. "My father is not as well as Daniela thought last night," Rico lied. "He slept all night and was vague this morning."

"The whole village is concerned about Totò Butera's health," the old man said.

Rico's eyes narrowed. He was tired and paranoid, he decided, perceiving every comment as a threat. "He appreciates your concern."

The man tipped his tweed cap, offered his compliments to Casey and left them alone. As soon as he was out of earshot, Rico muttered, "What were you doing talking to a stranger about the memorandum?"

Casey frowned slightly, surprised by his tension. "One of your relatives introduced me to him and his friends, then disappeared. We were talking about Pisciotta—not your family—when the subject of the memorandum came up. Actually, all the locals have pretty interesting theories about what happened to the papers. The others all deserted me when their lunch was served, but the old man said he would keep me company until you got here." She covered his hand with her own. "There's nothing to worry about, Rico. I would never endanger your father with carelessness."

He shrugged and looked away. He knew the nature of gossip. Yes, she had been very discreet, but the whole village, fascinated by the "very famous American journalist'' and her connection to old Totò Butera, would know by tomorrow that she was still hanging around days after she had expected to leave, and that she was asking seemingly innocent questions about Giuliano's memorandum.

He saw her notebook lying next to her glass of water. He picked it up and suggested she put it in her purse while they ate.

"I still can't get used to everyone staring at me," she admitted to him as she stuffed her notes in her purse and took another sip of water. "Now I know what you meant that first day when you told me that a blond woman only remains alone for a few seconds in Sicily. I've had company ever since Daniela dropped me off this morning."

Their meal of fried calamari and spaghetti with clams was as delicious as any Casey had eaten in Sicily. She noticed, however, that Rico seemed preoccupied, pushing his food around his plate and staring at the bread as if he expected it to speak to him. Finally she asked, "What's wrong?"

"Just tired, I guess," he mumbled.

She reached over to touch his beard-roughened jaw with gentle fingers. "Oh, Rico, I'm sorry. I thought you might like to eat in town, and I wanted to get out of the house for a while, but I should have realized how tired you'd be." She smiled tenderly at him. He looked like a tragic hero when he was exhausted. "Let's go home."

He agreed readily, paying the check and guiding her out to the car. He drove home at an unusually sedate speed, his mind occupied with a hundred conflicting thoughts. Sending her away would be like tearing out his most vital organ, yet he couldn't bear to risk her life by keeping her here. He tried to plan how he would explain things to her, but his mind clouded with pain and he could form no coherent thoughts.

"I have to talk to you," he said seriously as soon as they entered the empty house.

She looked at him in concern. "You're worried about your father, aren't you? Daniela was so optimistic when she came home last night. She thought I might even be allowed to see him by tomorrow.... I'm sorry, Rico. But he's old, and it will take time for him to regain his strength.''

"Yes," he said guiltily. *Tomorrow?* He couldn't think of a way to convince his sister to lie to Casey without involving her in this web of deceit and betrayal. He would have to get Casey away from the village and his family as quickly as possible. He ran his hands through his hair in agitation and took a shaky breath. He hated this—all of it.

"Rico, come upstairs and lie down," Casey insisted. "You look ready to pass out."

He let her lead him up to her bedroom. She turned down the bed and closed the shutters, throwing the room into shadows. When she would have left him alone, he seized her by the arm and closed the door behind him.

"Stay with me," he said huskily. "I need you right now."

Casey sank against him willingly, absorbing the restless fire of his kiss while his arms encircled her in a possessive embrace. This was what she had missed all her life, she thought as they sank into the mattress together. To be needed this desperately, desired this exclusively, to find such soul-deep delight and rich fulfillment from the touch of one special man....

"I'm staying," she said suddenly, wondering if he knew how permanently she meant it as his mouth covered hers again.

It was very late afternoon when Casey awoke. She was sprawled naked across the bed while Rico slept with his head pillowed on her stomach. One brawny arm cradled her thighs, and the other rested beside her as he held her hand loosely in his sleep.

She stared at the ceiling, breathing evenly in time with Rico, feeling her face flush as she remembered all the things they had done together in the soft shadows of her room. Always uninhibited and imaginative, he had been wild today, unlocking some hidden, primitive darkness in her that he then met with a savagery of his own.

She smiled faintly and touched his hair, her heart swelling with love, her loins aching in satiation. She remembered reading once that even a sensible woman might stay with a man who was bad for her if he was a good enough lover, and she had scoffed at the idea. Now she could believe it; now she could understand how what happened in the bedroom might bind a woman forever to a man, even if he wasn't what she needed otherwise.

Luckily for her, Casey thought, the problem didn't arise. Rico was such a good man—honorable, courageous, generous, forgiving and loving. He was such a pleasure to be with—teasing, intelligent, interesting, sincere, committed. And he was strong enough to embrace his pain, sensitive enough to feel pain for others. She could see how worried he was about his father, how shattered he was by the strange, secretive tale she had told him the night before about the mother he had loved.

Yet, today, in this room, he had shown her more tenderness, vulnerability and dark, tempestuous passion than she had ever imagined any man could. No matter what happened in his life, he made a special place for her and cherished her.

"Oh, Rico." She sighed languidly, running possessive hands over his broad, muscular shoulders. Hers to touch and enjoy, now and forever. She smiled sleepily.

She understood the complicated ramifications of her decision. This would mean a major upheaval in her life and career. *Who would have thought I'd wind up in Sicily? I always wanted a war zone, a place in the limelight, a chance to prove my mettle.*

Of course, Totò's story would help do that.... Her eyes flew wide open. She had to telephone *Sentinel!* Nolan would have told her editors by now that she was on to something hot and wouldn't be coming home until she got it. It would be morning in New York right now. She had better call in and explain herself.

She slipped out from under Rico, who grumbled a bit but didn't wake up. She covered him with the sheet he had kicked aside, picked up one of the pillows that had fallen to the floor and tucked it under his dark head. She brushed a kiss against his brow and left the room.

Rico was just waking up a half hour later when Casey returned to the bedroom, having called New York collect and evaded a lot of exasperated, demanding questions. She wasn't going to risk telling *Sentinel* about the memorandum until it was safely in her hands, so she had done a lot of verbal acrobatics in order to convince the magazine that she was hunting for something really important while neglecting to tell them what it was. She had also neglected to tell them that she would almost certainly be going free-lance after this story was over.

"Mmm. Where did you go?" Rico asked groggily, sitting up to kiss her when she perched on the edge of the bed.

She explained her phone call to *Sentinel,* pleased she could make him smile again while she described her editor's small temper tantrum. "He's promised to string me up by my hair if I don't turn in the story by next week." Casey rolled her eyes.

"You don't seem very worried," Rico commented.

"When he sees this story, he's going to kowtow to me," she concluded. "They all thought I'd give them some cozy account of an old bandit's memories, and instead I'm reeling in one of the most elusive mysteries of twentieth-century Italy." She rubbed her hands together and grinned playfully at him. Her smile faded when she saw how his eyes darkened. She took his hand and cradled it against her. "I would do anything to ease your pain," she said honestly.

He swallowed, his eyes filling with tenderness. "I have to talk to you."

"So talk."

He glanced at the way her robe parted to expose a considerable portion of milk-white skin and the swelling curves of her breasts. He half smiled again, ruefully this time. "Let's get dressed first."

She kissed him lightly, then watched with undisguised admiration as he slid off the bed and started collecting their clothes from the floor. He pulled on his jeans and fastened them while she watched. Then he handed her her slacks—the same practical trousers with big, loose pockets that she was wearing the first time he had ever seen her at the airport.

Smiling lovingly at him, glad that sex and sleep had finally removed that grim, haunted look from his face, if not the sadness, she shrugged out of her robe and started wriggling into her pants. He helped her fasten her bra, then bent down and scooped something off the floor while she slipped into her blouse.

"Did you drop something?" he asked.

"I don't think so," she murmured absently, buttoning her blouse.

There was moment of silence before he said, "This must be yours, Casey. It's in English."

She frowned and took the small slip of paper from him, wondering what it was. She read the two sentences printed on *Sentinel* notepaper and scowled.

Your father called again. He says he understands why you might not want to answer his messages, but he must speak with you. There was a telephone number printed below the words.

"Oh, brother," she said in disgust, remembering now that Nolan had handed her this note on the airplane, such a long time ago. She glanced at Rico and quipped, "Just when I thought it was safe to go back into my pockets."

"Why don't you call your father?" Rico asked in concern. "It sounds like he needs you."

"My father needs a therapist, a baby-sitter, or a keeper, but not a daughter, Rico."

"Why don't you call him from here, Casey? We can afford the charges, and—"

"No, thank you, Rico," she said dismissively, brushing past him.

"Wait." He grabbed her arm and pulled her around to face him. "I don't understand, Casey. I know you are bitter about how he hurt you and your family, I know he did things that were wrong and selfish. But he is still your father."

"He's my biological father, Rico, but he's also a rotten, lying, dishonest, scheming creep, and I have no room for someone like that in my life."

"When was the last time you saw him?"

She let out her breath in an exasperated rush. "I don't want to talk about this, okay?"

"No, not okay. Last night we discussed things about my parents that I didn't like hearing, don't like knowing. Now it is your turn."

She yanked her arm out of his hold. "Okay. You really want to know, I'll tell you. The last time I saw him was about five years ago. He was drinking heavily but still wouldn't admit he was an alcoholic. He wanted money from me for some investment scheme that was going to make him the most important man in America, and when I refused, he got abusive."

He took her hand, resisting when she would have pulled away. "I'm sorry. That's terrible. We need to be able to look up to our fathers." He paused, wondering how to make her understand. "But, Casey, that was five years ago. You don't know what has happened since then."

"The point, Rico, is that I don't *care* what's happened since then."

"Maybe he wants to make amends."

"Maybe he just wants to ruin another day of my life."

He sighed. "Casey, I know you have reason to be angry, reason not to trust him.... But we cannot turn our backs on our family. What else do we have?"

"Rico!" She jerked away from him and threw her hands up in exasperation. "I have plenty! I have my work, my friends, my life. I will get along without one lousy father."

"But will he get along without you?"

"Why have you suddenly become his champion?" she demanded irritably.

He looked at the floor, wondering the same thing himself. "His message sounds so desperate."

"He's *always* sounded desperate."

"I want . . . I want you to be able to forgive him," he admitted honestly.

"I'd rather just forget him, Rico."

After a long, uncertain moment, he nodded and turned away. Casey watched him while he finished dressing, wondering why she felt as though they hadn't actually finished this conversation. Could Rico really care so much that she had never forgiven her father? Could it possibly matter so much to him?

"What did you want to talk to me about?" she asked.

"Hmm?" He turned to look at her. What could he tell her? he wondered. That the son must forgive the father, the mother must forgive the son, and that she, Casey, must forget all about the story that would skyrocket her all-important career?

"I, uh…" He swallowed. He needed time to think. And to buy time, he had to get her away from the farm. "I have to get back to Palermo, to my job," he said slowly, beginning to weave his story. "You probably won't be able to talk to my father for a few days yet, and there will be nothing for you to do here. Why don't you come to Palermo with me?"

Her answer was to throw her arms around his neck, give him a beautiful smile, and say, "I'd love to come to Palermo with you."

While she packed her things, he called Daniela at the hospital, explaining that he had to get back to the city and he would take Casey with him until their father was well enough to come home.

"Papa would like to speak with Casey, Rico," Daniela said. "Why don't you bring her here this evening before you take her to Palermo?"

His heart pounding, Rico made up some flimsy excuse before hanging up. The he went up to Casey's room, packed his few belongings into his small overnight bag and carried it and her large suitcase out to the car. He concealed a sigh of relief as they drove away without encountering Paolo, who was due home at any moment.

Thinking it would amuse him, Casey read some passages aloud from Miss Winnifred's guidebook as they headed toward Palermo. It was more interesting than keeping her eyes closed, while still managing to keep them off the road.

"'*Mafioso*. A bold, valiant man,'" she read.

Rico grunted in annoyance.

"'*Mafia*. A Sicilian brotherhood that ensures the survival of the people by securing their persons and property through their own strength and influence, rather than trusting in the law and its officers.'"

"Ensures their survival?" Rico echoed incredulously. "What an ignorant—"

"'Blend a little boldness, bravery, valor, and add a dash of self-possession,'" Casey continued, "'and you have the essence of Mafia.'"

"This is making me very ill, Casey," Rico protested. "Next she will be putting them on white horses."

"'The *vendetta* (see entry) follows those who denounce or injure a member of the brotherhood, whether through physical force or through ignoring *omertà* (see entry).'" After flipping through the book, Casey informed Rico, "'The *vendetta* is a thoroughly Sicilian institution.'"

Miss Winnifred went on to describe the Sicilian passion for revenge with great relish, concluding that foreigners were hardly ever the victims of *vendetta*.

"Had enough?" Casey asked mischievously, seeing Rico shake his head in disgust when she risked looking up for a moment.

"Yes, quite enough," he replied. Casey started to put the book away. A moment later, sounding strangely hesitant, he said, "Wait. Just see what she says about *omertà*."

"Okay," she said, surprised by his request. She flipped through the book until she found the entry. "*'Omertà.* A code of silence, a code of honor. The quality of being a man.'"

She stared at the entry for a long moment, thinking of the brave struggle now going on in Sicily to change old ways. Finally, she said, "Winnifred was a real jerk, wasn't she?"

Rico didn't answer. She glanced up at him and saw his brow furrowed in an introspective frown. She quietly put the book back into her purse and closed her eyes, leaving him to his thoughts until they reached Palermo.

Rico's apartment building in Palermo was just what Casey expected of him. It was situated in a pleasantly quiet, older area of the noisy, bustling, violent, ancient city, on one of the few tree-lined streets still remaining in the *Conca d'Oro*— the Golden Conch Shell in which the city of Palermo rested, nestled between a surrounding semicircle of harsh limestone mountains and the spectacular Bay of Palermo.

"It was once one of the largest cities in the world, second only to Cordoba in beauty and wealth among European cities," Rico told her as he drove through narrow, stone-paved streets in the dying light. He added pensively, "But that was a thousand years ago."

At Casey's request, Rico gave her a quick tour of the old city center, although traffic made the drive last longer than expected. She had never seen such utter chaos and confusion rule city streets, not even in Manhattan. She watched disbelievingly, gasping in occasional shock, fear or amusement as drivers swerved recklessly in and out of insanely tight places, nearly knocking over vegetable displays, pedestrians and public monuments as they jockeyed for position. When Rico got distracted by Casey's questions, an impatient driver behind them nudged the Citroën's rear bumper none too gently and pushed them forward.

Casey noticed that Rico seemed to have forgotten whatever was on his mind as he entered the spirited fray that passed for two-way traffic here, shouting out the window, shaking his hands in anger and muttering Italian words under his breath in a distinctly unflattering tone as he observed other drivers.

The fruit seller outside Rico's elegant old apartment building greeted him enthusiastically and expressed enormous pleasure at meeting Casey. She immediately felt the speculative gazes of half the people on the street turn toward her when Rico pulled her suitcase out of his trunk and led her inside. No man, she was sure, could carry on an illicit affair with a foreign woman in Sicily.

They ascended to his apartment in an old-fashioned, coin-operated elevator. He lived on the top floor, and Casey admired his vast terrace and the wonderful view even more than the comfortable, colorful interior of his big apartment.

"I like it here," she told him.

"I'm glad," he said, slipping his arms around her as she gazed across the rooftops of his neighborhood.

He took her out for dinner. Casey ate hungrily, having worked up an appetite, silently worried that Rico ate little and seemed distracted.

He tried a dozen times to tell her his terrible story, but backed out each time. What would she think? Could she possibly understand? Could he make her understand? Rico sighed despondently and sipped some more wine, knowing that Casey watched him with troubled eyes, aware that she knew he was wrestling with a problem he wouldn't share with her.

On the drive home he said, as casually as he could, "Have you thought about going back to New York without the papers? I could send them to you."

Her eyes snapped open and she turned her head to look at him sharply. She couldn't make out his expression in the dark, but she noticed he kept his gaze uncharacteristically fixed upon the road. Her heart hammered and her eyes pricked with the hurt he had just inflicted. "Do you want me to leave, Rico?"

He cleared his throat. "I know you have deadlines, unfinished business with your publisher, other—"

"I want to stay with you," she said honestly. She wanted to say more but didn't trust her voice. She had never even asked, she realized, if he wanted her to stay. So she added quietly, "You haven't answered my question."

"Casey, I..." He swallowed the truth but couldn't force out the lies. "Do you want to stay?"

"Yes."

"Oh."

For two people who had always communicated so comfortably, they sounded ridiculously stilted. Casey didn't understand what was wrong. She tried again. "Are you worried about your father?"

Rico licked his lips. "I think he will be okay this time."

"Rico..." She took a deep breath and plunged ahead. "I love you."

He hit the brakes. She gasped, but there was no one behind them. She wondered if he had even bothered to look.

"Oh, Casey." He reached over to unsnap her seat belt, then took her in his arms and kissed her long and hard. "I was afraid.... I thought you... Oh, Casey," he muttered between the hot kisses he pressed against her throat, her shoulder, her lips. His hand slipped inside her blouse to caress the sloping curves of her breasts as his kisses robbed her of breath or coherent thought.

"Take me home," she panted, wanting to feel him inside her, wanting to nestle into his own bed with him, wanting to set fire to his fantasies tonight, as he had set fire to hers this afternoon.

"Yes," he murmured, still kissing her, "yes."

He drove home with a recklessness that surpassed even the *palermitani*. They began undressing each other in the elevator as it rose to the top of the building, and they made love on the floor inside his front door.

The second time was in his bed though, and it was even better.

* * *

Casey awoke the next morning when she felt Rico leave the bed. She heard him showering and dressing. She stole a few lecherous peeks, but she didn't bother getting up until she heard him go into the kitchen. She timed it just perfectly. He was pouring little cups of thick *espresso* just as she entered the sunny room, wrapped haphazardly in his bathrobe.

"Hmm." She moaned slightly when he kissed her good morning, then gratefully accepted the cup of caffeine he handed her. "I wish you didn't have to work today."

"So do I, *cara,* but there's a lot to do."

She leaned her cheek against her fist and wondered why he looked so gorgeous after a night of so much activity and so little sleep. She was sure she looked like a hag right now.

"What will you do today?" he asked, turning his back to her as he squeezed some *sanguinelli*—blood oranges—to make fresh juice.

"I thought I'd call Daniela and see if there's any chance of my talking to your father soon."

Heart pounding, Rico forced himself to say casually, "Oh, I will do that for you. I'm going to talk to her anyhow, and you might have trouble getting hold of her, since no one at the hospital speaks English."

"Okay. Let me know." She drank her *espresso,* then accepted the juice he handed her, wondering how long it would take her to develop fluency in Italian. She spoke Spanish well and had an ear for languages. With a good tutor by day and Rico's help by night, she could be proficient within a year, she hoped. "Maybe I'll play tourist for a day. I've got my own guidebook, and it's a little more current than Miss Winnifred's."

He frowned briefly. "Just be careful."

"Come on, Rico. I live in New York. I can handle myself."

"Ah, but you are not so noticeable in New York. Just watch out for purse snatchers. They are the greatest danger to tourists."

"I'll be careful," she promised. "No one's ever been so overprotective of me before." When he raised his brows, prepared to argue, she grinned at him. "Don't worry. I could learn to enjoy it."

She kissed him goodbye at the front door, thinking that she wanted to share every morning with him from now on. Of course, he hadn't actually asked her to move in with him last night. In fact, he hadn't done much talking at all, she remembered as she glanced at the rumpled sheets on his bed and hugged herself. She sighed and headed into the bathroom for a shower.

Despite certain omissions, she knew he was committed to her. He was about as good at hiding his feelings as a six-week-old puppy—especially when she touched him.

Something was terribly wrong, though, something to do with her, Totò and the memorandum. Perhaps Rico just couldn't resolve the startling things she had told him about his parents. Or maybe he didn't want her exposing his family secrets in *Sentinel*.

They would talk about it when he came home for lunch this afternoon, she decided firmly. She didn't like unfinished business, and there was a lot of it in her life right now.

She toured the city that morning, finding a special, ghoulish fascination in the catacombs where the Cappuccini monks, just as Miss Winnifred had promised, kept long-dead, dried-out, well-dressed bodies from previous centuries hanging up for visitors to look at.

"This is such a strange country," she muttered to herself as she left, shaking her head when a brown-robed monk offered to sell her a few grisly postcards of the catacombs.

She thoroughly enjoyed the other parts of the city she had time to see that morning. The exotic, red-domed, Arab-Norman architecture of Palermo's distant past, the more recent baroque structures, and the lush, tropical beauty of its gardens gave the embattled city a poignant, mysterious charm. Out of curiosity, she stopped outside the office of Mayor Leoluca Orlando, the great Sicilian reformer who was waging such a fearless battle against the Mafia, noting the bodyguards in attendance.

Most of all, however, Casey enjoyed the noisy, narrow, lively, colorful streets of old Palermo, with its thriving open-air markets for food, clothing, furniture and household items.

She stopped at a fishmonger's display on the way home and bought two absolutely disgusting raw octopuses, thinking she would give in and let Rico make her a meal out of this revolting substance. Sicilians could seem to do no wrong in the kitchen, so maybe it was worth the risk. In any event, it would at least put a smile on his face.

She returned to the apartment just a few minutes before she expected him back, noticing how everyone on his street stared at her. Some people were friendly enough to say hello, others simply watched her with undisguised curiosity. When she got to the front door of the apartment, she let herself in with the key Rico had given her, then took the octopuses into the kitchen.

She took them out of their thick paper wrapping, dumped them into the sink and stared at them. "No one on earth could make you edible," she said with certainty.

The phone rang, startling her. She hesitated. Then, hoping the caller spoke English, she lifted the receiver and said, "Um . . . *Pronto?*"

"Casey? This is Daniela."

"Daniela!" Casey said with relief. "How are you? *Where* are you?"

Daniela laughed. "I'm fine. I'm at the hospital."

"How's your father?" Casey said quickly.

"He's fine, too. He's grumbling, though, demanding to know why Rico hasn't brought you to see him yet."

"We've been waiting until he's well enough," Casey said with a feeling of enormous relief. Thank God Rico's father was better!

"Well, he has been asking for you since yesterday morning, so I think it is safe to say that he is well enough," Daniela said cheerfully.

"What?" Casey sat down without realizing it.

"Yes," Daniela continued, "in fact, if he behaves himself, I think he can probably come home the day after tomorrow."

"*What?*"

"Yes. He says he told Rico to bring you here, and I told Rico the same thing yesterday. Now Papa says my selfish brother is keeping the beautiful American woman all to himself."

Casey blinked several times. Her mouth worked, but no words would come out. Rico had lied to her. He had *lied*.

She had trusted him, and he had lied to her. She gave him love, and he responded with deceit.

Why? Why was he keeping her from his father?

"Casey?" Daniela said, sounding concerned. "Please, it is only a joke. My father is not offended. He just misses you."

"Of course, Daniela. I..." She took a deep breath, willing herself not to scream or cry. "Rico's not here yet. I'll have him call you as soon as he comes home and...make arrangements. Okay?"

"Certainly." There was a hesitant pause, and then, "Are you well, Casey?"

"I'll talk to you later, Daniela." Casey hung up the phone and stared at it. A moment later she heard a key in the lock, then the front door opened.

Chapter Twelve

The moment Rico saw Casey's face, he knew something was wrong. Her cheeks were flushed, and her blue eyes blazed with anger. She stood up very slowly, showing no sign of happiness at his arrival.

"What is it?" he asked, already suspecting.

"Daniela called. She and Totò would like to know why you haven't brought me to see him, since he's been asking for me since *yesterday morning*." She practically snarled the last two words.

"Oh," he said. What else could he say when the earth was crumbling away beneath his feet?

"Oh?" she repeated. "*Oh?* Is that all you can say? Why did you lie to me and drag me all the way to Palermo? You rotten, lying, deceitful—"

"Casey, please," he interjected, wounded by her words.

"How could you? How *could* you betray me like this? You know how much I want to speak to Totò, but you've done everything you could to keep me away from him!"

Angry beyond words, she picked up her notebook and threw it at him.

"I had to keep you away from him, away from the papers!"

"Why?" she demanded. "So I won't stain your precious family name? Doesn't it matter to you that your father *wants* the story told? Doesn't it matter to you that I've risked my professional credibility to stay here in order to tell his story?"

"My God, Casey, do you think I would play a game with this?" he demanded. "You don't understand. You have no idea what you risk if you keep looking for those papers."

"Now you sound like your uncle. For God's sake, Rico these are not the Dark Ages! I am perfectly—"

"No, you're not! We don't even know *who* is willing to kill to keep the memorandum secret forever. Too many people could have been implicated by Giuliano."

"Rico, it's been forty years. I seriously doubt that any one would still kill—"

"They killed my mother to keep it quiet, Casey!"

The silence that followed his tormented statement was deafening. Casey stared at Rico, her breath gusting in and out of her lungs in short, painful gasps. He looked stunned, as if *she* were the one who had just delivered such incredible news.

"What?" she whispered at last. When there was no answer, she continued, "No, Rico, no. She was killed in a hit-and-run accident. You told me." She waited. Still no response. "Rico!"

"Sit down."

"No."

"All right, keep standing," he snapped.

"I don't understand, Rico...."

He sighed and slumped into a chair. He had lost her, he thought bleakly. He had lied to her about this, and he didn't think she would ever forgive him. She had failed to forgive her own father for his betrayal.

"Last year, my parents decided to offer the memorandum to the authorities. My father contacted someone he had met through my brother in the days when my brother was investigating the Mafia. Papa met with the man, and the man met with his superiors." Casey closed his eyes. "A few days later, my mother was killed, and my father... My father had a stroke, and when the authorities contacted him again, he pretended to be a stupid old man who couldn't even remember having known Giuliano."

Casey stared at him. "Rico, your mother... That's sheer coincidence."

He opened his eyes again and studied his hands. "Sicily is a fabulous environment for coincidence. I would not like to see something coincidental happen to you, Casey."

"Rico, nothing will happen to me, I promise you." Seeing he wasn't even interested in her promise, she prepared to pursue the issue. Then she got distracted by another thought. "Why, after so many years, did your parents suddenly decide to turn over the papers?"

"Well, the old *mafiosi* who had helped my father escape from Sicily were dead, the *capo* with whom my mother had made her pact was dead.... My father disapproved of the 'young' *mafiosi*, running drugs, shooting children...." Rico swallowed. "But mostly," he whispered, "it was my fault."

"But you didn't even know about the memorandum," Casey said.

Rico's face darkened with shame. "My mother was influenced by all my... my preaching against *omertà* and Mafia and old ways. My parents wanted to..." He started breathing heavily, trying not to lose his control, the last remnants of his manhood, in front of her. "They wanted to make me proud of them, Casey."

Tears clouded his eyes, humiliating him, drowning him in his own guilt. "I killed my mother," he said brokenly.

"No, Rico, no." Casey crouched before him and took his face, his dark, beautiful, anguished face, between her hands. "You were right, Rico. Sicily can only have a future if people change the old ways, if they stand up against killers and extortionists. Your parents did what they thought was right. No one could have known what would happen, least of all you. You didn't even know what they were planning.''

"No one can win against them," he insisted, forcing each word out of his raw throat. "Honest people never win here.''

"They do, Rico. Mayor Orlando is still alive. And think of how many *mafiosi* went to jail after the maxi-trial.''

"And think of how many of them were back out on the street within a year. The trials changed nothing, Casey.'' A tear rolled down his cheek. "My father is right. Nothing ever changes here.''

"Then *we* will change it," she promised him, her eyes burning with tears for his pain. "Take me to your father.''

"No.''

"Please.''

"I don't have to, Casey.'' He took a shaky breath. "I know where the papers are.''

She gaped at him. "You *know?''*

"He told me yesterday.''

She grasped the lapels of his shirt. "Where's the memorandum?'' she demanded. When he shook his head, she said, "Rico, if you care about me at all, then tell me where it is.''

"Casey... I love you.''

Her heart near to breaking, because she hadn't wanted to hear him say it in such a terrible moment, even though she needed his love now to give her strength, she urged, "Then tell me.''

"No. I want you to leave Sicily and forget all about the memorandum.''

"I can't!''

"I won't give it to you, Casey. They killed her for it, and I won't let you die for it, too.''

"You don't know that, Rico. You're guessing. Thousands of people are killed by hit-and-run drivers every day. I've seen how people drive in this city—"

"I won't risk it! I won't risk your life just because you think I could be wrong about my mother's death," he said harshly.

"Rico, you can't say you love me, then say you want to send me away. You can't protect me by taking away my work. You—"

"God, don't you understand?" He shook her roughly. "If it weren't for me and all my modern ideas, my mother would probably still be alive, my father would be well and the woman I love wouldn't be risking her life to find some papers written by a bandit forty years ago!" He shoved her aside and stood up.

"Listen to me!" She held on to him when he tried to shake her off. "It's not your choice, Rico. The papers belong to Totò, and he wants to give them to me. If you won't tell me where they are, I'll rent a car and drive to Alcamo myself to ask Totò where they are. Do you understand? You can't stop it from happening unless you tie me up and lock me in here."

For a moment she thought he was considering the idea. Then he lowered his head. "And when you have the papers?"

"I don't know," she admitted. "It depends what they say. I…I was hoping you would translate them for me when I get them." At his incredulous look, she added, "But you don't have to if you don't want to."

"That's why you've stayed all along, isn't it?" he asked expressionlessly. "Not for me or my father, but for the memorandum."

She winced. When had ambition become one of her faults instead of one of her virtues? "I stayed for all three, Rico. I can't divide it up neatly. I stayed because I love you and didn't want to leave you, I stayed because I love Totò and thought he might be dying, I stayed because the memorandum is everything I've ever dreamed of, professionally." Seeing no change in his expression, she said desperately, "Damn it, Rico! I can't give you a pure answer. I'm sorry, I wish I could, but I can't. There's nothing pure about me or about this."

He looked sad. "There is nothing pure about me, either, though I used to believe..."

"You chose to fight, Rico. Now let me choose." She took a breath and asked again, "Where is the memorandum?"

He waited for the space of a heartbeat, then answered, "In my mother's window box. She wrapped the brown folder in thick plastic and buried it under the spices because... because the box was made by my father."

"My God, it's been under our noses all this time," Casey murmured in wonder. "Your mother was a smart woman. No one would ever think of looking there, and she could always keep her eye on it." She touched his face. "Oh, Rico, I'm sorry."

He avoided her eyes. "All my life, I cut spices for my mother from that box, never knowing that Giuliano's documents were hidden in the dirt."

"Why didn't your father tell me sooner?"

Rico sighed. "He invited you here because you represented a big, powerful, invulnerable American magazine. But when you arrived, he saw that you were only a woman—defenseless and unprotected. He liked you and was afraid you couldn't carry the burden he would pass on to you. My uncle's warnings increased his worries about who might be watching and listening."

He looked at her with a small spark of the fondness she was used to seeing in his eyes, and she soaked it up, desperately afraid she was losing him. He said, "Papa told me that you somehow convinced him to tell you, though. I suppose I am not even surprised."

"Will you take me to the farm tomorrow, Rico?"

"Please, Casey. Let it go," he pleaded, knowing it was useless.

"I can't." Her eyes begged him to understand.

The phone rang, breaking the charged silence with its shrill ring. They stared at each other, unresolved. "After I get off the phone," Rico told her, "I have to get back to work. Someone from the ministry in Rome is arriving this afternoon."

Casey nodded slowly, her chest aching. He answered the phone, and she listened to him speak briefly to the caller. Before he left, he said, "I lied to you, Casey—it's true. And if there was anything else I could do to keep you away from the memorandum, I'd do it."

"I know."

"I don't know if you can understand, but it's because I love you. I know you think anyone who loves you should want to help your career, but I can't do that when it's so dangerous."

When she didn't answer, he left quietly. Casey picked her notebook up off the floor, where it had rested ever since she threw it at him. She slumped into a chair at the table and stared at it blankly for a long time. Finally, with jerky movements, she wrote down the location of the memorandum and, out of habit, made a little sketch of the window box. She stared at it for a long time, too stunned for anger or sorrow.

Finally, she closed her notebook and stuffed it in her purse. Her mind was a jumble, and she couldn't seem to form a single coherent thought. What mattered most? Who was right? What was the right thing to do in this confusing place where moral boundaries seemed to constantly shift and change, where truth itself seemed like a mirage? Where the man you loved stood between you and your dreams while protecting you from his own nightmares?

"I need some air," she muttered. She grabbed her purse and left the apartment, going out into the brilliant Sicilian sunshine.

As soon as she left the building, she had a strong sensation of being watched. She tried to shake off her unease. Of *course* she felt watched. She had been watched with avid curiosity ever since she had come here. She glanced around her. The streets were very quiet now. The only people out and about toward the end of siesta were some old men playing cards, a fruit seller, a few people on their way back to work and a couple of teenage boys riding double on a Vespa motorbike.

The boys on the motorbike seemed to be following her. Casey glared at them and turned the corner, hoping they'd leave her alone. She had already had to shake off a couple of other admirers this morning, and she wanted to be alone with her thoughts right now. She smiled absently at a young couple who were just going into a cheese shop and she kept walking.

It all happened very quickly. She heard the motorbike suddenly speed up and approach her, then she heard footsteps. A moment later, she felt a sharp yank on her arm as one of the boys tried to snatch her purse. Anger overrode all other instincts. *This rotten kid is trying to steal my purse!*

She fought him, kicking, hitting, pulling on her purse strap as hard as she could, and—she was later told—screaming at the top of her lungs. The kid clearly panicked when he heard voices nearby. He socked her in the eye so hard she released her hold on the purse, fell down and hit her head on the sidewalk. Fighting unconsciousness, she heard the motorbike buzz away. A moment later, strong hands scooped her off the pavement, and several faces swam before her eyes while excited Italian voices penetrated her fogged brain.

"I've been robbed," she groaned disbelievingly. Then she passed out.

Rico rushed into the emergency room after dark, his heart in his throat. Casey awaited him placidly, surrounded by her new friends, sporting an amazing black eye and holding her prescription slips in her hand.

"You must be getting awfully sick of hospitals, Rico," she said apologetically.

His answer was a gentle but extremely fervent embrace. After he had stolen her breath with his kiss, while Casey's friends watched with unabashedly sentimental pleasure, he examined her injuries.

"How did this happen?" he demanded. He had returned late from a meeting only to find the apartment empty. He had thought Casey had gone to the farm without him, and he was changing clothes to go after her—whether to help her or stop her, he wasn't sure—when the phone rang. The call came from the emergency room at the university's hospital. They had been trying to reach him for about five hours, ever since Casey had been brought in, the victim of an assault.

As usual, things were very confusing. All of Casey's friends started talking at once, expressing outrage over the mugging, admiration for Casey's bravery, annoyance at the bureaucracy of the medical system, criticism that Rico hadn't arrived sooner and assurance that they had looked after her in his absence.

Casey stopped the flow of chatter by introducing everyone. "This is Calogero, the cheese seller. This is Marco and Giovanna—they're expecting a baby in October. They all helped me when I was mugged. Oh, yes, sorry," Casey said to the man she had forgotten to introduce. "This is Matteo. I think he's stabbed someone and is waiting to see if the guy lives. Something about a *vendetta.*"

"*Sì, sì,*" Matteo said, revealing a sparse selection of yellowed teeth when he grinned. He complimented Casey on her quick grasp of the vernacular and repeated, "*Vendetta, sì.*"

"I imagine the police will be coming very shortly for him, don't you think so, Rico?"

"Casey..." Nearly thirty-four years of experience had left him unprepared to cope with this situation. Finally, he said, "I love you."

The others understood that much English, and they expressed their sincere approval. At Casey's insistence, Rico wrote down the names and telephone numbers of the three people who had taken an unconscious Casey to the hospital, had explained her situation to the staff and had then kept her company all evening.

"I like it here," Casey told him as he carefully escorted her out of the hospital, having ignored her request to get Matteo's number, as well. He didn't want Casey seeing such a man again. "You know, in New York, people just ignore you when you're lying there unconscious in the street. But Calogero—what an awful name—and Marco and Giovanna rushed to help me. Where else would people give up half their day to help a stranger?"

"Well, Casey," Rico was forced to admit, "it doesn't always happen that way. You were just lucky."

"Well, they were nice, anyhow." When he asked if she had reported the attack to the police, she said, "Yes, a cop took my statement at the hospital. My friends explained everything for me, I mean, and I signed something. But the cop didn't seem to think we'd ever find my muggers."

"Casey," Rico began hesitantly, torn between wanting to protect her and wanting her to understand how dangerous this really was. "Are you sure it was just an ordinary mugging?"

"What else could it have been?"

"A warning, perhaps," he said quietly, helping her into his car.

"Oh, really, Rico. That's so...so melodramatic." A moment later she remembered what he believed about his mother's death. She reached across the car to touch him. "I'm sorry."

He covered her hand with his. "I want you to leave Sicily," he said urgently. "It's not safe for you here."

"Will you come with me?"

His silence was his answer. He couldn't say no, because he couldn't imagine living without her now. But he couldn't say yes, because, despite everything, he couldn't imagine leaving Sicily.

Casey understood his silence. So she said, "Then we'll just have to make Sicily safe for me. Because I'm staying with you."

He started the car, not sure what to say. "For days now, I have dreamed of you deciding to stay here with me. But now..."

"Now it's just a little more challenging. Oh! Careful on the turns, Rico, my head is killing me."

He sensed her optimism and was baffled by it. Normally, he was the optimistic one, but he had never felt so defeated in his life. "What do you think we should do?"

"I think we should go to the farm first thing in the morning and get the memorandum." When he started to protest she said, "Listen to me. I've thought about this all day. It's not because I think they'll make me a big-shot investigative reporter. It's because this will eat at you the rest of your life if you don't expose the memorandum.

"This isn't like protecting some poor farmers in the Belice Valley who've stolen some water, Rico. You can move the moral goalposts in a situation like that because you believe you can do some good in a no-win scenario. But the men who wanted your mother to keep Giuliano's memorandum secret were killers. You even think they killed your mother. So long as you keep the papers hidden, so long do you protect them. That's the real nature of *omertà*, Rico, protecting evil with silence because you think that by doing so, you're protecting me. But you're not, because we would live under that shadow forever then. We would be victims for the rest of our lives."

"This isn't America," he warned her. "They kill cops, magistrates, politicians and journalists here, Casey."

"Then we have to stop them, one battle at a time. No one can be free while truth remains a power currency here. You said yourself that Sicily would only be free when the code of silence was destroyed." She grasped his arm. "Rico, you'd throw away your whole life if you gave in now. Think of everything you've done, everything you could do."

"I'm thinking of you lying dead somewhere," he said brutally, turning the car sharply again.

"If they already know we know where the memorandum is, we have no choice, Rico. If we don't get it now, we'll belong to them forever."

Omertà, he thought. To be a man.

No. He would be trapped forever in the cycle of submission and retribution. She was right.

And because he knew she was right, because, in his terror for her, he had probably known all along what they would have to do, he said, "All right. We'll get it first thing in the morning, and I'll tell you what Giuliano wrote."

Aware that it might be suicidal, she unbuckled her seat belt so she could gingerly edge across the seat to kiss him. "You are the best man I've ever known," she told him.

She had been right to trust him, she thought. Everything was a compromise here, and she had often questioned Rico's moral flexibility. But she had come to realize that he dealt with every situation individually, and that he tried to do the right thing every time. His loyalty to his family, and now to her, came first, and sometimes it clouded his vision. He would have been silent forever to protect her, but she had made him see a deeper, stronger obligation. And in so doing, she had finally discovered what she could give him in exchange for all the things he gave her.

The elevator in his building made her so sick that she threw up when she reached the bathroom. "Concussion," she apologized groggily to Rico. He locked her in the apartment after asking his next-door neighbor to sit with her, then went to Palermo's all-night pharmacy to fill her prescriptions.

He knew she was right, and it was cleansing to believe he was going to do the right thing tomorrow. He didn't know what would happen afterward, what they would do with the papers, or how he would live with the things he had learned, but he knew that the woman lying in his bed right now was able to help him find his way again when he got lost. And that, he thought, was what he had always longed for.

He held her all night long, shielding her against the darkness around them and using her as a shield against the darkness within him. When morning came, he knew he was bound to her as irrevocably as he was bound to this island.

The drive out to the farm west of Palermo was quiet and tense. They spoke very little. Rico wrestled with his own demons, smoking one cigarette after another. Casey tried to gather strength and ignore her aching head.

The farm seemed deserted when they arrived at last. Daniela was at the hospital, Paolo was gone, the children were still staying with their relatives and even the hired farm workers were nowhere in sight. It was just as well, Casey thought. She didn't want anyone asking why she and Rico were digging through his mother's sacrosanct window box.

Casey had never been around the east side of the house, which couldn't be seen from the drive, the courtyard or the garden. Rico helped her climb over a couple of piles of stone and duck under a couple of fig trees. When they rounded the side of the house, Rico stopped in his tracks. Casey bumped into him, righted herself, then looked where he was looking.

"No!" she cried.

There was a huge pile of dirt on the ground in front of the window box. Lovingly tended spice plants lay all over the ground in obscene disarray, withered and dying, their roots exposed to the merciless Sicilian sun.

"Someone's been here," Casey said hoarsely, her voice sounding like a stranger's.

Rico rushed forward, but Casey stood rooted to the spot, disbelieving, shocked, appalled. Rico looked inside the window box. "There's something in here," he called.

Hope sprang cruelly to life inside her, despite her common sense. No one who had done this would have left behind the precious memorandum. "What is it?" she heard herself ask.

Rico reached inside the box to retrieve his find. He pulled it out and dusted it off. He turned slowly toward her. "I'm sorry, Casey. It's your notebook."

"What?" She stumbled forward and seized it from him. Tattered and smeared with dirt, it was indeed her notebook. It had taken the place of Giuliano's memorandum inside Loredana Butera's window box. "No," she croaked, hurting unbearably from the defeat.

She opened the notebook. Almost everything was still intact, with the important omission of her final interview with Totò, her written speculations on the location of Giuliano's memorandum and her sketch of the window box with the notes she had written after Rico had told her where his mother had hidden the papers.

"It's as if...as if it never happened," she murmured, too shocked to feel anything yet.

"Except for this," Rico said angrily, indicating the devastation of his mother's window box.

"And this," Casey said suddenly. She pointed to a sentence written on the last page of her notebook. She hadn't written it. It was in Italian. "What does it say?"

Rico read it and answered, "It says, 'The agreement is annulled.'"

Chapter Thirteen

They know you are here.

The phrase Rico's uncle had uttered that day in the *trattoria* echoed again and again in Casey's brain as she accompanied Rico to the hospital in Alcamo.

The wizened old man had been so right about the need for discretion. The whole village knew Casey wrote everything in her notebook and kept it in her purse. She couldn't even count how many people had asked her about her interest in Totò and Giuliano. The moment Totò had begun to brag about the important American journalist who had come to interview him, someone must have heard about it, then waited and watched. It would have been easy for that person to have a couple of teenage hoodlums snatch the purse from her to find out what she knew.

Or had the purse snatching been a coincidence? Such things were very common in Palermo. Perhaps the boys recognized they had stolen something important when they saw the notebook, and they turned it over to some big shot that same evening.

They know you are here.

The agreement is annulled.

Casey shivered.

"I'm sorry, Casey," Rico said again, seeing her quiver in her seat as she stared bleakly out the window of the car. He knew she would never forgive him for this, and he couldn't blame her. If only he had told her the location of the memorandum as soon as he had learned it, if only he had come here with her yesterday afternoon when she had asked him to.... *If only.* He sighed unhappily.

She had been uncharacteristically silent ever since they had discovered her notebook in the ruined window box. He had given her some heavily sugared *espresso,* afraid she was suffering some kind of shock after watching her sit in the kitchen for twenty minutes, staring dully at the table without saying anything. She had only spoken enough to insist they go see his father immediately.

The crushing weight of disappointment made her look fragile, paler and more exotic. He hated himself for having caused it, even as he felt a flood of relief. The memorandum was gone forever, and Casey was still alive.

Nevertheless, he ached for her pain. "I'm sorry I made you lose the memorandum."

"Oh, Rico," she said irritably, "will you stop trying to take responsibility for everything that happens in the universe?"

He blinked at her in surprise. "I'm not. I just—"

"Oh, you're not? Let's see. You personally are responsible for supplying water to Sicily, and for every dry town or thirsty farmer in the country. You personally were responsible for your parents' decision to turn the memorandum over to the authorities, and then you were responsible for your mother's death at the hands of a hit-and-run driver in Palermo. It was all because of you that Totò invited me here after I wrote begging him for an interview, and it's your fault that someone got to the memorandum before I did—after I let them steal the notebook in which I had written down the hiding place." She gave him an exasperated look. "Have I left out anything else that is totally and entirely all your fault?"

"But . . . aren't you mad at me?" he asked weakly.

"Keep your eyes on the road," she snapped. "Of course, I'm mad at you! But I'm more mad at them. Damn it, am I supposed to blame you for what they've done? Am I supposed to blame you for not knowing how badly someone else wanted the memorandum, for not guessing they would find out where your mother hid it, for not realizing they would come here after I was mugged? I mean, *I* thought the mugging was unrelated, so should I just blame you so I have someone to be mad at?"

"Well, I . . . No, but . . ."

"You were right and I was wrong," she said.

"About what?"

"This *is* a war zone." She nodded her head emphatically. "Honest people have just lost another skirmish, but I intend to strike back."

He thought he might have a heart attack. "What are you talking about? Are you crazy? You can't play with these people, Casey! They killed—"

"So you keep saying. I don't want to seem insensitive, Rico, but has it ever occurred to you that you and Totò have been overreacting?"

"There are informers everywhere," Rico said vehemently. "My father believed—"

"That someone told someone else he was planning to hand over the memorandum to the authorities. I love your father, Rico, but he's not a very logical man. He thought he was protecting the family by clamming up after your mother's death, then he brought an American journalist right into his home, apparently thinking that would look perfectly innocent."

She shook her head. "You'll never know for certain, Rico, so you'll just have to learn to forgive yourself. You've lived with shadows too long to shake them off easily, but I'm convinced your mother's death was just a senseless accident. After all, nobody has tried to hurt me. Those kids yesterday wouldn't have even blackened my eye if I would have just let them have my purse." She touched her bruised eye tenderly. "Whoever took the memorandum took it without doing anything violent to the family. It doesn't make them good guys, it just means they didn't want to kill for it . . . if they didn't have to."

"I . . . I want to believe," he said wistfully. She could almost convince him.

"'The agreement is annulled,'" she quoted thoughtfully. "Rico, I think they didn't even know what your father was planning to do last year until they read my notebook."

"Now you are guessing," he said critically.

She shrugged. "Maybe."

"How will you strike back?" he asked uneasily.

"With my work. If I study hard, I should be able to understand Italian within a year or so, but you'll have to help me a lot. Then I'm going to write a book about Giuliano. I told you how little accurate, updated reference material there is in English, didn't I? I'm going to change that. Then I'm—"

"You're staying?" he asked incredulously. He braked suddenly, stopping the Citroën in the middle of the road.

"Rico!" Casey gasped as a car nearly rear-ended them. Other cars started honking vigorously. "Are you nuts? You'll get us killed!"

"Did you say you're staying?" he demanded.

"We can't just sit here—"

"Casey!"

She met his gaze. One look into those yearning, passionate, liquid dark eyes made her forget the chaos around them. "Of course I'm staying. You've always said you can't leave, so how could I?"

"But you've seen . . . I mean, today . . . You . . ."

"I told you I love a challenge, didn't I?" she said tenderly. Had he really thought she would leave him because she'd lost the memorandum? "And Sicily's safe for me now, isn't it?"

He made one of those expressive gestures. "*Not* if you go around writing books that attack—"

"Could we argue about that later?" she murmured, edging closer to him.

"Casey, life is very hard here," he said, trying to suppress the racing joy in his heart as he looked at her. She had to be crazy to want to stay, as crazy as he was.

"Then why do you stay?" she asked knowingly.

"Because life is also very pleasurable here," he admitted, believing she knew.

"You told me once that I'd have to suffer with you to really understand. Believe me, Rico, I'm suffering right now. I wanted that memorandum the way most women want a child." She added on a whisper, "And I'm starting to understand."

He stared at her for a long moment, finally believing it. She would stay here with him, in this devastated, dramatic, voracious land, in this land that ate up your heart and soul. She came to him with no illusions, knowing and understanding the life he offered her, and she would stay because she was a fighter as he was. And because they loved each other, powerfully, irrevocably, as his parents had.

"You should know," he said huskily, ignoring the sounds of traffic all around them and the shouts that came through the open windows of the car, "that we are not a permissive society. You won't be able to just move in with me. You will have to marry me."

"I guess I can live with that," she murmured.

They kissed gently, needing tenderness to seal their pact, tasting the sweet wine of love on each other's lips.

She made him believe again. Things *could* change here, but it would take courage, more courage than he had expected, all the courage he would be given by this woman he loved. He felt a familiar surge of optimism grow inside him—new plans, new hope.

"Oh, Casey," he murmured. "To think you almost went to South America instead of coming here."

She held him tightly, aware of how much had been missing in her life until she had come to Sicily and found him.

When someone bumped their rear fender insistently, Casey finally said, "We should get moving."

"Yes," he agreed, taking one last sip from her soft lips before putting the car in gear and continuing the journey to the hospital.

Totò was in fine fighting form by the time they reached the hospital. He was arguing ferociously with one of his cousins about a soccer match, Rico explained to Casey, disagreeing with another about politics and teasing a young niece and nephew. Casey helped Rico clear the room of his relatives, ignored curious stares from Totò's fellow patients and sat down with the old man to tell him what had happened.

Totò was stunned, but less dismayed than Casey had expected. "I'm sorry, Totò," she said. "I practically drew them a map in my notebook."

He patted her hand. "You could not have known," he said. "The tentacles of the octopus—"

"I'm sorry, too, Papa," Rico interrupted, not wanting to hear that phrase again.

"You," Totò said severely, "have a lot to be sorry about."

"Totò," Casey began, not wanting him to chastise Rico.

"But you had to protect her," Totò continued, "as Mamma and I had to protect each other. I understand that."

"I'm afraid I can't mention the memorandum in the article, Totò. I can say that Giuliano showed it to you that night in 1947, but *Sentinel* won't want me to write about all of this—" she made an encompassing gesture "—when I can't produce the memorandum. It would look too much like cheap sensationalism."

"So the article, after all, will be just the memories of a dying bandit," Totò said wistfully.

"Yes. I know you wanted more," Casey said sadly.

"*Sì.* I wanted to clean the slate before I died." He was silent for a moment, then shrugged. "As my wife used to say, 'God gives with one hand and takes with the other.' He has taken the secret Loredana guarded all her life to keep me safe, but he has given me the mother of my grandchildren."

"What?" Casey said.

He shook a teasing finger at her. "Don't think an old man's eyes are too weary to notice when his own son falls in love."

"Papa," Rico interjected, "this isn't—"

"How much longer do you think I will live?" Totò cried vehemently. "A man wants to see all his children married and settled before he dies."

"Yes, Papa," Rico said resignedly. He rolled his eyes apologetically at Casey.

"You have found the wife," Totò continued, gesturing dramatically. "Now maybe it would not be *too* much trouble for my busy son to get to work on the grandchildren before his old father gets much weaker?"

"We'll work on it, Papa," Rico promised, grinning at Casey's flabbergasted expression.

"Daniela can teach her some of Mamma's recipes—"

"Now just a darned minute here," Casey said. "Kids are fine, I can see your point, Totò. But *cooking* is an entirely different matter. That's what pizzerias are for. I do *not* intend to spend all day over a hot stove the way Daniela does, do I make myself clear? I have a career, I have work to do—'' She broke off as she realized something. "Oh, my God, Rico, I left two octopuses sitting in your kitchen sink yesterday afternoon.''

"They'll be pretty ripe by now,'' he said mournfully.

"I'm sorry. It just slipped my mind.''

Totò held up a hand, insisting they get back to a more interesting subject. "So you are going to continue your career here? How?''

"I'm going to resign from *Sentinel*,'' she explained. "Why keep waiting for them to send me to a war zone when I can get married in one?'' She winked at Rico. "And I'll go free-lance, selling articles to magazines and press services. But mostly,'' she concluded, "I want to work on a couple of nonfiction books. One about Giuliano, the bandit king who brought us all together.'' She smiled at them both and added, "I'll need your help, of course, Totò. That's when I'm going to tell what happened to the memorandum,'' she added firmly.

"And what else?'' Rico asked curiously.

"There's a lot to write about here,'' she said thoughtfully. "Mafia, shifting moral values, changing times, *omertà,* beautiful countryside and exotic cities, centuries of conquerors, and, of course, Rico, water shortages.'' She nodded and added, "I'd like to write something about truth as a power currency. If I can get anybody around here to give me a straight answer, that is.''

"So, you have finally found a woman that matches up to Mamma, eh?'' Totò said.

"It looks that way,'' Rico conceded, looking at Casey through heavy-lidded eyes.

It was a look that made her squirm and long to be alone with him. "We've got a lot to do, Rico,'' Casey said suddenly. "Those kids who stole the notebook also stole my passport, my traveler's checks and a lot of other things I'll need before I go back to the States to quit my job and move out of my apartment.''

He nodded. "I guess we should go to the American Consulate in Palermo. I'll go with you. It can be a little confusing.''

"Yes, I'm sure it can," she responded dryly. So what else was new? She said goodbye to Totò and headed for the door, giving the two men a moment alone together.

"Rico, Rico," Totò whispered. "I'm so sorry, my son. Sorry for the secrets we kept from you, sorry for putting this woman in danger. Are you ashamed of us, because Mamma made a pact with them, because I kept my silence?''

"I could never be ashamed of you, Papa. I've always been proud of who my parents are. You couldn't do anything to make me ashamed, and you don't have to do anything to make me proud." Rico smiled for a moment, hoping Totò would live long enough for his grandchildren to know what a remarkable man he was. Then he leaned over and kissed the old man's forehead. "Besides, the son must always forgive the father," he said simply.

"As God must forgive each of us when we face Him," Totò added sagely. "Go now with your woman. And I will sleep, as old men should when the sun is high and the air is still.''

"I'll be back tomorrow, Papa, to take you home," Rico promised.

He left the room and joined Casey outside. Just as they were leaving the hospital, Daniela returned from having lunch in a nearby restaurant with one of her many cousins.

"Casey! There you are!" she cried. "I was hoping you would come today!" She stopped in her tracks and exclaimed, "What has happened to your face?''

"Oh." Casey touched her eye self-consciously and said, "It's a long story, Daniela. I'll tell you later.''

After a few moments of obligatory fussing about Casey's health and comfort, Daniela said, "I have a message for you."

"For me?" Casey asked, frowning.

"Yes, your mother called the house last night."

"My mother?" Casey repeated incredulously.

"Your magazine gave her our telephone number when she told them it was urgent."

"What's wrong?" Casey immediately felt Rico's hand at her back, supporting her, there for her.

"Oh, nothing, I think. I would have given her Rico's telephone number, but she had made a mistake about the time difference and called us in the middle of the night. I didn't want her to wake you, so I wrote down the message."

How like Daniela, Casey thought, to take a message in a foreign language in the middle of the night rather than risk waking Casey from a sound sleep. "Thank you, Daniela," she said, embracing her impulsively. Daniela returned her hug with that warm ease that was so typical of her family.

"Here you are. I hope it makes sense," she said, handing a note to Casey. "I didn't understand some of the words and your mother had to spell them for me."

Casey read the note twice and then folded it carefully, when Rico saw the mist in her blue eyes, he asked, "Is something wrong, *cara?*"

She shook her head and said huskily, "My father asked her to call, since I haven't returned any of his messages. He didn't know I was in Sicily." She took a deep breath and continued, "He's in a rehabilitation program now. Oh, Rico, he's been sober for three years. He's already made amends to my mother, and he wants to see me to make amends, to ask me to forgive him."

Rico touched her soft cheek and smiled tenderly, feeling the quiet strength of her happiness. "And do you think you can forgive?"

She slid her arms around his neck and met his warm, welcoming kiss. "I'm definitely learning how to forgive," she whispered. "I have a very good teacher."

* * * * *

Author's Note

I've tried to portray Salvatore Giuliano's story as it is documented, straying from the truth only when describing his interaction with my fictional characters. However, contrary to my heroine's statement that there are no recent sources in English about Giuliano, I did discover an excellent one while researching this book: *King of the Mountain: The Life and Death of Giuliano the Bandit* by Billy Jaynes Chandler.

Bestselling author **NORA ROBERTS** captures all the romance, adventure, passion and excitement of Silhouette in a special miniseries.

THE CALHOUN WOMEN

Four charming, beautiful and fiercely independent sisters set out on a search for a missing family heirloom—an emerald necklace—and each finds something even more precious... passionate romance.

Look for THE CALHOUN WOMEN miniseries starting in June.

COURTING CATHERINE
in Silhouette Romance #801 (June/$2.50)

A MAN FOR AMANDA
in Silhouette Desire #649 (July/$2.75)

FOR THE LOVE OF LILAH
in Silhouette Special Edition #685 (August/$3.25)

SUZANNA'S SURRENDER
in Silhouette Intimate Moments #397 (September/$3.25)

Silhouette Special Edition

presents

SONNY'S GIRLS

by Emilie Richards, Celeste Hamilton and Erica Spindler

They had been Sonny's girls, irresistibly drawn to the charismatic high school football hero. Ten years later, none could forget the night that changed their lives forever.

In July—
ALL THOSE YEARS AGO by Emilie Richards (SSE #684)
Meredith Robbins had left town in shame. Could she ever banish the past and reach for love again?

In August—
DON'T LOOK BACK by Celeste Hamilton (SSE #690)
Cyndi Saint was Sonny's steady. Ten years later, she remembered only his hurtful parting words....

In September—
LONGER THAN... by Erica Spindler (SSE #696)
Bubbly Jennifer Joyce was everybody's friend. But nobody knew the secret longings she felt for bad boy Ryder Hayes....

SSESG-1

SILHOUETTE·INTIMATE·MOMENTS®

IT'S TIME TO MEET
THE MARSHALLS!

In 1986, bestselling author Kristin James wrote A VERY SPECIAL FAVOR for the Silhouette Intimate Moments line. Hero Adam Marshall quickly became a reader favorite, and ever since then, readers have been asking for the stories of his two brothers, Tag and James. At last your prayers have been answered!

In August, look for THE LETTER OF THE LAW (IM #393), James Marshall's story. If you missed youngest brother Tag's story, SALT OF THE EARTH (IM #385), you can order it by following the directions below. And, as our very special favor to you, we'll be reprinting A VERY SPECIAL FAVOR this September. Look for it in special displays wherever you buy books.

Silhouette Books®

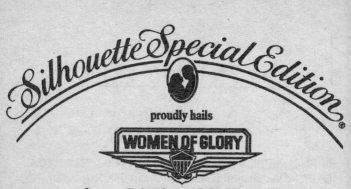

Silhouette Special Edition®

proudly hails

WOMEN OF GLORY

from Lindsay McKenna

Soar with Dana Coulter, Molly Rutledge and Maggie Donovan—
Lindsay McKenna's WOMEN OF GLORY. On land, sea or air, these
three Annapolis grads challenge danger head-on, risking life and limb
for the glory of their country—and for the men they love!

May: NO QUARTER GIVEN (SE #667) Dana Coulter is on the brink
of achieving her lifelong dream of flying—and of meeting the man who
would love to take her to new heights!

June: THE GAUNTLET (SE #673) Molly Rutledge is determined
to excel on her own merit, but Captain Cameron Sinclair is equally
determined to take gentle Molly under his wing....

July: UNDER FIRE (SE #679) Indomitable Maggie never thought
her career—or her heart—would come under fire. But all that changes
when she teams up with Lieutenant Wes Bishop!

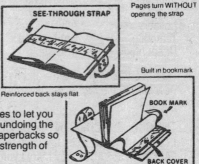